Spiked Punch

A Maddie Sparks Mystery, Book One

LESLEY A. DIEHL

CAMEL PRESS

Kenmore, WA

CAMEL PRESS

A Camel Press book published by Epicenter Press

Epicenter Press
6524 NE 181st St.
Suite 2
Kenmore, WA 98028

For more information go to:
www.Camelpress.com
www.Coffeetownpress.com
www.Epicenterpress.com
www.lesleyadiehl.com

Cover design by Scott Book
Design by Melissa Vail Coffman

Spiked Punch
Copyright © 2023 by Lesley A. Diehl

Library of Congress Control Number: 2023936018

ISBN: 978-1-68492-125-6 (Trade Paper)
ISBN: 978-1-68492-126-3 (eBook)

To all those generous individuals who have found room in their hearts for a furry companion and given them a forever home, I thank you. As does Spike.

ACKNOWLEDGMENTS

THE MADDIE SPARKS MYSTERIES are set in the Butternut Valley of Upstate New York. It's where I make my home, as charming a location in real-life as it is in this book. Its residents are equally fascinating. I can't think of better inspiration for a cozy mystery.

CHAPTER 1

I HADN'T HEARD THE DOORBELL RING, nor anyone enter the house, but when I went into my office, I found him standing over the desk reading the screen on my computer. He must have come in the front door while I was upstairs in my bedroom. I read shock along with disappointment on his face.

"What is this? For God's sake, Mom. What is wrong with you?" Without letting me reply, he held up a pudgy hand and paced back and forth in front of the desk in my tiny office off the living room. "Oh, I know, I know. You're getting older and you have too much time on your hands. You're bored. But can't you find something different to read?"

"It's not a book, at least not yet." I reached out, hit a key and made the screen go blank.

"You mean you wrote this?" His mouth dropped open in astonishment.

I nodded. I hadn't intended for him to see what I was working on because I knew my son wouldn't approve. Geoffrey, my oldest, was a lovely man, kind, generous, and he put his family first, the kind of son a mother would be proud of. And I was. But he was a private person when it came to his personal life. He didn't like off-color jokes, and I'd never heard him say the word "sex" or allude to anything sexual, not that I expected my children to engage in conversations with me about "bedroom activities," Geoffrey's words, when referring to intimate relationships.

"Well, this certainly isn't one of the usual cozy mysteries you've been churning out for the past decade. These people are . . . . This is . . . ." He sputtered and couldn't seem to find the words. I decided I'd help him.

"Love? Excitement. Passion? Romance?" Now why did I use those words? I was working on a romance novel which explained some of his reactions.

"No, no, no. Not from a woman of your age. You're a lovely older woman, so sweet and elegant with your silver hair pulled back in a simple bun. You look your age, not all made up and wearing tight jeans and low-cut blouses. I can't believe this is something that interests you."

That was part of Geoffrey's issue with my writing about romance that included sex. He didn't think of women my age as interested in anything but crocheting and daytime soap operas on TV, gliding quietly into life beyond this one. I have, without meaning to, cultivated an image of a woman working by spending my time writing. My social life consisted of little other than having lunch with a few women friends. I had led such a quiet existence. I was changing, and I promised myself my newest writing interest was just the beginning of a more active, outgoing lifestyle.

"Really, Geoffrey? Here. Read it again. It's about love." With a keystroke I opened the page again.

"I don't want to see that. Delete it." He turned his back on the computer.

"No. I am not deleting this work. I think it's rather good. A man and a woman expressing their love for each other. It's contemporary romantic suspense."

"I'm not familiar with romance novels at all, but this is something better kept private, not spread all over the page."

"Yes, well. Don't you think what I do or write in my own house is private?"

He looked down at his feet and muttered something.

"What did you say?"

"As long as you have no intention of continuing this or of ever publishing it."

I knew what was at the root of Geoffrey's uptight attitude toward overt expressions of emotion whether it is physical intimacy and love, real or written. It had to do with his father, my ex-husband. Don't get me wrong. Geoffrey adores his father. What he didn't adore was his understanding of what his father was: a philanderer, a man who cheated on me throughout our marriage. In Geoffrey's mind there was a clear separation between his father as father and his father as unfaithful husband.

I laughed. "I'd have to find a new agent. Mine doesn't represent this genre. She prefers stories set in small towns, no sex, no violence."

I really wanted a change in my writing career. Once I retired as a librarian for the library in our village, I began writing cozy mysteries. I had published over fifteen books, all set in a charming upstate New York village similar to the one I lived in. The stories featured my bright, funny and plucky protagonist and her gentlemanly fiancée who tripped over conveniently located bodies and quickly found the killer. Of late my writing was not as fulfilling or exciting as when I first started writing cozy mysteries. In years I was a senior, but thoughts of love and the physical expression of love filled my head. My bed was empty, and I felt the same. I wanted to try something new and see what I could do now with my writing life. Maybe it wouldn't work, maybe I was too old to be conjuring up scenes of love, but I was determined to let my imagination fly where it wanted and see what happened.

I reached out and touched Geoffrey's arm. "I'm still the same mother you've always known. I'm just expressing another side of myself. I love you, Geoffrey, and that will never change. You know that, don't you?"

"Sure, Mom. You're my rock and always have been."

"Right back at ya, my dear."

"The family likes the mysteries you write. I'm sure they and others would prefer you continue to write them."

I wasn't certain any of my family had read my work, but I appreciated his attempt to compliment me on my mystery writing, aware that he was trying to encourage me to return to it, something with which he was familiar and comfortable. "I'm glad."

When this work was published, if it was published, it would be under another name, not under Maddie Sparks, my name in real life and the one I used for my cozy mysteries. The people in the Upstate New York village of Butternut Falls where I had lived most of my adult life, knew me as the woman who wrote those funny cozy mysteries. It was a reputation I enjoyed. Our town of less than two thousand people was small enough that everyone knew everyone else and knew about everyone else. This new identity was one I intended to keep to myself.

The scene I'd created was passionate. It gave me goosebumps of desire writing it, and rereading it sent warm tinglies up and down my body. It was a lovingly crafted scene of desire, the kind I knew appealed to women readers. It certainly appealed to me. Reading romances was something women of various ages in my village did. What they read they kept mostly to themselves and told only their closest friends.

"So let's not tell anyone about this right now. If this got around town, who knows what people would think," Geoffrey said.

I put my fingers to my mouth and moved them across my lips as if I was zipping my mouth closed.

A look of relief crossed Geoffrey's face. "Good. That's settled."

He meant, "Good, then you're done with this kind of writing." I wasn't but now was not the time for me to contradict him.

"Let's have a nice cup of tea and you can tell me what you stopped by for." I steered Geoffrey out of my office into the kitchen, filled the kettle with water and flipped it on.

"Oh, nothing much. Checking on you."

He never checked on me. Something was up. I rummaged around in my pantry and located the package of cookies I'd bought a while back. The "best by" date had long passed. Stale, but they were all I had. I'd been so wrapped up in my writing I'd not gone to the supermarket for at least a week. I had to set up a better schedule for writing, not simply one where I wrote nonstop for hours and fell into bed exhausted with no time for shopping or feeding myself in a healthy manner. And I had been neglecting my friends and family as well as trips to the fitness center.

Geoffrey pulled out a chair and dropped himself onto the seat with a groan. He'd added weight to his large over six-foot frame. The chair squeaked as he sat. He also looked a little ragged to me, his brown hair longer than usual and his tie crooked. His mussed appearance gave me pause. Something was on his mind. He reached for a cookie and popped it whole into his mouth.

"Love your cookies, Mom." The man was buttering me up for something.

I made a dismissive "pssst." "What do you want?"

"Why do I have to want something? Can't I stop by and see my old mom for a chat?"

"No, you cannot. You ignore me most of the time probably because I don't cause you any trouble. When you do turn up, I know you have something on your mind."

He reached for another cookie. I slapped his hand. No son of mine is too old to have his hand slapped.

"No more cookies until you get on with it. Besides, you're putting on weight. I think I should have a talk with Abigail. Have her put you on a diet."

"You do that, and I'll tell the family what you're up to." He nodded his head toward my office. "The turn your writing has taken."

"It's not a 'turn.' It's another genre."

"Why can't you go back to your little mysteries?"

"They are not 'little' mysteries. They are cozy mysteries, and, for a time, they sold well."

"So there, then. You're making money from them. Why change?"

"Cozy mysteries make money, not necessarily my cozy mysteries like they used to. Besides, I'm bored and ready for a change."

"Well, join a knitting club or something."

"I said I'm bored, not boring."

"Mom, these little, sorry, I mean these clubs are what all women your age do. Why not you?"

I gave him one of my "are you daft" looks. "It's as if you don't know a thing about me. When have I ever knitted?"

"Well, whatever women your age do then."

"I have no idea what women my age do. I only know what I do." And what I surmised women liked to do regardless of age: read about a man yearning for them.

"But I'll bet you're happy to be settled into a life free from the hassles of work and family responsibilities, dabbling away at your writing."

Sometimes I worried Geoffrey was the dimmest wick in the candle factory. Didn't he know that no matter how old one is, there are always family responsibilities? I didn't expect him to understand how a person could age and not feel old. That I'd let him learn on his own. But family? Family was forever. Sometimes I wasn't sure if that was a good thing or God's way of reminding us we could never just coast into old age.

"What did you say you stopped by for? And don't tell me for my cookies."

He looked up from the table and gave me one of his disingenuous smiles.

"I came to offer you a job."

"I'm a terrible keyboardist, I'm not personable when I answer the phone, and I never took a bookkeeping course. Sitting at a desk for hours will make my back stiffen up. There's no way I could be of use to you in your business."

Geoffrey and his wife Abigail ran a local business, Sparks Real Estate and Property Management. I understood the real estate part of the business but didn't get the property management bit. Were people now incapable of taking care of their own properties and had to hire someone to oversee their houses, garages, and lawns? It sounded boring, so I kept my nose out of it. They were self-supporting, so that was a good thing. Actually, the business seemed to be doing well.

"We have all the office help we need. We lost one of the people who we used to keep an eye on houses for people who are on vacation, and we need someone to replace him."

"'Lost' as in you can't locate him?"

Geoffrey shot me an annoyed look. "Don't be ridiculous, Mom. David Gardner is out on sick leave. He fell down the basement steps of a house he was looking after and broke his leg. He'll be back to work in a month or so, but until then, we could use someone to take his place."

"Me? You think I can do the job?" Well, I could, of course, but why would I want to? I glanced toward my office and thought of the half-finished scene on my computer. "I don't have time."

Geoffrey caught my look. "Now I thought we finished that. I think you'll find this fun. And it's easy. You pick up the keys to the residence from our office, read the specs for the job and then stop by the house. It takes little time to do a walkthrough, checking each room and the basement, sometimes the garage and any outbuildings."

"Dogs. What about dogs?"

"Homeowners don't contract with us to care for their dogs while they're gone. They take them along or board them at a boarding facility."

"You're certain of that because I don't fancy being bitten by a dog or chased around the property by one."

Geoffrey clapped his hands together in happiness. "So, you'll do it then?"

"No way. I've got a lot on my plate like writing a novel, a house to keep up and neighbors to look in on. I'm a busy woman. Why don't you hire someone for a few weeks to replace Mr. Gardner?"

"That would be you."

"Pay?"

"I thought you'd do it as a favor to Abigail and me."

Ah, ha. Now I got it. "You think you can get me for free, no pay for roaming through other people's property and snooping around their houses."

"It's not snooping. It's professional residential management work."

"Well, it's settled then." I took my final sip of tea and set the cup in the sink.

"You'll do it?" Geoffrey looked ecstatic enough to have won the lottery.

"I'll do it for a week."

"I need you for more time than that."

"A week, Geoffrey, until you find someone else to do the work." I grabbed his cup and the cookies from the table, signaling our conversation was over.

"You'll have to stop by the office tomorrow for training."

I pushed him toward the front door. "How much training does it take to insert a key in a lock, peek into a few rooms and then lock up?"

"A few hours and then you'll be on your way. I wouldn't want anyone to think we were sending people into the field with no training." Geoffrey gave me a smile, walked down the front steps and got into his car.

Training? A few hours? What was I letting myself in for?

I removed our teacups from the table and found room for them on the top rack of the dishwasher which I hadn't run for days. Too busy writing. I leaned against the counter and my gaze travelled around the kitchen and adjoining living room. I needed to vacuum as well as dust, but all I could think about was my manuscript.

Besides, who ever saw my house? Before I retired as a librarian in our local library and reinvented myself as a mystery writer, friends and I got together for dinners or on the weekends for card games, but few of my old crowd remained in the area. Many had moved closer to children who had relocated, or they chose Arizona or Florida for a milder climate.

As harsh as the winters were in this river valley at the edge of the Adirondacks, I had no interest in moving anywhere else. I'd saved my money to buy this little house fronting a small trout stream in the village I'd raised my sons in. The downstairs fitted my needs perfectly—a kitchen open to the living area. I'd enlarged a closet off the living room and created an office large enough to fit in a desk and bookcase. Upstairs were three bedrooms, a master with attached bath and two other bedrooms with a bath in between. The master bedroom overlooked the backyard and into a giant spruce tree at the edge of the stream. Back downstairs the kitchen door opened onto a deck where I often sat to have my morning coffee.

I turned to gaze out the back window over the sink. It was raining. Again. And more rain forecasted for the rest of the week. The potatoes I'd planted in my garden were probably rotting from all the moisture. Well, I certainly wasn't going to run out there in this downpour to see how the vegetables were faring. Again I considered the house. I should clean. But I couldn't work up the interest. Instead the siren song of my writing drew me back to the computer and I again took up writing my contemporary romance about Katherine Modley and the man she loved. I had decided on a title for my work, one I was certain would grab the attention of readers. I wanted to call it *Love Again*, the story of two people separated for decades by family conflicts.

Outside the summer storm intensified and the tap tap of my fingers on the keyboard added to the sound of raindrops on the roof and against the windows creating a rhythm that drove my story forward. Now this was fun and satisfying. An hour later, a smile on my face and a martini in my hand, I settled onto the couch to watch the six o'clock news. Not a bad ending to a dreary Monday. Life was good especially since I had an appointment tomorrow to have my hair dyed and styled. Afterall, I was no longer the woman who wrote cozy murder mysteries. I thought champagne blonde would be a good color for me. And I should include a makeup consultation as well as purchase some more fashionable and youthful clothing. Besides drafting a different story, I was also going to change my outward appearance with new hairdo and clothes.

The phone rang. It was Abigail.

"I'm so delighted you're willing to pitch in for us. You have no idea how much this means. Stop by the office tomorrow at nine and we'll begin your training."

"Can't. I'm busy."

"Doing what? Geoffrey said you've finished your mystery series."

"What else did he say?"

"Oh, nothing much, that you're playing around with a new writing project. You must be so bored."

"I am. That's why I'm busy tomorrow."

There was a moment's silence on the other end of the line. "You're not making any sense. Geoffrey said he was worried about you."

"I've got a hair appointment."

"But I thought you did your own hair and besides, what is there to do? You wash it, dry it, and pin it back in a bun. You've worn it that way for as long as I've known you."

"Not any more I don't."

"What then?"

"I'm going to try something different."

"A shorter cut?"

"You could say that."

"Well, after your hair appointment then."

"I'm going into the city."

"City?"

"Just up to Utica, to get my hair done but also to shop in the malls there."

"By yourself?"

"Yes, by myself."

I hung up before she could react. Utica was only thirty miles north of here, but I was going to make a day of it. I'd lied to her about going alone. I was asking Buff my personal trainer from the local fitness club to come with me for my hair appointment and shopping for clothes. I'd also asked his girlfriend to accompany us. Both were tan, blonde and fit, and dressed well. I'd seen them at the toney Billinghouse Restaurant in nearby Stone Side, a town of over 15,000 people, only ten miles away from Butternut Falls. Buff and his friend could give me a few pointers on clothing. What better way to spend the day than in the company of two attractive people who could help me find a fresh look for myself. The woman whose taste had always been impeccable although a bit dated was going for a make-over. The feeling was almost as good as making love with a handsome man. I said almost as good. Nothing could compare to the feeling of muscular arms around . . . . Inspired, I went back to my writing.

CHAPTER 2

ABIGAIL LOOKED UP WHEN I ENTERED the real estate office two days after Geoffrey had visited me and asked me to work at property managing. "What have you done to your hair?"

"Not even, 'Hi, Mom. So good of you to do this for us.'" I tossed my coat onto one of the desk chairs and gave Abigail a hug and a smack on the cheek.

"Well, of course we appreciate what you're doing, filling in for a few weeks or so."

I held up a finger to stop her from continuing. "I told Geoffrey I'd do this for a week. A week. That's it."

The door to the inner office swung open, and Geoffrey stuck his nose out, a cup of coffee in his hand with a crispy cruller balanced on top of it. "We expected you in here yesterday."

"Give me that." I grabbed the cruller from his hand and took a bite of it.

"Hey, that's the last one." Geoffrey plopped down into a one of the waiting room chairs and looked on jealously as I ate the pastry.

"I brought in healthy snacks for the office." I handed Abigail a bag. She opened it and peeked inside.

"Wonderful. Carrot sticks." Her tone of voice and the dip of her mouth downward said the snack was anything but wonderful or my effort at wholesome eating appreciated.

Geoffrey groaned. "Snacks for rabbits, maybe."

"Snacks for all of us who need to eat healthy."

She removed the plastic container from the bag and opened it. "Oh, goodie. There's a container of ranch dressing to dip them into."

Geoffrey continued to frown at the veggies, but Abigail munched enthusiastically on the carrots and dressing.

Abigail was now approaching her late forties. I was her age when I gained almost ten pounds, weight I was still packing around thirty years later. I knew she and Geoffrey found it difficult to eat well because of their busy schedules. I was acting like a mother of young kids with worrying about their health and eating habits. I needed to watch that as they were grown adults. And just as I did not want Geoffrey telling me what to write maybe I should think about telling them what to eat.

"I can give you the recipe. It's homemade." If I could convince her to try easy but wholesome recipes, both of them would benefit.

She looked up from her crunching. "Your hair looks good, and you look years younger."

"Thank you, dear. I tried someone new to do my hair and make-up. There's nothing like a refreshed look to make a woman feel good. I'll give you his name if you like."

"Your sweater and pants are a little tight for a woman your age, however. What gives?" Abigail said.

"A healthy lifestyle." I said even as I swallowed the last bite of the cruller. "So, let's get crackin' with this training thing. I've got things to do this afternoon."

Geoffrey gave me a penetrating look. "Some writing, perhaps?"

I returned his look with the kind only a mother could give a son.

Abigail took a final bite of her carrot stick, then handed the container to Geoffrey. "At least try one, dear."

He shoved her hand away, picked up a ring binder from the desk and handed it to me. It was labeled "Training Manual" on the front. "We have seven properties that we need you to stop by this week."

Seven? Hmmm. that seemed doable in a day or so. Pop in for a look around and then leave. How hard could that be? I flipped through the manual.

As it turned out, according to the training manual, this property management thing was going to be more time-consuming than I thought. First, I was required to read over the specifications of what the property owner had contracted for, then go to the property, let myself in, do what the contract required with a check list in hand, leave a copy of the checklist in the house to let the owner know when I'd stopped by and what I did, then lock-up, walk the perimeter of the property looking for signs the property hadn't been broken into and the wires to the house were undamaged, verify that the lawn and gardens had been maintained by the landscaping company, then drive back to the office and leave off a duplicate of the checklist and any notes taken while on the site. Reading the list sent my heart racing and left me breathless, and not in a good way.

I looked up from the training manual. Geoffrey gestured to a chair.

"Take a seat, Mom. You'll need to read the manual carefully. There will be a short quiz on the materials covered there."

"A quiz? Look, you two, I'm doing this for nothing, as a favor to you. And what I don't understand is why your customers don't have a neighbor look in on their places when they're gone. It would save them money."

Abigail gave me a startled look "It's an imposition on neighbors and friends."

"I do it for the Bromley's who live next to me and go on winter vacation each February for two weeks. I see it as a neighborly thing to do."

Abigail clucked her tongue. "And there's always the possibility of something going wrong and the property owner having to sue a friend."

"Or there have been instances where a family member was sued when the relative overlooked an electrical issue and the house burned down." Geoffrey added his own cluck to that of his wife.

"Wouldn't the fault be the house owner's and not their relative's?" From my perspective people seemed much too litigious of late.

"We're covered by insurance if anything happens to the property while we're responsible for it." Abigail smiled.

"I assume your insurance covers the person hired by you to do the management work?"

"Well, certainly. We'll give you time to read and study the manual and then, when we return from lunch, you can take our test." Geoffrey went back into his office and came out pulling his suit coat on. "We'll be back in an hour or so."

"Hey. I'm hungry too."

"You just ate a cruller. Here. Have a carrot stick," said Geoffrey. "While we're gone, you can answer the phones for us."

"Where's your secretary?" I asked. Abigail and Geoffrey had hired a new person to replace their old secretary who retired last fall. I'd only met Tanya several times, a pleasant enough young woman, slim with long brown hair and big brown fawnlike eyes that made you want to put your arms around her and hug her.

"She's on her coffee break, as usual." Abigail rolled her eyes and followed Geoffrey out the door.

"Isn't there a training manual for phone answering?" I said to their retreating backs.

"Don't be silly," said Abigail, waving to me. "Everyone knows how to answer the phone."

I looked at the manual before me. My heavens, this had to be over a hundred pages long. And there was a test on the materials? I would have torn out my hair over having to study this garbage, but I remembered as I reached for a lock to pull that yesterday, I had had my hair cut in a perky but sophisticated short bob. I'd also had it dyed a luscious champagne blonde. The procedures had taken a large whack at my credit card, but intent upon updating my look, I'd used the card to purchase the basics of a more "fashion-forward" wardrobe (that was Buff's girlfriend's word for the apparel I bought). The transformation made me look like a hot granny, mature but doable. I ran my hand over my short, sassy haircut.

I might as well get to it. I began to flip through the pages. Whoever wrote it needed a proofreader. Punctuation errors, misspellings, poor grammar. The durn thing was unreadable. I rummaged through the desk drawer looking for a pencil, found one and, like the writer I was, I began to make corrections. I spent half an hour on it when I stopped myself. This wasn't my job. Annoyed, I tossed the manual on the desk, but wondered how I could get through it without being caught up in the errors. Lie to Abigail and Geoffrey and say I'd read it? Not an option. There was that stupid test. I chewed on the pencil as I mulled over the dilemma but was saved from making a snack of the eraser by the ring of the telephone on the secretary's desk. I looked up and down the street through the office windows, but there was no sign of a secretarial sort of person in sight. I shrugged and answered the phone.

"What?"

"Who is this? Is this the property management office?"

"Yes. Who wants to know?"

"I don't have much time. I was supposed to leave two keys. Oh, never mind. You know. Anyway, I found my second key, and I don't feel comfortable leaving it lying around, so come over here and pick it up, would you?"

"Huh? I don't understand. I started working here this morning."

"Look. I need to leave now. Get over here to pick up the extra key."

"It will have to wait until the owners return from lunch."

"But it should be done now. Right now!" I heard a shuddering intake of breath and then a slow exhale as the individual seemed to recover control. "It will only take a minute or so. It's the red house on the east end of Main Street. You can't miss it. Please." Demanding followed by pleading.

I held the receiver away from my mouth and uttered a word I'd never write in one of my cozy mysteries. Come to think of it, it wasn't a word I'd put in any book even my steamy romance. I imagined all my characters, whether in or out of bed, clothed or naked, in the middle of making love or escaping through a bedroom window, possessed large vocabularies which didn't necessitate the use of smutty words. Not that my vocabulary was small, but sometimes my emotions overwhelmed me enough that a few lewd words spewed forth. Heavens knows where I learned them. Or from whom. Maybe that guy I picked up while driving cross-country with my college roommate. Such fun.

"What did you say?" asked my caller.

"The hitchhiker. His name was Barry, I think. Or Larry. Could be Ralph."

"Are you going to help me?"

"Fine. I'll be right there."

I disconnected and stared out the window. Had I ever learned the hitch hiker's name? I shrugged before grabbing my coat. Or I could have imagined the whole episode. But his face was so clear in my mind as was the image of his tight tee-shirt pulled over pecs that bulged when . . . Dang, I was writing again. Sometimes when my writing mind took over, I found it hard to direct my thoughts back to the real world. When I wrote cozy mysteries, dogs, cats, teacups, country cottages, and treelined woodsy paths drew my attention. Now it was heaving bosoms, rippling muscles, and sighs of abandonment or groans of satisfaction. I had been guilted into helping Abigail and Geoffrey, but instead I wanted to be in front of my keyboard. I shook myself back to the present. I'd made a promise to them and helping the poor soul who was having property issues fell under the heading of helping.

I had no way of locking up, but unless a thief wanted to cart off office furniture in broad daylight down a village street, I wasn't worried anyone would burgle the place. I grabbed the training manual for reference in case I ran into something I needed to look up, tossed it in the back of my car and pulled away from the curb with a squeal of my tires. I did put the "Closed" sign in the window of the business. I could be at the house in under five minutes, the advantage of living in a small village with little traffic.

Geoffrey and Abigail's office was located on Main Street, north of the only traffic light in Butternut Falls. All the commercial businesses were located up and down Main Street. The remainder of the small community consisted of a few short streets that ran parallel to Main and a few others north and south of Main Street. The village streets were all shaded with old maple trees. There had been a fountain at the junction of Main and the county route crossing it in the center of town, but the fountain had been removed decades ago and recently discovered stored in the loft of a nearby barn. There were plans to refurbish it, and the local beautification committee was trying to raise the funds to renovate the crossroads and fountain. If the town found the money, the addition of the old fountain would add to the already charming street.

The businesses on Main Street included a bank, post office, diner and pizza place, two insurance firms, a styling salon, and beyond the firehouse, a general store of the sort that had sprung up in small towns. The school was located a block beyond, soccer fields across the street. The lawyer's office in town had closed several years ago as had the antique shop. Not many businesses, but what there were met the village's needs, and Stone Side, the small city nearby, was a mere fifteen minutes' drive away. Most people did their shopping there. For more extensive shopping we went farther north to Utica or Syracuse or took the two hours plus drive to Albany. We had four churches in town, and all held

Sunday services and offered events such as pot luck suppers and thrift fairs. In most nearby villages, the churches had shut down and were sold, to be used as private residences or they sat abandoned and were eventually demolished.

Ours was a thriving town, and we were proud of it. It was beautiful, quiet and served as the bedroom community to Stone Side's hospital and two colleges as well as other businesses that employed the residents of Butternut Falls. Who wouldn't want to live here? The houses were well-maintained, some large mansions lovingly renovated as well as small cottages like my own. And the school and property taxes were far less than those in nearby cities.

I had parked in front of Geoffrey and Abigail's business, but the house I'd been called to was located at the other end of Main Street. I checked my rear-view mirror to see if there were any cars behind me. If not, I could pull a U-turn. Just my luck I spied several cars, one of which honked its horn at me.

Dang. I'd have to go down the street and pull into the firehouse's parking lot to turn around there. As I approached the intersection, the signal changed to red before I could go through. I wanted to get to the house, grab the key and be on my way. I drummed my hands on the steering wheel as I waited for the green. The cinnamon from the cruller made me burp. I chided myself for taking it from Geoffrey. I'd done it to save him the calories, but I should have let him finish it to deal with the issue of its fat and sugar content tomorrow morning when he weighed himself.

The signal turned green. I went through and turned into the firehouse lot to make my U-turn back onto the street careful to make certain there were no trucks exiting the firehouse. The sign in front of the lot read "official use only" but everyone in town used the lot to make their turns after they stopped at the post office to pick up the mail. If a state trooper caught them, they'd be fined, but troopers rarely drove through the village. We were too small a town for a police department and depended upon the state police or the county sheriff's department if we needed help, but we were a law-abiding lot here, few crimes of any sort.

After I completed my turn and was headed back in the right direction, I heard a siren behind me. Oh, no. This was one of those rare occasions where a trooper was in town, and he was signaling me over. I pulled to the curb and watched him exit his cruiser, clapping his wide-brimmed hat on his head. I recognized him. Trooper Tommy Turner. He and a sheriff's deputy had attended a village meeting this past summer when residents had noise complaints against a family around the corner from me. He seemed nice enough and sympathetic to our concerns, but there was no noise ordinance in the village so there was little authorities could do.

I rolled down my window.

Trooper Turner gave me a big smile. "You know why I stopped you, right, Ms. Sparks?"

"Uh . . ."

"Oh, you remember. You said you'd sign a copy of your latest book for my daughter's birthday." He shoved the book at me along with a pen.

"Shari," he said.

I personalized the book to Shari and felt relieved. I'd dodged a bullet.

I handed the book back to him. One of my fans. "I hope she likes it." I returned his smile.

"Oh, and a ticket for using the firehouse lot to make your turn."

I took the ticket. "How much is this going to cost me?"

"You can plead your case in front of the judge, and it could be dismissed."

He tipped his hat and walked to his car. When he turned to get in, the smile remained on his face. Mine slipped a bit.

I wouldn't have been in such a hurry if I wasn't running an errand for Geoffrey. I shrugged my shoulders. A business expense. I'd make Geoffrey pay the ticket.

I carefully pulled into the street and headed back toward the traffic signal which, of course, turned yellow when I approached it. The car behind me honked his horn, so I stuck my head out the window and yelled. "I'm not running a yellow light just because you're in a hurry."

I recognized the driver as our mayor. I gave him a friendly wave. No sense in crossing another official today.

I glanced at the real estate office as I sped by. It appeared empty. The "Closed" sign still hung on the door.

Driving over, I realized the caller's comment about "two keys" made sense. The manual indicated that each property owner should leave two keys to the property with the company, one for the office, the other for the employee doing the walk-thru of the premises. My caller had handed my son only one key, promising to find the other one, and he must have located it just now. No problem. I could grab the key from the owner and get right back to the office.

I checked my watch. It had taken me longer to arrive than I originally estimated it would. I glanced in the rearview mirror to make certain my hair was neat and rushed up to the front door. I knocked and waited, knocked again and waited. The third time I banged hard with my fist. Still no response. I turned the knob. The door wasn't locked, so I opened it enough that I could stick my head in.

"Sparks Properties. Hello. I'm here." I stepped inside the entryway which opened into a living room and beyond to the kitchen. There was a stairway to my left and a hallway behind it. I peered around the open stairway and down the hall. At its end I could see a home office, but there was no one in it. On the other side of the kitchen was a door, which had to lead to the garage. I walked into the kitchen, opened the door and peeked in. A small red car sat in one of the two bays. The property owner must still be here.

I called out again. "Hello. I'm here to pick up the key." I thought I heard a sound upstairs. Why didn't the owner answer my call?

Convinced someone was upstairs and might need my help, I took the stairs to the second floor and poked my head into the first two bedrooms which were empty as was the bathroom. It was then I heard a scuffling sound coming from the third bedroom at the end of the hall.

"Hello. Anyone there?" This was beginning to creep me out. I was in someone else's house, permission to invade the domicile given over the phone by someone I didn't know. I turned and fled down the hallway. Before I could descend the stairs, I heard the scuffling sounds again. Was the guy in the bedroom hurt or had he suffered a stroke or heart attack? I couldn't leave without making certain no one needed help.

"I'm coming in," I opened the door to the third bedroom and realized the fellow lying on the floor didn't care if I had invaded his privacy. He was dead, a knife in his chest.

CHAPTER 3

"**Y**OU SAY HE'S DEAD? HOW DO YOU KNOW THAT?" A sheriff's deputy met me on the front porch of the house after I had called 9-1-1.

"He's got a knife in his chest and there's a lot of blood." I gripped my hands together to keep from shaking.

"So, you're guessing."

The deputy was tall, thin, with a butch haircut. His thin lips were set in a hard line of disapproval. I guessed his age at around forty. Young whippersnapper.

"I'll show you the body." I turned to enter the house, but he reached out and grabbed my arm.

"If there is a dead body in there and he's been murdered as you believe, then I don't want you back in the house."

"I don't think he can hurt me."

He gave me a dirty look. "It's not for your safety. You'll mess up the crime scene more than you already have."

I gave a hmmph. "I touched nothing except for the front door-knob. Oh, wait. I also opened the door leading from the kitchen to the garage to look in."

"What I don't understand is what you're doing here. You told the emergency operator that you didn't know the man in the bedroom or the homeowner. That means you're trespassing, and I'd like to know why." His accusatory tone made me feel defensive which washed away most of my shock at discovering a body.

"I'm working as an interim property manager for Sparks Real Estate and Property Management, my son's and daughter-in-law's property management company. The owner called and said he had another key which the business needed, so I rushed over here on their behalf and at the request of the house owner. I mean, I assume it was the homeowner who called."

"So that's something else you're guessing about. You'll have to wait in your car until I or another deputy can question you further."

"Whatever you say." I went back to my car and watched the surly deputy enter the house. I was relieved to get away from him. Then a crime scene van pulled up and several personnel in coveralls also entered. I waited, then another county sheriff's car parked in front of me. A female officer got out, glanced my way and then walked the perimeter of the property. She met the skinny deputy in the front yard, and the two of them went in the house. I continued to wait, finally deciding I should call Abigail and Geoffrey to tell them what had happened. I was still too keyed up over what I had seen to sit in my car, so I paced back and forth in front of the property while I made the call.

Abigail answered the phone. "Where are you?"

"There was a call from one of your clients who needed to see someone from the agency ASAP."

"You left the office unattended and open."

"I took the training manual with me so no one could steal it."

"That's not the point." Abigail sounded flustered at my behavior. "Your secretary not back yet?"

"No."

"Then blame her for the office being unattended and put Geoffrey on the phone. I need to tell him something."

"You can tell me."

"Fine. If I'm right, you lost one of your clients. You'd better mark the Basset case closed. He's not having a good day, In fact, I'm certain he's dead."

I heard a bang from Abigail's end of the line, then Geoffrey came on the phone. "Sorry. Abigail dropped the phone and said something about someone being dead. Who is this?"

"Your mother. Sorry. It's my fault. I told her the Basset guy in the red house at the end of Main Street is dead."

"Heart attack?" asked Geoffrey.

"No. A knife."

"Are you okay, Mother?" asked Geoffrey.

"I've been better, but I think you'd better see to Abigail. Get her a glass of water or something. I'll be back to the office as soon as I can."

"Can't you come now?"

"I can't. I'm waiting to be questioned."

"Why would they question you?"

My suspicious deputy yelled at me and signaled me to return to my car.

"I'll get back to you." I disconnected and trotted over to the deputy. "I almost gave up on you." I slid my cellphone into my purse.

The deputy shot me another of his disapproving looks. "I thought I told you to wait here, that I had questions for you. Who were you talking to?"

"My son and daughter-in-law."

"Why?"

This guy was getting on my nerves. From my perspective, his abrupt and suspicious manner toward me wasn't doing anything to get to the bottom of this murder.

Before I could tell him my thoughts, an unmarked car pulled up behind mine and drew our attention. A fellow who looked to be in his mid-sixties got out. His hair—and he had a full head of it— was silvery gray, and he was taller than the deputy and dressed in a dark suit which fitted him as if it had been tailored for his body, a body which filled out the suit jacket with the right amount of bicep definition. The jacket was unbuttoned, and I could see that he did the pants justice too. They rode low on his hips and "muffin top" was not a word I'd apply to his flat belly. Who was this dude?

"Oh great. Here we go." The deputy's thin lips got thinner and tighter with the presence of what his expression said was an intrusion into his crime scene.

"And you are?" the man in the suit asked me.

"Possibility the murderer, sir. She appears to have been the last one to have talked with the victim." The deputy heisted his pants up and settled back on his heels, staggered back and forth then regained his balance. If he thought the pose made him appear authoritative, he was wrong. He looked like a kid playing grown-up.

"That's speculation on your part, buddy. I talked to someone on the phone before I got here, but I can't tell you if it was the man upstairs with the knife in him." I gestured to the house.

"I'm guessing some kind of a domestic argument." The deputy crossed his arms, and he gave me a smug look.

I ignored his comment. "And who are you?" I asked of our newcomer.

"I'm the interim sheriff for the county, Acting Sheriff Montgomery."

Polite as well as handsome, I thought.

"You look a little, uh, mature to be holding the position. Shouldn't you be in Florida or Arizona on a golf course?"

He laughed. "Good one. You're right. I retired from a county further north of here, but when this county lost your sheriff to an automobile accident, they pulled my sorry butt out of mothballs and here I am." He tipped his broad-brimmed hat to me and held out his hand.

I shook his hand and introduced yourself. "Madeline Sparks. Your deputy here seems to think I had something to do with the scene in there. I did not. I found the body, but I heard something upstairs, so someone may still be in the house."

"Let's take a look at the scene." Sheriff Montgomery started toward the house, but the deputy remained rooted in place, scowling at me.

"Should I arrest her?" The deputy reached for his handcuffs.

Montgomery turned with a look of disbelief on his face. "For what?"

Deputy Jumping-to-Conclusions gestured with his head toward the house. "You know. Murder."

"Unless I missed something, she had nothing to do with this. She said the guy was stabbed, but she doesn't have a drop of blood on her. The killer probably does."

Well, well, I thought to myself. The county got a smart one on its hands. Too bad Montgomery was only a temp in the sheriff's position.

"I do need to talk to you, Ms. Sparks, so if you don't mind waiting while I take a look inside . . ."

"No problem. May I call my son and daughter-in-law back to tell them I won't be returning to the business for a while?"

"Of course. I'm sure you understand I can't invite you into the house."

"I get it. I'd leave more deposits from my body and further complicate the crime scene." I gave him my pleasantest smile and connected again with the office.

The deputy stood rooted to the spot until Montgomery yelled at him "Are you coming, Deputy Stevens?"

"Maybe he can't stomach all the blood?" I said. Montgomery heard me and chuckled. The deputy gave me another scowl. I shrugged and called Geoffrey.

"Where are you, Mom?" asked Geoffrey. "We're worried about you. I was about to drive over to Basset's place to see what's happening."

"Stay where you are. I think some officers will be there soon to question you."

"Us? Why would they question us?"

"Think about it. One of your clients has been murdered, and they want to know what I was doing on site. I told them I worked for you."

"Oh, right. Can't you explain to them and leave us out of this unpleasant situation?"

"A man is dead, a man who signed a contract with your business and then called it for help of some kind. You are involved. Period." I disconnected.

Another few minutes and Sheriff Montgomery came out the front door with something in his arms. As he got closer to me, I identified the object as a large orange, quite furry cat.

"I found this guy in the bedroom closet." Montgomery petted the cat on its head while it purred loudly.

"I'll take it off to the animal shelter. They can dispose of it." Deputy Stevens reached for the cat who let go with a hiss and unsheathed claws to the deputy's hand. "He bit me!"

"Don't be silly. He scratched you because he heard what you said." I gave the cat a pat on the head and the animal purred louder and rubbed its head against my hand.

"He's a cat. He can't understand what humans say. I like dogs anyway." The deputy kicked his foot through the grass in disgruntlement.

"Maybe that's why he doesn't like you." The sheriff looked at me, one eyebrow raised in an unspoken question.

I reached out for the cat. "I'll take him home with me until we can decide what we should do."

"Now, about asking you questions? It's going to rain soon. We could go to the sheriff's department, but that means a drive for you." He looked at the sky which had darkened, and lightening flashed in the west.

"Another thunderstorm rolling in. Seems like it rains every day," I observed and added, "Fancy a cup of tea?"

He nodded.

"Follow me, and I'll put on the kettle."

Another nod, and I was on my way to talk with one of the handsomest men I'd seen in a decade.

Sheriff Montgomery removed his hat, placed it on the table inside the door and settled himself on my couch while I put on a kettle for tea and placed a bowl of water and left-over chicken breast on a paper plate on the kitchen floor for the cat.

The cat looked up at me with intelligent eyes, produced a meow I interpreted to mean, "Thank you," and gobbled up the food. He lapped up half the bowl of water and then jumped into the sheriff's lap and began to lick his fur.

As if reading my mind, the sheriff said, "You referred to the cat as a 'he.' You're assuming the cat is male?"

"Seems right, doesn't it?"

The sheriff nodded while the cat turned himself around and around on his lap, then lay down and resumed his purring.

I handed the sheriff a cup of tea and set a plate of cookies on the coffee table in front of him.

"Have one. They could be stale. I haven't baked this week." To be honest, I hadn't baked since the youngest of my children left for college and that was years ago. I was not known for being domestic.

The sheriff gave me a penetrating look.

"Okay, okay. They're not homemade. I don't bake much. Better dunk it in your tea or you might break a tooth." I then added when the intensity of his look didn't change, "Right. I don't bake at all now that there's only me in the house, Sheriff Montgomery."

"Call me Zack."

"Maddie."

He sipped his tea, ate one of my stale cookies and was in no hurry to interrogate me. His gaze traveled around the room and came to rest on the hand-carved liquor cabinet which stood along the wall at the bottom of the stairs. "Beautiful. As is the decanter."

A man with taste and manners. Instead of plunging into questioning me, he sat on my couch admiring my décor and drinking tea like an English gentleman.

"My mother gave me the brandy decanter. It was her father's.

My grandfather went to sea at an early age, rose to captain a ship and that decanter with the wide bottom was his."

He moved the cat off his lap, got up and crossed the room. He reached for the decanter. "Do you mind?"

"No, of course not."

He picked up the bottle. "Heavy and with a thick base. It would take quite a roll of a ship to topple this."

"The liquor cabinet came from Hong Kong."

He smiled, set the decanter down and resumed his seat on the couch. The cat resumed his seat on the sheriff's lap. After another sip of his tea, he leaned forward. "You get a good look at the body?"

"No. I saw it on the floor when I looked through the door of the bedroom, then I heard a noise," I nodded at the cat, "and worried the person responsible for the fellow lying there might still be in the house, so I ran."

"Very wise."

"Thank you." I hesitated a moment. "I couldn't help but see the knife in his chest and all the blood. It's only an impression because I didn't take a closer look, but I don't think I knew him."

"But you say he was the person who called you on the phone."

"No. I don't know that. I assumed it was. Who else would have called the office?"

"Time of death might tell us something."

I liked that he said "us."

"Time of death is never very exact, so . . ."

He shifted the cat out of his lap and for the first time, the look on his face turned from a friendly and charming authority to one that said, "police officer trying to solve a murder." "Now how would a lovely lady like you know that?"

"Listen, Zack, uh, Sheriff Montgomery. I write murder mysteries and I must do research for my work, so I know lots about murder, killers, victims . . ." I stopped midsentence when I saw his mouth quiver and then erupt into a smile.

"Sorry, Maddie. I know you write mysteries. I wanted to see if you'd admit it to me."

"Why not? They're durn good tales."

"My wife, now deceased, used to read your books. I read a couple of them also, although I don't have the time for reading for pleasure, if that's what you can call murder mysteries."

"I'm afraid most of my work was written with a mature female audience as its target but I am glad there's one man I've met who reads them." I thought about my recent work and realized my target audience still was the mature woman. I also wondered what Zack would think of me writing sex scenes.

"A good story is a good story." He leaned further forward on the couch.

"Sorry. What? My mind wandered."

"Did it?"

I wriggled uncomfortably in my chair. "Sure. I mean after all that happened today."

"Well, I guess I should be going anyway. I may have to talk with you again."

I jumped up from my chair. "Oh, I didn't mean to chase you away." And I didn't. I was enjoying his company. He was smart and a treat for the eye.

"I need to stop at the office to talk with the rest of the officers and see what the coroner knows."

I wanted to kick myself. The crime scene, gruesome as it was, hadn't tired or distracted me. In fact, it was the most energizing event in my life lately, discounting my newly found interest in writing love scenes, of course. I was just getting to know the sheriff and considering making him the model for the love interest in my work-in-progress, my writing, I mean.

"But," he held up one finger, "if you're free tonight, how would you like dinner at the Billinghouse Restaurant?"

CHAPTER 4

After Zack left, I paced from my front door to the kitchen door, excited about tonight's dinner date, and unsettled about the murder. I should call Geoffrey to see how he made out when the authorities came to visit him and Abigail. The cat, which Zack had left sleeping on the couch, lifted his head for a moment to eye me, then resettled into purring which drifted away into light snoring. Zack hadn't said a word about who should take care of the cat. It was likely the cat belonged to the dead man, or it had wandered into the house and gotten trapped inside the bedroom closet. Maybe I should call the shelter. Instead, I called Geoffrey and Abigail at the office. No one answered the phone, so I called their house.

Geoffrey came on the line. "Mom? I was about to phone you. The police left a half hour ago, so we closed the office and came home. I'm having a drink, and Abigail has gone to bed with a headache. What a grueling experience. Those cops treated us like we were suspects."

"Sorry to say but both of you are suspects. Me, too."

"But I'm a respected businessman."

"You're suggesting businesspeople don't kill anyone?" I asked. Sometimes Geoffrey could be somewhat nearsighted, family and business before anything else, even something as overwhelming as murder.

"I'm your son, for heaven's sake. You can't believe I'm responsible for Basset's death."

"Of course, not, dear, but the terrible truth is that it's the police's job to question anyone associated with the victim."

There was silence at his end of the line.

"Geoffrey, are you still there?"

"Yes, yes. I was refreshing my drink. Your problem, mother, is that you've spent so much time writing murder mysteries that all you can think about is the case and not about those who are victims."

"You mean like Mr. Basset?"

"I do not. I mean like innocent citizens who get caught in a police web of suspicion."

"You, you mean." I heard ice cubes tinkle through our connection. I could use something a bit stronger than tea myself.

"I mean unsuspecting citizens like Abigail and me and the people in this town who had nothing to do with the murder."

"That's a lot of folks, and you don't think any of them capable of murdering Mr. Basset? Amazing. You'd prefer to believe it was a demented bum who wandered into town and happened to pick his house and then call your office on the phone. That seems a stretch to me."

"Why don't you stop by tonight after dinner, Mom? Then we can talk."

"Uh, I'm busy tonight."

"Busy? Doing what? Not writing that story of yours? We're family and being harassed by the police. Don't you think you owe us your support?" Geoffrey's voice took on an accusatory note.

"I do support you, dear, but not tonight. By the way, do you know if Mr. Basset had a cat?"

"I don't know about any cat. Why?"

"Because now the cat found in his bedroom closet is living with me. I don't know if he was Basset's cat or belongs to a family in the neighborhood. I'm going to check that tomorrow. Someone may be missing their cat."

"Why all this fuss over a cat?"

I looked at my watch. "Gotta run. I'll be in touch tomorrow. Tell Abigail I'm sorry about her headache."

Zach would be here in less than two hours to pick me up for our date, and I had no idea what to wear. It was fortunate I'd done shopping while in the city. Buff and his friend had helped me pick out some clothing including a cranberry red dress with a neckline that fit well yet was a bit daring. Dare I wear that on my first date? Of course, I would dare. Zack had reacted favorably to my make-up and hair color and short, swingy bob. And who knows? Maybe there wouldn't be another opportunity to wear the dress. Maybe he wouldn't ask me on a second date and the dress would hang in my closet like a forgotten moth-eaten sweater.

The cat meowed, got up and stretched, then stared at me. Did it want to go out? Was the cat hungry? I was prepared for neither of those events. Back on the farm when I was growing up, we had cats, but they were barn cats, there to keep down the rat and mouse population, not really pets. I grabbed my purse, jumped in my car and drove to the store. I was unclear what supplies were necessary, but with the help of the clerk at the dollar convenience store, I came home with a litter box and the stuff to fill it, dry and canned cat food and a selection of toys.

The cat devoured the food, used the litter box and ignored all the toys no matter how hard I tried to coax it into chasing or leaping at the stuffed mice, fish, or feathers on a fishing pole. Could a new place have traumatized the poor thing? I looked at my wall clock and realized it was after five and the vet clinic had to be closed. I'd call in the morning for an appointment to have the cat checked out.

I'd dallied too long at the store and in trying to play comforter/play partner to my feline guest. In case he or it got hungry while I was out, I filled a bowl with dry food and headed up the stairs to jump into the shower. I'd shimmied into my dress and checked my hair and make-up in my bedroom mirror when I heard the cat let out a loud yowl. I rushed down the stairs, assuming it was lonely or distraught or . . . sitting in front of the door, looking at it. The doorbell rang. My date! I hoped the fancy designer deodorant I bought wouldn't fail me. I was as nervous as a . . . well, you know, a cat. Cat and I answered the door together. I smiled at Zack. The cat began a loud purr and wrapped itself around Zack's legs, weaving in and out in a frenzy of adoration. Why didn't Zack take the cat? The animal adored him. Why had I become its foster parent?

Zack handed me a bouquet of flowers. So sweet.

"You look, uh, breathtaking." He stepped back and took my hand spinning me around and making the skirt of my dress swirl out to reveal another of my assets, a new pair of shoes.

"I'll put these in water." I grabbed a vase from under the sink, arranged the bouquet in water and set it on the table. The cat jumped up and began nibbling at the flowers.

"Didn't you feed him?" Zack grabbed the cat and placed him on the floor.

"I did. He thought the flowers were for him, I guess." I gave Zack the once over, in a friendly way, of course. He was dressed in tan slacks, a brown sports coat with a thin, light blue stripe in it, white shirt and blue tie. He smelled as good as he looked. A woodsy scent, very masculine. Of course, the yumminess of his appearance provoked my writer's imagination, so I removed his jacket and was about to unbutton his shirt when his voice interrupted my thoughts.

"Are you alright?" asked Zack. "You've got a funny look on your face."

"Fine. I'm fine. Just worried the cat might get sick eating the flowers. I'll put them in my bedroom and close the door. "Back in a jiffy." I grabbed the vase and ran up to my room.

Back in the living room, I threw my gray shawl around my shoulders, and Zack and I started out the door. The cat meowed what sounded like "Goodbye." Its amber eyes stared up at me as if cautioning me not to stay out too late.

"Did you hear something?" I asked Zack, He shook his head. I shook mine. Cats don't talk, and I don't speak felinese. What was happening to me? I must have been more upset about seeing a dead body than I thought.

IT WAS TUESDAY NIGHT, so the restaurant wasn't busy. Zack had reserved a table for us overlooking the back garden bathed now in the golden light from a sun low in the sky. The afternoon shower had left drops of rain on the flowers and leaves causing them to sparkle like gems.

"You look as if you want to ask me a question, Maddie."

"I do. A silly one."

"Not about the murder then, is it?"

"It's about the cat. We both have referred to the cat as he. Is it a male? I mean, how can you tell or are you guessing?"

A red blush crept over his cheeks. "I didn't examine him if that's what you're asking. I'm just guessing. The cat seems like a guy, I guess."

"Well, I'm taking it or him to the vet tomorrow for a check-up."

"Is he, uh, the cat hurt?"

"No. I think he misses his human or where the cat lived, or he may have witnessed the murder and it left a scar on him, emotionally speaking, that is. My friends who are cat people say cats can be extremely sensitive."

"Listen, you don't have to do this. Like the deputy said, we can take the cat to the local shelter."

I tapped my nail on my water glass. "That doesn't seem right. If the cat is grieving for the human who cared for it, tossing it in a cage would be cruel. I'll see if the cat is microchipped. If not, I'll visit the neighbors to determine if it belonged to Mr. Basset or was someone else's pet."

"You're a good person, Maddie." He reached across the table and squeezed my hand.

"I'm older than you, you know, by quite a bit, I'd guess."

He leaned back and scrutinized my face. "Are my intentions so obvious?"

"Are mine?"

"Nope. I can't read you at all. I was surprised you accepted my dinner invitation."

"I was kinda surprised you asked me out."

"You are a beautiful, mature woman, Maddie Sparks. And I'm a mature man with good taste. Let's leave the age difference at that."

The waiter came and we ordered wine. While we perused the menus, I looked up and said, "About sixty-five?"

He smiled across the table at me. "Close enough."

"Yeah. I'm around there, too."

And I was around sixty-five, plus a few years or so. I couldn't care if he was thirty-five. I could tell the guy liked me. I could also tell he was enough of a seasoned police officer to know I was lying about my age, and he didn't care. Neither did I.

The remainder of the evening flew by. We covered family issues. His wife had died several years ago, and he had one daughter now living with her husband in Seattle, Washington.

"I don't get to see her but once a year and I miss her." He sipped his wine and looked out the window. I could see his eyes were full of unshed tears and understood there was more to the story, but I would not push it unless he was ready to talk. He cleared his throat and asked, "What about you? I understand Geoffrey is your son, but are there other children?"

"Yes. One. A younger son, grown. He lives nearby also, but Geoffrey is the one I see the most. My husband and I are divorced, have been for years." I hesitated. There was more I could have said also, but I left it for another time.

"And writing murder mysteries? How did you get into that?"

"I suspect the same way you got interested in murder in your line of work."

He looked startled, drew back and seemed about to deny there were similarities between writing about murder and it being one's profession. I jumped in before he could say anything.

"It's a puzzle, don't you think? An important one. For you, the most important one to solve so that the victim's families know what happened and the criminals pay for the crime. For me, it's much the same. Who would do such a horrible thing? As someone said once about mysteries, writers of them create a world where there's always a happy ending and the criminals pay for their deeds." I paused to gather my thoughts. "Well, there's a difference. In real life, some crimes go unpunished, the criminals never found. That's the part of your job I couldn't tolerate. It must be sad."

"As you well know from all the research you must do, criminals are not smart people. Most of the time they meet a just end." He reached across the table and took my hand. "This case may be one of those where I don't get my man."

"I doubt that."

"Thanks for your vote of confidence, but that's not what I mean. I may get pulled from the case before it's wrapped up. My assignment is temporary until the election in the fall."

"Oh. That's too bad."

"But we can still see each other if you'd like."

I did like. I liked very much.

We ordered coffee and split a dessert, my concession to having stolen that cruller from Geoffrey this morning.

When Zack dropped me off at the end of our evening, he walked me to the door and gave me a peck on the cheek. What a sweet man. And so sexy too.

I CALLED THE LOCAL VETERINARY CLINIC the next morning and made an appointment for the cat that afternoon. While I gulped down a cup of coffee and ate a piece of toast, I called the sheriff's office and asked for Deputy Stevens but was told he was out on a case.

"Is there anyone there who was at the murder scene yesterday who I could ask a question of?" I could have talked with Zack, I suppose, but I didn't want him to think I was too eager to contact him or too nosy about the deceased.

"What is this in reference to? Do you have information pertaining to the crime?" asked the officer on the other end.

Well, rats! Now I'd gotten myself stuck in police bureaucracy.

"No. It's about the cat."

"Cat?"

"The one in the bedroom."

"Just a minute."

Oh, oh. Worse than bureaucracy. Now I knew the person thought I was a crazy calling.

"Oh, look. Never mind." I disconnected.

My phone rang not a minute later.

"There's phone ID on all calls coming in here, you know." It was Zack.

"I didn't."

"You can talk to me any time you want." His voice was filled with friendly innuendo.

"I didn't want to talk to you." Well, I did, but not for the reason he was implying. And here I thought he would think I was going too fast in our relationship, or whatever it could be called.

"Oh, I see." He sounded disappointed.

"It's not that I don't want to talk to you. I do, but I was calling about the cat."

"Is there something wrong with him?"

"Other than being hungry all the time, I don't think so."

"Good."

"I wanted to know if Deputy Stevens saw any evidence of a cat living in the house. Litter box, food bowls, toys? Or did you?"

"I didn't. I'll ask the deputy when he returns. He's out in the field.

So, you're trying to determine if the cat belonged to our victim."

"From everything I've heard and not being a cat owner myself, I understand cats don't belong to anyone. Rather they allow humans to take care of them."

He laughed. "Well, you might be the cat's new servant."

I chuckled.

There was an uncomfortable silence on the line.

Zack cleared his throat. "Uh, would you be insulted if I invited myself to tea again this afternoon? I mean, assuming you'll be home."

"About four?"

"I'll bring cookies."

"That'll be the only way you get something to eat with your tea."

We said goodbye, then I got back on the phone and called Geoffrey's office to see how he and Abigail fared with questioning by the police.

Abigail answered. "A skinny deputy came by yesterday and questioned us. He was so rude."

"I know who you mean. He was first to respond to my call. His name is Stevens."

"He said he might have more questions for us. He acted as if we knew something about Basset's murder. As if."

"Don't worry, sweetie. It's just police procedure to get information about the victim."

I heard Abigail give a sigh of relief.

"That's reassuring, Mom. I guess research for your mysteries has provided you with information about such investigations." Abigail paused for a moment and then asked, "Did you take the training manual from the office?

"Yes, I have it in my car."

"I assumed you had a chance to study it last night."

I didn't want to tell her I'd spent the evening out with the county sheriff. "Sorry. I was so exhausted after finding Mr. Basset that I went to bed early."

"Well, if you could get around to it today and then pop into the office for the test, we can proceed with more house inspections."

"Uh . . ."

"You aren't going to back out of this, are you, just because you found a dead body your first time out? Summer is prime time for vacations and people count on us to manage their properties."

"I'll stop by this afternoon. Is Geoffrey there?"

"I'll put him on."

"Hi, Mom. What a day yesterday was. I hope today's better."

"I'm sure it will be. I have confidence the authorities will find the killer."

"Do you?"

"Yes. The county has a new man on the job as sheriff. I met him yesterday. He seems very competent."

"You met him?"

"Yes. At Basset's house." Before Geoffrey asked too many questions and I said too much about the acting sheriff, I said, "Got to go, Geoffrey. I'll see you this afternoon."

Next, I wanted to talk to Mr. Basset's neighbors to determine whose cat I was fostering and then it was off to the vet followed by a stop at the property management office. If I had time before Zack stopped in for tea, I would spend it writing. Whew! What a day I had ahead of me. I jumped into a pair of slacks and my new blue flowered blouse and set out to track down the cat's owners, er, parents or hired help, or whatever.

When I rang the bell at the place north of the Basset house, no one answered. The garage door was open and there was no car in it or in the driveway. I walked past the victim's house to the neighbor on the other side, an older woman who was working in her front yard cutting back her climbing roses. Her hair was short, white and curly. She had tied it off her face with a blue bandanna and wore a loose tee-shirt and faded jeans. She looked up from her work when I called hello.

"Darn roses are getting out of hand. I should git rid of 'em. I'm known around here for my winning roses at the county fair, so I've got a reputation to uphold. I wish the durn things didn't bite."

"Well, don't let me stop you. I'm Maddie Sparks. I have a question you might be able to answer."

"Hi. Jane Tremble. I thought you looked familiar. I've seen you around the village, haven't I?"

"Yes. You look familiar, too. I'm surprised we haven't met before."

"You're that writer, aren't you? And you were here yesterday, weren't you?"

Interesting. If she noticed me what with all the police presence and other people hovering around the house, she might be astute or, like me, nosy enough to have seen other things of interest.

"I was checking the property. I work for my son and his wife. They own the local real estate and property management company."

"I wondered. I saw you drive up and go into the house."

How much should I tell her? Did I confess I was the one to find the body? She appeared to be a hardy, country woman. Her hands looked rough from hard work, and, despite her small stature, she gave the impression of someone who wasn't easily upset.

"I was the one who found the body."

"Did you now? Listen, uh, Maddie. I've worked up a sweat here. How about an iced tea? We can sit on my back deck. It's shady back there and you can ask your question and tell me all about yesterday."

"Cat," she said, as we sipped our tea. "Well, I'm not sure he had a cat. There are always cats wandering through this neighborhood. People should keep them indoors. Safer for the cat, you know. So, you're taking care of a cat that was hiding in the bedroom? Have the authorities questioned the animal yet?" She grinned at her joke.

I shook my head. "I've got to see if any of the deceased's relatives or friends knows if the cat was his. If it wasn't, then it lives somewhere else, and someone is missing their pet." I opened my mouth to ask another question, but Jane read my mind before I could ask it.

"I do keep an eye on the neighborhood as you must have guessed, but I never noticed a cat at his house. As for friends and relatives of his, I saw few people come to his house. He wasn't a very friendly gent. Always yelling at the kids in the neighborhood for making too much noise. Kids make noise because they're kids. He never participated in block parties. The man kept to himself. I always said hello to him when I saw him outside, but he barely replied and never stopped to chat. I got the message. I left him alone. Most people around here did." She nodded toward my glass.

"No, no. I'm fine."

"There was one thing, however. Yesterday I was surprised when your car drove up to his house, but you weren't the first one to stop by. There was another person who pulled into his drive before you came by."

"I don't suppose you saw the make of the car, color, license plate?'

"It was a black sedan and there was writing on the side. Come to think of it, I thought it was from your son's business, but I got distracted when my phone rang. I guess your son came by before you, huh?"

Did he? I wondered why.

CHAPTER 5

I'D RUN INTO A DEAD END in my inquiries about the cat unless I wanted to ask the neighbors across the street and farther down the block.

"Quiet street," I said to Jane as we were saying our goodbyes on her front lawn.

"Everyone here works days, so you won't find them home at this hour. I can ask around about the cat if you like."

That would save me a bit of work. "Sure. Let me give you my cell number." I jotted the number down on a slip of paper from my purse and handed it to her. "Let's do tea some afternoon."

"My gardening owns me as I bet your writing does you. I don't get a chance to get out much. I wanted to join the historical society here in town, but I always miss their meetings."

"There's one this coming Thursday afternoon. How about I stop by and give you a ride?"

"You're a real peach, Maddie."

And Jane could be a font of information about folks around here. She might remember something more about Mr. Basset or locate the person who would claim the cat. Besides, I liked this woman on contact and wanted to get to know her better.

Despite Zach volunteering to bring the cookies to our teatime this afternoon, I decided I should be a better host than that, so I stopped by the store and bought a dozen of their chocolate chip cookies which were close to homemade. They were better than anything I could put together in the few hours I had left before Zack came by. I had promised myself I would get at least five hundred words in on my writing this afternoon, and I was determined to stick to that pledge. It had been four or five months since I began a new project, and just because this one was in another genre didn't mean I could be less disciplined than when I wrote my cozy mysteries. I also had the appointment with the vet and then a stop at Abigail and Geoffrey's for that test. Time would be tight, but I'd fit everything in.

My fingers danced over the keyboard until I came to a scene where my protagonist and her soon-to-be lover were to have one of their lovemaking encounters. I wanted something jazzy, exciting, different. Let's see. He could make love to her while she perched on the back of the sofa, like making love on a kitchen counter but much more comfortable for this older couple. Would that work, I wondered. The way to find out was to try it. I was short while my protagonist was tall, so I grabbed the step stool from the back room, placed it behind the sofa and climbed up on it, placing my derriere onto the sofa back. It felt like it might work. I arched my back as if my lover were bending over me and . . . toppled backwards onto the sofa, my legs in the air against the back cushions, my hands at my sides. There was nothing to grab onto to get myself upright. A more agile and younger person could have extracted herself by throwing her legs over her torso and doing a backbend onto the couch. But that wasn't an option for someone my age. I hadn't been that flexible for decades. Because my protagonist was an older woman, I assumed she might not be as spry as a twenty something gal. Unless I made her a retired circus performer, she could wrench her back, or she might pull her partner down on top of her resulting in injury to both. I lay with my shoulders against the seat cushions, my legs in the air and stared up at the ceiling.

The rush of blood should be good for thinking, but the pain in my neck blocked my creative juices.

I heard the front door open and someone yell, "Hello."

It was my granddaughter who came into the living room and looked startled to see me in my strange position.

"Yoga?" she asked.

"No, Sara. Help me up from here. I'm stuck."

She came around the couch and stared down at me.

"What are you doing, Grammy?"

"Writing."

"Wouldn't it be easier at your desk?"

"Don't be impertinent. Give me your hand and pull or push or roll me onto my side. Anything."

Sara gently swiveled my legs to one side while also taking my hand and sliding me across the seat cushions. I lay on the couch and struggled to catch my breath.

"I like to try out any moves I'm not familiar with before I put them down on the page."

Sara ran into the kitchen and returned with a glass of water.

"What's this?" I pulled myself to a sitting position.

"Water."

"There's a chilled bottle of white wine in the fridge."

Sara returned with two wine glasses and the bottle.

"You are old enough to drink, aren't you?"

"You know I'm over twenty-one. What about you, Gram?" She poured the wine and held up her glass in a toast.

"Me too. Cheers." Nothing like a cold, white wine when you discover you were right about a scene that includes a passion between the male and female characters.

"So, are we celebrating your not putting yourself in the hospital, or is there something else afoot here?" Sara was my one grandchild, Geoffrey and Abigail's daughter. My other son wasn't married. Sara took after no one in the family although her parents worried she was more like me than not. She did not look like me. She was tall and slim with shiny golden hair and long, graceful fingers. If she reminded anyone of me, it was in her endless curiosity about life. Like her parents, I worried her inquisitiveness would get her into a situation that took some doing to get out of. That had been my experience over the years as I stuck my nose into too many places it shouldn't be. I did manage to extract myself from those messes, even from a bad marriage to a man I was passionate about and who was passionate about anything in skirts.

I took another sip of wine. What the hell. I needed to share my interest in writing a hot, sexy novel with someone who could appreciate it. Sara was just the person.

I got up from the sofa, slowly because my back felt a little tender, went into my office and grabbed my laptop from my desk. "Read this."

"Oh, Gram. Another cozy? You don't need me to critique your work. There are plenty of folks who love your characters, setting and convoluted plots."

What she didn't say was that she found my cozies yawners.

"This is different. Try it."

I watched her as she read. A blush crept up her cheeks making them rosier than usual, but she didn't lift her gaze from the screen. Her breathing became shallow and quick. Then she gasped.

"Too much?"

Sara looked across the coffee table at me, her eyes wide and round. There had always been love in those eyes, but now her look was filled with something I couldn't identify.

"Oh, Gram. This is . . ., this is . . ."

"Spit it out, will you. It's racy and provocative. Right?"

"Right, right. And I love it."

I sank into my chair and felt a tear roll down my cheek. "That's what I needed to hear."

"Dad said you were working on something else, and he implied he'd read a bit of it and said it was awful."

"He would think this was terrible, wouldn't he?"

She nodded. "Sometimes I wonder if I'm adopted. My parents are so uptight about sex. Do you know where they got that attitude?"

"Well, not from me, dearie. Maybe from your grandfather." Although, given his philandering ways, I doubted that.

"Is that why you divorced him?" The question seemed to tumble out of her mouth. "Oh, sorry, Gram. That's none of my business, is it?"

"You might as well know the truth. Other women." I waved my hand in the air as if I could somehow erase my words or swat them out the window. "Everything turned out fine in the end." Why was I telling Sara a lie? Things did not turn out well, not for him, not for me and not for his second wife. But Sara had no need to know that.

"I never met my grandfather. "

"No, but you have your mother's parents. They've more than made up for missing one grandfather."

Sara jumped off the couch and grabbed me in a hug. "And you, Gram. You're the best grandmother there ever was. You're smart and talented, funny and beautiful, even more beautiful now that you're doing your hair this new way. And now I find out you're sexy, too."

For a moment it appeared my granddaughter was thinking about what I wrote. "Oh, you're not assuming I do the things I write, are you? This is not autobiographical."

"It could be. You need to get out there and have fun. It appears you're capable of it."

"Having that kind of fun requires a partner," I said.

"I'm sure you'll find someone." Sara's tone was teasing, and her eyes twinkled with merriment.

"Around here? The men my age are either in a retirement facility or over there." I pointed toward the village cemetery.

"Why do you assume you need to find someone your age? How about a younger man?"

The doorbell rang. I looked at my watch and realized the

afternoon had gotten away from me. Had Zack arrived early? He was a younger man. Why not?

"Are you expecting company, Gram?"

"A friend is supposed to stop by for tea. Sit tight. I'd like the two of you to meet."

I swung open the front door, expecting to see Zack's smiling face, but instead he looked grim.

"Bad day at the office?" I reached for his hand and pulled him in the door. "I have what you need. Come in and meet my granddaughter. Sara, this is our acting county sheriff, Zack Montgomery."

Zack removed his hat and stepped into the living room. Sara popped off the couch and put out her hand. She raised one eyebrow at me in a suggestive manner.

"We're having wine instead of tea. Or would you prefer tea? It won't take a minute."

"I forgot my contribution to the afternoon, the cookies." He looked embarrassed, as if not bringing the cookies was a major social faux pas.

"Cheese and crackers go better with wine, anyway. How could you know there was a change in menu?" I gestured for him to take a seat on the couch.

"I'll have to take a pass on the wine," he said.

I put my hand over my mouth and gave a little giggle. "How silly of me. Of course. You're working."

Zack continued standing, nervously fidgeting with the brim of his hat. "It's not that. Well, it is, but there's something I need to tell you."

"Please sit down. If you won't have wine, I can make us a pot of tea."

Zack sat on the edge of the couch and continued playing with his hat brim. "We're questioning Geoffrey for Basset's murder."

"What?" Sara and I spoke as one.

"I know this is a bad way to tell you the news, but . . ."

"A bad way? It's the worst way. And it's absolute rubbish. My son can't even kill a spider in the bathroom. Abigail has to do it.

He'd never kill anyone. Never! Now get the hell out of my house." I pointed at the door he'd just entered.

"I'm sorry, Maddie," he said, "I was doing . . ."

"I know. You were doing your job, but your job puts us at odds right now."

He held out his hand to me. I ignored the gesture. He frowned, set his hat back on his head, arose and left.

After the door closed, I ran over to it and kicked it with my foot. "Ouch. I think I broke my toe." I hopped around the room on one foot. Damn. It did hurt, almost as much as having to toss Zack out of my house.

"Sit down and let me look at it, Gram. Then I think we should call Mom to see what's going on."

The landline in the kitchen rang. It was the vet's office informing me I'd missed my appointment earlier this afternoon.

"Uh, something came up."

"Would you like to reschedule?" asked the perky sounding voice at the other end of the connection.

"I'll get back to you." Abrupt and not as pleasant as I should have been, but the cat could wait. Right now, I needed to see about Geoffrey. I grabbed my sweater from the hook next to the door and looked around for my car keys.

The phone rang again.

"I'll get it." Sara started toward the phone, but I pushed past her and hobbled over to it.

It was Abigail. "We were about to get in touch with you," I said.

"I'm at the county jail. I didn't know what to do, so I called our attorney. The authorities have been questioning him. They think he killed our client, Mr. Basset." Abigail's voice quavered.

"I know. The sheriff just left here. I booted his buns out when he told me."

"Why would they think he killed Mr. Basset?" She began to sob.

"Listen, can anyone hear you, Abigail? This isn't something you should talk about within earshot of the authorities."

Her sobbing turned into accusatory yelling. "You can't believe Geoffrey is responsible for that horrid man's death, can you? What kind of a mother are you?"

"Please don't scream at me through the phone. I'm trying to tell you not to talk with anyone at the jail. Do you think Geoffrey knows to keep his mouth shut?" I rethought my question. No. Geoffrey was a blabber. Pressure from authority figures could make him confess to crimes he'd never heard of committed a century ago.

There was silence on the other end of the line, then Abigail's voice came through in a whisper. "When they took him, he said he could explain everything, the argument with Mr. Basset and his visit to the house before you found the body."

"But he went off with you to lunch while I remained in the office. That's how I took the call. Didn't you tell them you and Geoffrey were together?" My newest friend Jane told me she had seen the company car at Basset's house, but she had to have been mistaken. He couldn't have gone to Basset's house. And what's this about an argument?

Abigail said nothing for a moment. "Geoffrey dropped me off at lunch, said he had an errand to run, and asked me to pick up a sandwich for him."

"But he came right back, right?"

"Well, soon enough. He told me when he returned that he had stopped by Basset's house. He knew I'd learn about the visit because he talked to the postal carrier when he was there. That must have been how the authorities found out about his presence at Basset's. I always thought the post office hired nosy carriers."

Our acting sheriff knew his business. Clever of him to talk with the carrier who delivered mail in the mornings in Basset's neighborhood.

"I don't think the carrier was being nosy, Abigail. If the sheriff's office talked to him, he had to tell them what he saw on his route." Why didn't I keep my mouth shut? I knew my reasonable approach to the situation was the last thing Abigail wanted or needed to hear right now.

There was a muffled noise at the other end of the connection as if Abigail had placed her hand over her phone. "Our lawyer arrived. I've got to go."

Sara leaned into me, trying to pick up what her mother was saying. "What's going on?"

I explained to her what had happened and then added, "I think we should go down to the county jail. Your father is going to need more than a real estate attorney to get himself out of this one."

After Sara assured herself that my toe was not broken but merely bruised from my having kicked the door behind Zack, she insisted upon driving to the jail. Unlike either of her parents, she was always a level-headed young woman, and I appreciated that. Between the two of us I was certain we could sort this out and get her father home. I knew Geoffrey was incapable of doing harm to anyone, except for occasional comments that hurt people's feelings. He sometimes spoke without thinking, and that had to have been what his tiff with Basset was all about.

We found a parking place right in front of the jail and hurried into the building where we encountered an officer in the brown and tan uniform of the county.

"Please state your business." He blocked our entrance to the offices.

"I'm here to see my son. There's been a terrible mistake. He's been detained for a crime he didn't commit." I heard myself speak and realized I sounded like one of the characters in my novels.

"Name?" he asked.

"Mine or his?"

"Let me handle this, Gram." Sara stepped in front of me and looked up into the officer's face. "You don't remember me, Stan? We were in the same class in high school."

His face reddened and he scuffled his feet around. "Yeah, but my job is to take down names and ask your business."

"Don't be so officious, Stanley Angeletti. You know my father is Geoffrey Sparks. My gram and I are here to see him."

"You can't, I'm afraid. He's being interviewed."

"And my mom? Where is she? She called us from here. And don't tell me you don't know who I'm talking about. She was the chaperone at the senior prom who found you and your date kissing behind the fake sand dune." Sara turned to me. "The prom theme was "A Beach Paradise." Sarah paused and turned to face the officer again. "And both of you were drunk."

I held up one finger. "Oh, right. I remember that. It made the local newspaper. You should be ashamed with your background to wear that county police officer's uniform. You must have hidden your criminal history to have been hired as a sheriff's deputy." I was kidding him, of course, but it made him uncomfortable, which might work to our advantage.

"Uh, I'm not a deputy. I'm a guard, Mrs. Sparks."

I turned to Sara. "They have no standards for hiring personnel here, do they?"

At that moment, Zach emerged from behind the door that led to the back of the jail.

I huffed when I saw him. "That's an example of what I mean. No hiring standards at all."

Zack held out his hand to me. "Maddie, I know you're furious at me, but I can explain." He tried to draw me aside, but I heard Abigail yell from the end of the hallway to my left.

I rushed to her and put my arms around her. "Where were you?"

"Mom." Sara joined in on the embrace. "Are you okay? What's happening with Dad?"

"Ask him." Abigail pointed with a trembling finger at Zack. "He's the one responsible."

I turned on Zack in a fury. "You said he'd been taken in, but you didn't say you were the one who took him in."

"Tell me the truth, Gram. Is this the guy you were seen with the other night in the Billinghouse restaurant?" Curiosity, not anger filled Sara's eyes.

"So, it's already around town, is it?" I asked.

"You're dating this man?" asked Abigail. "Your son and I won't have it. We won't."

"Abigail, I'm over thirty years older than you are."

"Yes, and you have about fifty years less sense. Is this the reason you got your hair and make-up done and bought new clothes? He must be years younger than you."

"Mom, sit down a minute, would you? This is not the time to sort this out. We need to focus on Dad." Sara led her mother to a bench located further down the hallway. I followed.

"You got yourself all gussied up for that man. How could you?" Abigail slumped back on the bench.

"That's not what happened. I . . ." As I began to explain, Geoffrey emerged from the back of the jail led by his lawyer. Mr. Pembroke, and a uniformed officer.

"We need to talk, Maddie." Zack took my arm and directed me away from Abigail and Sara.

Geoffrey saw me with Zack and yelled, "What are you thinking, Mom? He's the reason I'm here. Whose side are you on?"

"Yes," said Abigail, coming to life again and jumping up from the bench she had used as a fainting couch.

"Gram," said Sarah.

"Mrs. Sparks," said Stanley the guard.

"Maddie," said Zack.

"WILL EVERYONE PLEASE SHUT UP SO I CAN THINK?" My loud voice, one I had mastered years ago breaking up fights when my boys were kids, silenced all of them.

I held up my hand hoping I could keep them quiet. Everyone closed their mouth. I withdrew my phone from my purse and tapped a contact.

"Who are you calling, Maddie?" Zack whispered.

"Richard. He's Geoffrey's younger brother and a criminal defense attorney."

Zack smiled as if he approved. How dare he act supportive of my actions? I wanted to punch him for being so sensitive and caring.

Chapter 6

I WALKED AWAY FOR PRIVACY TO TALK with Geoffrey's younger brother. "Hello, my dear. Sorry to bother you, but we've got a situation you could help with." I explained to Richard, who lived in the next county east of here.

"I'll be there in less than a half hour."

I heard a noise at his end of the connection. "Richard, are you laughing?"

"Well, yes. Sorry, Mom, but Geoffrey is the last person I'd believe was capable of killing someone, unless you count boring a person to death with stories about his golf score."

We ended the call, and I walked back to Geoffrey and his lawyer.

"Mr. Pembroke, the family wants to thank you for your time, but I've called my son Richard who is a criminal defense attorney."

The worry lines in Pembroke's face smoothed in an expression of relief at the news. He gave Geoffrey a pat on the back, a hardy handshake and bolted for the door.

"You can use the room down the hall to wait for your attorney." Zack gestured toward an open door. "I'll lead the way. Walk with me, Maddie."

He leaned close to me. "I don't think I'm too young for you." His voice was low and inviting, not at all sheriffy.

"I don't think that's the problem. It's your duplicitous nature that I find aggravating."

"Explain." He seemed puzzled by my characterization of him.

"You try to become my friend, but then you take my son into custody for something he had nothing to do with."

"I don't see the two as connected. I am the sheriff, at least for now. What do you expect me to do?"

"Don't show up at my house after the arrest and think you're getting tea from me."

"I wanted to tell you in person what happened, so I took advantage of our tea arrangement."

"You didn't even bring the cookies you promised." I stopped midstride and stepped toward him, giving him my best you're-a-bad-boy look, the one that always made my children back down.

He didn't flinch. "That's why you're so angry? Because of the cookies?"

I watched the side of his mouth twitch in a small grin.

"Okay, Maddie. I get it, but there's evidence, you know."

Now I was interested. I needed to retain my relationship with this guy, especially if I could find out more about the Basset case and what they had against Geoffrey. What was I thinking? I couldn't butt into a criminal case. I was a writer, not a detective, wasn't I?

"Big deal. Geoffrey stopped by Mr. Basset's house, and they had some kind of a disagreement. Property stuff, I'd guess."

"There's more."

"Like what?" I moved closer to Zack and gazed up at him, trying for a look of innocence. It didn't work.

"You know I can't tell you that, Maddie, so don't try to wheedle it out of me with feigned naivete."

"How about tea and homemade cookies?"

He shook his head.

"Wine, cheese and crackers?"

He shook it again.

"Pot roast?"

"No."

"Steak?"

"Nope."

"I pay for a dinner out?"

"Uh, uh."

I tapped my foot and thought for a minute.

"How about sex?"

He blinked and opened his mouth, then leaned close enough that his mustache tickled my ear. "Are you sexually harassing an officer of the law?"

"Yes, I am. How about it?"

"I could charge you and arrest you. If I had a pair of handcuffs on me, I'd slap them on your wrists." His eyes twinkled.

"But you don't, so borrow Stanley's. He's got a set."

"Maddie, you are shameless."

"Yes, I am. I'm trying to help my son."

He stepped back and gave me a hard look which I might have worried about had the twinkle gone out of his eyes, but it did not.

"So, this conversation is about your son and not about us?"

Well, of course it was about Geoffrey. But now he didn't believe I found him the least bit attractive, although I did and I would jump into bed with him in a second if . . . well, if things were different.

"This is a stupid conversation." I turned away and grabbed Geoffrey's hand. "Your brother will be here soon. Until then, don't say a thing to the cops, especially to this guy." I gestured with my head toward Zack. Out of the corner of my eye I saw that smile again. The man was so, so, annoying. And he was something else that I didn't want to think about right now.

Zack directed us into a small, windowless room that smelled of old varnish. It contained a table, four chairs and another two folding chairs against the far wall. The tabletop was made of pressboard and had gouges in places. A recording device sat on the table, but I spotted no one-way mirror. I shot Zack a questioning look.

"This isn't our interrogation room. We confer with people here."

"So, Geoffrey isn't being charged then?" I asked.

"Not at this point. No. Have a seat everyone." Zack pulled back a chair for me, but I chose to take the one on the other side of the table. I resisted resting my arms on the tabletop. It looked sticky.

We all remained silent until there was a knock on the door, and it opened. Richard, my attorney son stepped into the room. "So, what's this I hear about murder and my brother?"

Richard was handsome, smart and his smile showed off even, white teeth, the result of braces when he was younger and good oral hygiene, or so I suspected, in adulthood. Although there was a time pre-divorce when I thought his father was a looker, I liked to believe Richard took after me and not his father. He had his father's blue eyes and light brown hair which flopped boyishly over his forehead reminding me of his father's when he was Richard's age. But Richard was reliable, honest and steady. If I needed anything, I knew Richard would come through for me. He honed this already appealing image by working out, volunteering for various local, regional and state organizations and told me he had a shot at being considered for head of the state bar association. I wouldn't be surprised if he tried a run for a seat in the state legislature. For a criminal defense attorney, he was well respected by his colleagues and his reputation was untainted by the usual belief that criminal defense attorneys got the guilty off. Although Geoffrey respected and loved his brother, I knew he also was jealous of his success, and Richard made him nervous.

"I didn't do it" Geoffrey jumped out of his chair and grabbed his brother by the arm.

"Of course, you didn't, brother." Richard's tone was reassuring, exactly what Geoffrey needed right now.

Geoffrey let out a sigh of relief to hear his brother didn't think he was a killer, but I suspected he was at the same time offended that Richard's tone implied absurdity at the thought Geoffrey was capable of anything more serious than a parking ticket.

"Tell me, sheriff, what is going on here?" Richard sat his brief-case on the floor and settled into a chair at the end of the table, legs crossed in an attitude of relaxation as if he was entertaining visitors in his living room and not listening to the case against his brother in a county sheriff's department. He picked at a piece of nonexistent lint on his silk and wool blend trousers. As his mother, I could see he was on high alert, but feigning noncha-lance. In college, Richard had been torn between becoming a lawyer or an actor.

Zack explained about the murder and the circumstances sur-rounding the suspicion that Geoffrey could have been involved.

"I can explain what I was doing at the house." Geoffrey once more popped out of his chair.

Richard shot him a stern look and gestured for him to sit down. "Say nothing."

Zack finished his story, indicating the timing and circumstances of Geoffrey's visit to the house warranted picking up Geoffrey and questioning him. I searched the expression on Zack's face. It didn't convince me he thought Geoffrey was guilty. Hmm.

Richard was quiet for a moment, then he stood and bent down for his briefcase. "Let's go, everyone." Zack didn't try to stop him. "You've got no case, you know, so until you do, I assume you won't be bothering the family again." He shook Zack's hand, then steered Geoffrey and the rest of us out of the room.

"Maddie." Zack stepped in front of me as I started to follow my sons, granddaughter and Abigail out of the room.

I stopped. What did he want now?

"Now that all of this is taken care of, can we reschedule our tea?'

The man was incorrigible. He'd taken my son into custody and questioned him about a murder, and he thought we could go on as if nothing happened?

"What do you think?" I stepped around him, then turned my back on him.

Outside, I caught up to everyone.

"We need to talk." Richard may have meant a conversation between Geoffrey and him, lawyer to client, but I intervened.

"Oh, yes, we do. I want an explanation, Geoffrey, for why you didn't tell me you dropped by Basset's place the day he was killed. C'mon, everybody. My place. I've got cookies and tea."

"This conversation should be between Geoffrey and me." Richard used his lawyerly voice.

"Geoffrey will tell everyone what was said anyway." I grabbed Sara's hand and pulled her toward the car.

"Mom always gets what she wants, doesn't she?" I heard Richard say as Sara and I got into the car.

Not always, I thought. I wanted Zack to be what I fantasized him as, not as the sheriff who wanted to arrest my son for murder.

BACK AT MY HOUSE, EVERYONE SETTLED IN with a cup of tea although I didn't divulge that there was wine in my cup. Geoffrey reached for another of my cookies, but Abigail pulled the plate out of his reach. I shot her a supportive smile for tending to Geoffrey's weight issues, but then replaced it with a scowl when she took two more cookies for herself.

The cat presented himself at the top open staircase and yowled.

Everyone glanced up at the landing.

"What is that?" asked Abigail.

"It's a cat. I think he's hungry. I'll be right back." I scurried to the kitchen cupboard to get a can of cat food.

"Oh, good heavens. First, she gets herself tangled up with that sheriff and now she's adopted a cat. The woman is coming unhinged." Abigail wrung her hands in despair.

I carried a dish of cat food to the landing and placed it in front of the cat.

"There now. He's all settled. I didn't want him to get worked up with so many strangers in the house." I gave everyone a reassuring smile, hoping we could move on from the cat to Geoffrey's problem.

Geoffrey sank back into the couch. Richard opened his brief-case and took out a legal pad. "Now . . ." He clicked his ballpoint pen to take notes.

I interrupted. "What were you doing at Basset's house?"

Abigail was as eager as I to find out what her husband was up to the morning of the murder. "There was no need for you to check on either the house or him. The paperwork was all in order, and no visits to the property were necessary until next week."

"Well, that's not strictly true, my dear." Geoffrey set down his cup. "Mr. Basset's check for management of his property bounced the morning I tried to deposit it at the bank. I called him after I opened the office, but I got no answer at the house, so I thought I'd pop over to his place at lunchtime and talk with him about the check."

Abigail reached out and tapped Geoffrey's hand. "That check was written last week when the papers for managing his house were signed. I thought you were going to take it to the bank then. Why did you delay? That's not like you. You're always so careful about these things."

Geoffrey looked embarrassed. "I, uh, I was distracted."

"By what?" Abigail knew Geoffrey was almost never distracted from business responsibilities. And on those rare occasions when he was, Abigail reminded him or tended to the matters herself.

Geoffrey's face reddened. I wasn't the only one who saw how nervous he was. All of us turned our gazes to him waiting for his answer.

"It's a long story." Geoffrey spoke in a whisper.

I banged my cup into the saucer. "Well, speak up and get on with it, would you? Richard charges by the hour, and I'm sure he sees this teatime as billable."

Richard nodded.

"It started with the afternoon you went home early with a head-ache." Richard turned to Abigail. She nodded. "I was in the office with Tanya."

Richard looked puzzled.

"Let me elucidate." I plunged in before either Geoffrey or Abigail could answer. "That's the secretary they recently hired at the business. I don't think you've met her—young, shapely, probably not too competent. Why did you hire her, Geoffrey?" I had wondered about Geoffrey's motives in taking her on in the office, and I now suspected the worse. Had Geoffrey developed a wandering eye? Not possible, I told myself. Still . . .

"She's very personable, great with people." His face continued to redden, and Abigail took notice. "Could I have a drop more tea, Mother?" He held out his cup to me.

"I'll get it." Sara went into the kitchen to heat up more water.

Abigail twisted her head to one side and gave Geoffrey a questioning look. "You're having an affair with Tanya, aren't you?" She jumped up from her place next to Geoffrey, spilling her tea and knocking the cup to the floor. It broke when it hit my hardwoods. I sighed. There went my matching set of Le Moge cups. Now there were only five of them.

I rushed into the kitchen and returned with a broom. "Don't be absurd, Abigail. Geoffrey and Tanya?" I'd always seen Geoffrey as a faithful man. Family was important to him.

I guess all wives want to believe their husbands are desirable to other women. In this case, infidelity might have looked better to Abigail than murder. She let forth a sob and tears ran down her cheeks. She grabbed her purse off the couch and ran toward the door.

"I didn't, Mother," Geoffrey said to me.

What I feared was not that Geoffrey had been messing around with Tanya. I knew him better than that. Instead, I worried he was covering up for something Tanya did. He was the kind of man who would see her as an innocent and want to rescue her. Both my sons had big hearts, from the time they were kids when the house was filled with stray cats, dogs, turtles, and a tubful of fish that Geoffrey had helped his friend Bunny steal from a fellow fishing in our creek. The kids grabbed them, thinking they would put them back into the creek that night. My boys flirted with vegetarianism from time to time.

"I know, and Abigail will too. Go home and talk with her. I'm sure Richard will drive you, won't you, dear?"

Throughout Geoffrey's story and Abigail's horrified assumption that Geoffrey was having an affair, Richard had sat quietly in my overstuffed armchair, soaking in the events. No wonder he was such a good lawyer. He got stories out of his clients by making himself invisible, sitting back and memorizing every word, every look, every gesture, tucking them away in his brilliant lawyer's brain. I settled back on the couch and picked up my cup. Empty. I got back up and headed into the kitchen to open the back-up bottle of wine in the fridge.

"I thought Richard was taking me home." Geoffrey started to rise from the couch.

"I'll stay for a small glass of the wine." Richard gave Geoffrey an encouraging smile as if they were kids once more in school, chatting about boyhood pranks.

"Of course, dear, then you can give Geoffrey a ride home, right after he tells us what he's hiding about Tanya. And while you're at it, would you open this for me?" Giving Geoffrey something to do might calm him. I handed him the wine bottle and a corkscrew.

"Hiding? About Tanya? Nothing." He struggled with the corkscrew then popped it out of the bottle.

I pulled two wine glasses out of the cupboard—Sara shook her head when I held up the bottle—poured each half full of wine and handed them to my sons. I considered my empty cup but decided not to pour myself anymore. I filled my cup with tea. "No one believes you had anything to do with Basset's death."

Geoffrey took the glass and dropped onto the couch once more. I watched as the wine sloshed in the glass.

"Drink it, dear. Don't bathe my furniture in it." I slipped off my shoes and curled my legs under me. "About Tanya . . ."

Geoffrey took a tentative sip of the wine. Then tipped the glass and gulped half of it.

"Better?" I asked.

He gave a slight tip of his head.

"Mr. Basset was Tanya's father."

CHAPTER 7

RICHARD ARCHED ONE OF HIS EYEBROWS in an isn't-that-interesting look.

Geoffrey slouched further down into the couch. Any lower and he would be underneath the seat cushion. "This whole thing is such a mess. I guess I need to talk to someone about it."

"We're listening." I leaned forward. Too bad Zack wasn't here. He'd be interested to know more about Basset and about Tanya's connection to him.

Richard sat forward in his chair, clasped his hands together, and gave Geoffrey a sweet smile. Richard was good with sweet smiles.

Geoffrey sat up straighter and took another substantial gulp of his wine. "I don't drink much, you know. I hope I don't get sloppy drunk."

Richard and I exchanged looks. He nodded. Now was the time to do what Richard and I often did to pull the truth out of his brother. Although he was the younger child in the family, Richard often stepped in to support me when my acerbic approach failed to extract information from Geoffrey. It was good training for his future position of attorney. We worked together well, a kind of good cop, bad cop approach. I was, of course, the bad cop.

"The last time you got drunk was the night before you married Abigail. Case of bridegroom nerves, I guess." I recalled Geoffrey's buddies returning him home—he was still living here with me—and dumping him in his bedroom, then leaving it to me to sober him up. Mothers still came in handy even for sons grown into adulthood.

"I was always grateful to you for taking care of me."

"And I was always grateful you chose someone like Abigail to marry, a motherly type of woman, more maternal than I ever was."

"You were a wonderful mother." Geoffrey leaned over and patted my hand. A tear worked its way down his cheek.

"Thank you, dear, but get on with your story before you start slurring your words and no one will understand what you're saying."

"Like after my bachelor party, huh, Mom?" He gave me a toothy grin. I shot a warning look at Richard who seemed about to burst into laughter.

I'd made a mistake plying him with wine—one small glass was all the plying it would take, and I knew it—in hopes he would relax and spill his story about Tanya and her father.

"You're prevaricating, Geoffrey."

"No, I'm not. I'm a little tipsy."

I snatched the wine glass out of his hand. "You were saying about Tanya and her father?"

"Well, he's not her real father. Well, I mean, he is her real father, but he was no kind of father to her."

"What are you trying to say?"

"She didn't know who her father was until several years ago when her mother told her the man who she knew as her father wasn't her biological father, a man who had abandoned her and her mother when Tanya was a toddler. She's spent much of her adult life trying to find him. She tracked him down here."

"When was that?" I asked.

"About half a year ago."

Richard crossed his legs and asked the question that was on my lips. "Had she approached him to tell him who she was?"

"She was trying to work up the courage to talk with him, but she was so angry that he had left her and her mother that I convinced her she should calm down before she approached him and figure out what it was she wanted from him. I think she saw me as a father figure because it seems I was the one she felt comfortable confiding in."

"But you hired her only months ago. Isn't that fast for her to trust you with her story?" I had doubts about Tanya's character beyond her inability to function as a secretary. Doe eyes couldn't fool me for long.

"What can I say? I guess I'm the kind of guy who wears a sign across his forehead that says, 'Tell me your troubles.'"

I never saw Geoffrey as the father confessor type of man. He may have wanted to believe he was, but I knew of no one else, not even his wife and daughter who saw him in quite that light. He was an adoring husband and loving father, but not the kind of person others went to for advice. Something was off here, and it smacked of Tanya tapping into Geoffrey's kind nature and his need to be viewed as an individual to be trusted with a secret. She wanted something and had used Geoffrey to get it. What was it? She was clever enough not to come on to him sexually. Instead, she flattered him with her pose as a naïve and brutally treated young woman needing help.

"But she did go see him, didn't she?" I was guessing, but Geoffrey confirmed my suspicions.

Sara slipped her hand into her father's and laid her head against his shoulder. She adored her father and knew he was incapable of killing anyone. "It's going to okay, Daddy."

He slid back into the couch once more, relaxed and comforted by his daughter. He patted her hand and gave her a tiny smile.

I worried that if I continued to confront him about Tanya it would nix the rest of his story. He always thought I was negative about people he found charming, like the girl he dated in his first year of high school. When she was caught with some items from the general store, merchandise she did not pay for, he stepped up and took the blame. I never trusted the little minx, and only later did Geoffrey discover she had another boyfriend, a fella who sold the shoplifted items to make money for booze. Don't get me wrong. Geoffrey was not stupid, but he liked to believe the best about the worst people. I don't know where he got that trait. Not from me.

He seemed to take encouragement from Sara's support. "Okay. Fine. Yes. She pulled herself together and went to the house to talk with him several times. At first, he denied being her father, but he came around. It appeared the two of them were establishing a relationship and then, without warning, everything changed. He told her he didn't want to see her anymore. She was so upset. I told her I'd talk with him and try to find out what was going on. She didn't want me to mix my business with her personal problems, but it was time I intervened on her behalf."

"You stuck your nose in where it did not belong and became a suspect in his murder." As I had suspected. My son being his usual kind, naïve self. Tanya had used his generous nature to get him to intercede for her.

"He was a horrible man, you know, Mother."

"Yes, but he didn't deserve to be killed for being less than a stellar example of humanity."

"Tanya wanted to try to mend fences, to get to know a father she'd never had, and he tossed her out."

Well, now, that was believable, but it was possible she had other motives. Daddy's money perhaps?

"You didn't tell anyone about you and Tanya, did you? You didn't blab to the cops, did you?" I shot Richard a look of alarm that the authorities suspected Geoffrey because of something he said to them.

Richard had the same worry. He shook his head and sighed.

"Your relationship with Tanya is something the police will find very interesting, especially the secrecy," I said.

"Tanya trusted me to keep her confidence." Geoffrey's face registered stubbornness.

"Well now her pappy is dead, murdered. He rejected her as a child and after he'd led her to believe they could establish a relationship, he tossed her away again. She had strong motive to . . ." I stopped midsentence. I was conjecturing and only making Geoffrey more upset.

"Mother! She wanted to get to know him, the poor kid."

Did she go back for a final showdown, this time with a knife? I kept my thoughts to myself.

Geoffrey muttered something else.

"What?" I asked.

"That's not all to the story." Geoffrey wriggled uncomfortably on the couch. Sara continued to sit close. This was a new interrogation technique: Sara comforts, I threaten, Geoffrey confesses.

Richard and I both waited, he patiently, me eyeing the wine bottle lustfully.

"I wanted to protect her because I think she's in danger."

Was this a story she had used to entangle Geoffrey in whatever her scheme was?

He held up his hand before I could plunge in with one of my negative comments.

"I'm not even certain she realizes the danger, but the other day as I was emerging from my office, I overheard a man say to her as she sat at her desk, 'Stay away from him or you'll regret it.' The fellow left when I stepped out of my office. I asked her who it was, and she said it was no one important. 'It sounded like he was threatening you,' I said. She told me it was a misunderstanding."

Hmmn. Tanya wasn't a schemer as I thought. Perhaps she was as naïve about people as Geoffrey.

"I guess the guy could have been Hiram Barley." Geoffrey said.

Richard looked up from his laptop. "Who is Hiram Barley?"

"Basset told me he and Hiram Barley were in business together, but they'd had a falling out and dissolved the partnership. I don't know the details."

"When did you find out all of this?" I was puzzled Geoffrey knew so much about Basset.

Geoffrey slipped down into the back of the couch. "Oh, you know. When he signed the contract to have us check on the property while he was gone. He said he was leaving for a trip."

"Pleasure, business? What kind of trip?" asked Richard.

Geoffrey shrugged. "He looked as if he didn't want to say more so I didn't pursue it."

"Unfinished business between former partners, do you think?" I directed my question to Richard.

Geoffrey gave an innocent blink.

"You think Hiram would hurt Tanya?" I asked.

"I was worried." Geoffrey slid further down into the couch. He looked defeated.

"I can see why. We don't know the terms of the will yet, but Barley might have stood to get his hands on some money from the former partnership if there were no heirs to Basset's estate. Scare off the daughter, kill his former partner and the money might be his," I said.

"It depends upon the terms of the dissolution," said Richard. "We need to find out if Basset had a will, and if he did, who the estate went to at his death."

"I'll bet there are more people who had reason to want Basset dead."

"Why do you say that, Mom?" asked Richard.

"I talked with one of his neighbors. She told me no one liked him much. He was a loner, but when he made his presence known, it was to harass his neighbors. An unpleasant man."

Geoffrey blinked, looked first at Richard, then at me. "I didn't find him so bad. I mean except for the Tanya thing, and it's understandable that he might have been shocked at her showing up suddenly."

"Nice of you to say, Geoffrey, but he's dead. Someone didn't like him." I grabbed the bottle of wine and splashed some into my teacup.

"I could use a little more, Mom." Geoffrey held out his wine glass.

"I don't think so, my brother. You've had a difficult day. And so has Abigail. Until the police find the real killer, you can expect them on your doorstep daily. Let's go. Abigail could use your support." Richard arose and held his hand out to his brother.

"Abigail is mad at me."

"She has every right to be, you keeping secrets from her." I followed them and Sara to the door. "Come back later," I said to Richard in a low voice.

"As soon as I've gotten Geoffrey calmed down."

And they were gone, my two grown sons, so unlike each other. I sometimes wondered if they were from the same father. I knew they were, but how different they had turned out.

I looked in despair at the empty wine bottle. I hadn't another in the house. There was scotch, but I knew better than to start on the hard stuff after wine. Sigh.

I explored the fridge for the making of a sandwich and found left-over cheese, but what kind? Blue cheese or was it cheddar that had aged too long? The bread in the cupboard was moldy, and when I grabbed a handful of crackers, they bent in half instead of breaking. What was I left with? I opened the freezer door. Ah, goodie. Chocolate ice cream. All was right with the world despite the recent murder and the cops' suspicion Geoffrey was somehow involved in it. I took a bite of the sweet, creamy delight and decided I could dismiss my worries, at least until Richard returned. There was a quarter of the pint left, a tiny serving for a hungry gal. I'd have to eat fast if I didn't want to share my meager treat with Richard. I took a giant spoonful, then another. The doorbell rang. Richard. I scraped the sides of the carton on my way to open the door. Brain freeze.

Richard stood in the doorway, fiddling his keys between his fingers. "C'mon, Mom. I'm taking you out to dinner."

I hid the empty ice cream carton and my spoon behind me. "Oh, darn. I just ate."

"Ice cream is not eating."

"How did you know?"

He reached into his jacket pocket, extracted one of his pure white handkerchiefs and swiped at my mouth. "Chocolate, I assume?"

I dumped the empty carton in the waste basket by the door, grabbed my sweater off the chair and followed Richard out to his car, a late model Mercedes, of course.

"The Billinghouse Restaurant okay with you?"

I remembered the last time I was there had been with Zack. Our evening had been perfect, the beginning of friendship, romance and more.

"I don't think so. The food seems good, but I get indigestion the next day."

"How about Rabbit's Run then?"

The food there was wonderful, but I hated the name. It made me think the chef chased bunnies around the backyard all day to serve them up in a cacciatore that night.

I shook my head. "Here's an idea. We'll run into the supermarket, grab a roast chicken and a salad to go. We can bring it back here and talk with privacy."

"Should I stop at the liquor store and buy another bottle of wine?"

"If you want one, go ahead. I think I'll stick to club soda." I gave a quiet and what I hoped was a ladylike burp.

Richard looked at me. "Club soda suits me. I have to drive home tonight."

"You could stay."

"I've got work piling up on my desk and a court appearance early tomorrow."

"I miss having you around, you know."

He chuckled. "I miss you too, but I know you're busy with your writing."

I said nothing.

"Aren't you? Busy writing, I mean?"

I nodded. Telling Sara what I was writing should have been confession enough for me, but I wanted to share my newly found writing interests with a man. Maybe not Richard, but it would be nice to run my scenes by a male. Like Zack.

The chicken had just come out of the supermarket's oven. It was hot and the skin crispy. The smell must have wafted upstairs when we carried our take-out dinner into the house because my feline visitor began yelling from my room. Hungry again, I surmised.

"I'd better bring him down." I scampered up the stairs and returned, cat close on my heels. Richard, the cat and I ate the entire bird, paired with a green salad. The cat refused a serving of salad.

"Coffee?" I asked after we had cleaned up the dishes together and the cat curled up on the couch to clean his face.

Richard looked at his watch. "I've got time for a quick cup."

He seemed happy to have spent the evening with me. We rarely got together even though we were a mere hour or less apart. I knew his work kept him busy, but I wondered if the man ever had time for a personal life. Ah, well, I thought as I made the coffee and Richard worked at his laptop in the living room, his work was important. When I entered the room with the coffee, I heard him on his cellphone.

"Great. See you in an hour then."

He tapped off and looked up when I set the coffee on the table. His face flushed, and his gaze didn't quite meet mine. Ah, not work then. Did I dare ask him?

I handed him his cup and resumed my seat next to him on the couch.

He cleared his throat, took a sip, and this time he met my look squarely. "I might as well tell you."

I tried to look surprised. "Tell me what?"

"Mom, you're not particularly good at hiding your thoughts and feelings. What do you know?"

"I know nothing about your personal life."

"I guess the same is true about my knowing about yours, but I've got a suspicion from your behavior around the county sheriff that there's something going on there."

"And you don't approve?"

Richard laughed. "As if what I thought would change you. He seems an interesting fellow. How long have you known him?"

"Hey. How did this conversation get sidetracked to me? Weren't you about to confess something about what's going on with you?"

He looked smug at being able to divert attention from himself. He crossed one leg over his knee and settled back into the couch. "Not much to tell. I've got a date later tonight."

I leaned forward excited to hear the news. "Tell me everything."

"If I did, I'd be late for my date." He took the last swallow of his coffee and arose. "I do have to run."

I walked him to the door and hugged him. "I'll guess I'll be seeing a lot more of you because of this murder case. We'll have time to talk every now and then."

"That should give you lots of opportunities to pry into my personal life." He gave me that same teasing smile from when he was a child.

"I never pry." I smiled also, letting him know I was kidding. I was good at getting information out of people. Maybe that's where Richard's ability in law came from. "Richard, do you think we have anything to worry about with Geoffrey?'

"Of course not, Mom. You know Geoffrey."

Did I? Did a mother ever know her children once they were grown and had lives of their own. But Geoffrey? A killer? Never.

After Richard left, I grabbed my laptop and settled back on the couch to work on my manuscript. As I typed, images of Zack filled my head, making it both more and less difficult to create the scene between my protagonist and her beau, less difficult because my image of her lover was inspired by my interest in Zack. I transposed those feelings onto my writing. But it was more difficult to write when all I wanted was to close the laptop, call Zack and tell him I forgave him and that he should drop by. And make it quick.

I had overreacted a bit when he told me about Geoffrey. He could have called or had someone else let me know, but he'd been kind enough to tell me in person although he had forgotten the cookies. But he had remembered we were having tea together. He had the broadest shoulders I'd ever seen on a man. And his mouth. I envisioned those lips touching mine then becoming more demanding . . . . A cold shower? Did that work to dampen the flames of lust? It sounded darn unpleasant, and I wasn't about to replace that warm glowing feeling with cold water. I decided to have a nightcap of brandy, scroll through the books on my ereader to find one not too sexy and go on up to bed. I poured a hefty shot of brandy from my grandfather's decanter and, snifter in hand, I was about to turn off the front porch light when a knock on the door startled me. I checked my watch. Ten o'clock, but too late for visitors. I set the brandy on the liquor cabinet, took out my cellphone, my fingers prepared to dial 9-1-1 if necessary. I pushed aside the curtains covering the narrow windows at the side of the door and peaked out. A familiar face presented itself to my gaze, but not one I was eager to allow in my house ever again.

CHAPTER 8

D AN, MY EX-HUSBAND PEAKED IN through the door side windows, trying to get a glimpse of me.

"What are you doing here?" I called through the door. "Not that any reason would allow you in."

"Maddie, sweetie. Let me in for a minute. I have something urgent to tell you, something that will change our lives."

I hadn't seen Dan in years. When I tossed him out twenty years ago, he moved to Stone Side, and although it was only fifteen minutes away, it was large enough that our paths never crossed. And he had no good reason to come back to this village, calling it "nowheresville" when he left. I thought I spotted him in the supermarket once, but I slipped down a far aisle. He wasn't someone I wanted to say "hi" to. The man who stood at my door was older, his hair thinner and grayer, but he was as handsome as ever. Age hadn't diminished his sex appeal. He remained fit and trim, his blue eyes wide with longing.

"Please, sweetheart. I need to talk to you."

I gave in to his pleas, knowing I'd regret letting him through my door. He'd always had a hypnotic effect on me. He knew what to say so I would forgive him anything. Being great in bed was one of his many charms. Being a faithful husband wasn't one. Neither was being a good father to our sons. He was never around when we needed him like the time Richard broke his leg climbing a tree. We lived in the country then, five miles out of town, and Dan had the car, off to visit one of his women, I suspected. I called our nearest neighbor, but she wasn't home. The ambulance service in the area was sketchy so that when I called 9-1-1, the operator told me she would try to get help to us but couldn't promise how long it would take. Between Geoffrey and me, we carried him to the road leading into town and flagged down a car to give us a ride to the hospital. Dan never showed up until the next day with the excuse that he never received the message I'd left at the real estate office where he worked at that time. Where had he been that night and the following day? In some other woman's arms. I don't remember what his excuse was that time because there were so many excuses, so many promises to do better, so many times he found his way back into our bed with his usual sexual allure.

Following high school I had enrolled in a small college in the Midwest and Dan and I met in English class. He was smart, I had to give him that, and I felt flattered that this charming and bright guy seemed attracted to me. We married after graduation. Dan enrolled in medical school at the University of South Dakota, and I worked at a restaurant near campus as a waitress to put him through medical school. He flunked out the first year, but enrolled in a less demanding area, journalism. He certainly had a way with words. He'd charmed me, hadn't he? He replied to an ad in the Butternut Falls newspaper, a weekly in a small village in Upstate New York and worked there as a staff writer for five years until the newspaper folded. By then we had two kids, I was working part-time in the local library and taking night courses to earn a Library Science degree. I knew Dan could never be faithful to me or be a provider or support for our family. As many women of my generation did, I felt I could not divorce him while the boys were still in school. I filed for divorce the day after Richard graduated from high school.

And now I had invited this man back into my life by giving in to his request to talk with me. No good would come of this, I was certain.

I opened the door. Dan leaned against the door jam and gave me that slow, easy, lop-sided half-smile of his. Against my better judgement, I felt the old warmth spread through me. I stepped back and let him into the house. He reached out for me. When his hand touched my waist, electricity shot through me and with it the memories of how he had cheated the family out of a real father.

I pushed his hand aside, crossed my arms over my chest and blocked his way into the room.

"How about a cup of coffee?" He jacked up his smile by several hundred watts.

"It's too late for coffee."

"Maddie, I'm desperate. I could use your help." He dropped the smile, and I could read the fatigue in his eyes.

"C'mon in. Have a seat. I'll get you a glass of water."

"Thanks." He smiled again, but this time he left off the suggestive stuff.

I let him settle on the couch in the place the cat had abandoned. Cat liked Zack, but he shot up the stairs when Dan entered the room. The cat had great taste in men. I ran a glass of water, handed him the drink and took the chair across the room, far enough away that he couldn't touch me. "Okay. What's up?"

"Belinda threw me out."

"Threw you out?" I chuckled. "Well good for her." My chuckle turned into full-fledged laughter so overwhelming that I found it difficult to catch my breath. Tears ran down my cheeks.

"Go ahead, Maddie. Laugh at me. You know you're covering up your hurt at what I did to you. And the fact that you still love me."

His words cut through my laughter, and rage burned through my body. I rushed toward the couch and jumped on him. He was wrong. My reaction to his situation wasn't laugher covering hurt. It was laughter covering rage. I yelled at him using words I didn't realize I even knew and pounded on him with my fists. He held up his hands to ward off my blows, then stood, grabbed my arms and flung me to the floor. And that's when the door opened, and Zack walked in.

Zack threw himself between me and Dan, pulled back his arm and punched Dan in the face. Blood spurted from Dan's nose. He tried to stem the blood flow with one hand and ward off Zack's continued assault with the other.

I picked myself off the floor. "Stop it, both of you. It was my fault, Zack. I started this."

"Let me finish it. What man attacks a woman in her own house? Who the hell are you, fella?"

"He's my ex." I grabbed Zack's arm and pulled him away from Dan. "I just want him to leave."

"You don't want to press charges?" Zack asked.

I shook my head. "I want him gone. That's all."

"Press charges? I should press charges against you. And at one time this was my house. I paid for it." Dan had taken a hanky out of his pocket and held it to his bleeding nose. "And I also want to press charges against you, whoever you are. You assaulted me."

"He's the acting sheriff for this county."

"That's even worse. A law enforcement officer attacking private citizens for no reason."

"Shut up, Dan. Better yet leave, would you?" I hooked my arm through Zack's.

Dan's eyes squinted as his gaze traveled between Zack and me. "Oh, I get it. The two of you have a 'thing' going. He's your boy toy."

I took a deep breath and gazed up into Zack's blue eyes. "Yes. We have a 'thing,' and we'd like to get working on it now. Get the hell out of my house, or I'll have Zack throw you out, and then I will press charges against you."

"This is not over, Maddie."

"It was over years ago, Dan."

He took a final swipe at his nose, tossed the handkerchief on the coffee table and left.

"Did he hurt you, Maddie?" Zack pulled me to him, and I relaxed against his chest.

"He did all the hurting of me he's ever going to do when I wised up and tossed him out over twenty years ago."

Zack gave me a penetrating look. "You're sure you're okay."

"Yup. But what are you doing here, tonight at this hour?"

"I was working at headquarters and kept thinking about you. I wanted to come over so we could talk. Besides, I have something for you I didn't get a chance to give you this afternoon."

"What?"

"Oh, dang. I must have dropped the package when I pushed through the front door. Wait here a minute."

He left and soon returned with a white box. I recognized it as a pastry container from Decker's bakery.

"Cookies." He opened the box and held it out to me. "See?"

The cookies inside were broken into pieces.

"You didn't forget to buy them for our afternoon tea."

"There's not a lot I'd ever forget about you, Maddie."

We stared at each other for a moment, then we both eyed the cookies.

"They can still be eaten," said Zack.

"I'll make tea."

WE TALKED UNTIL ONE IN THE MORNING when Zack yawned and stretched his arms. "It's not the company, but it has been a long day, and I've got work in the morning. You must be exhausted, too, Maddie. It had to have taken a lot out of you to hear your son was a suspect in a murder. Not easy for a mother."

The topic of the murder hadn't come up all night, but there it was once more between us.

"You don't think Geoffrey had anything to do with Basset's death, do you?"

"So far, he's still part of our suspect pool. He had an argument with Basset the morning he was killed."

"Geoffrey argues with words, not with his fists. He's not a physical person. I can't remember a time when he had any kind of row at school or in college. Geoffrey is not made that way. That he felt the need to confront Basset on behalf of Tanya was surprising." Oops. Had I given away more than I should have about my son and his secretary? Ah, well. I'd said what I said. "You haven't had the opportunity to ask what was said during that altercation, have you?"

"And I won't, not with his lawyer keeping him away from me. Sorry, Maddie. But you must know how these things go." He arose and headed toward the door.

"I do. I have to say I'm happy Richard was available to intervene. I know it makes your job harder, Zack, but these are my boys." I paused at the door. "I suppose you're already on top of this, but there are other strong suspects, you know."

Zack said nothing but looked interested in what I was about to say.

"Basset had a business partner." I stopped there and said nothing about Tanya, but I suspected he already had found out about her.

Zack didn't indicate whether he already knew about the business partner or ask me how Tanya might have figured into Basset's murder. "What's the connection, do you think?"

"Check Basset's will?"

"Will do when I find it."

I touched his hand. "I should have guessed you were ahead of me." Well, of course he was. He was a professional crime fighter. I was . . . What? I wrote murder mysteries, but this was nothing like writing. My son's freedom and reputation were at stake. Real life, not fiction, not fantasy. Could I be of any help to Zack? Did I want to be?

Zack nodded and then paused on his way out the door. "Your ex is interesting."

"Let's not go there now. This evening turned out better than I expected, and I'd like to keep it that way."

"If he comes back, call me."

"Oh, he'll be back, maybe not tonight. He has something he wants to talk with me about."

Zack leaned back into the open doorway and gave me a peck on the cheek. I grabbed his arm and pulled him into me. "You can do better than that."

And he did. The kiss was electrifying. My entire body trembled with desire.

"How's that?" he asked.

"Better."

"Just 'better'?"

"We can work on it in the future."

He smiled down at me. "I'm glad you think there will be a 'future' for us."

With a nod of his head, he walked to his car, got in and drove away. The future couldn't come soon enough for me.

I AWOKE THE NEXT MORNING TO A BUZZING IN MY EARS and the feel of wet sandpaper being drawn across my cheeks. I jumped out of bed and dislodged a furry animal from my pillow. He narrowed his yellow eyes at me and resettled himself on the bed.

"Where did you disappear to last night? I could have used your claws to fend off my creepy ex-husband."

At the word "ex-husband" he growled.

"I couldn't agree with you more."

He turned and pushed his head into my hand, then began loud purring.

"That's better. How about breakfast?"

His eyes widened with interest.

"Followed by a visit to the vet," I said under my breath. The purring ceased. He hissed and turned his back on me, the universal cat sign for disgust.

"How did you understand what I was saying?"

The cat looked over his shoulder. Once again, his eyes grew

large and round, and he tipped his head to one side.

"Oh, ho. So now you're trying to look cute and innocent. Well, forget what I said. Food first, then we'll negotiate the rest of the day's activities."

The negotiating wasn't easy. When I brought out the cat carrier, he ran by me, up the stairs and crawled under my bed. I tried to tempt him out with tuna, but he wouldn't move, so I shoved him out from underneath with a broom. He ran back down the stairs. I followed, slamming my bedroom door closed. I checked my watch. I had made the vet appointment today at ten. I had fifteen minutes to find the little bugger, coax him into the cat carrier and drive him to the clinic. I looked everywhere downstairs, but he was nowhere, not under the couch or the chairs or in any of the corners. I dropped onto the couch, exasperated and thinking I'd never get him into his carrier.

"Okay, buddy. I give up. I'll have to call in help. You win for now." I grabbed the carrier to put it into the closet. It felt heavy. I looked in. He was sitting in the back. I was certain the look on his face said he'd fooled me. "I'll go to the vet on my terms," his expression seemed to say.

I shut the carrier and left with fewer than five minutes to spare before my appointment.

The howling began when I placed the carrier onto the passenger's seat of my car. It continued all the way to the clinic.

"He's kind of mad," I told the tech who showed us into the examining room. "I think he thought he'd outwitted me by hiding in the carrier when he thought I'd given up bringing him here, but I spotted him and slammed the door."

"Yeah, well, there's no outwitting a cat. You got lucky. I'll take him back and we'll see if he's chipped. You can wait here."

A few moments later, the tech, whose name badge read "Terri" carried him back into the room. The guy was all purrs and gave her chin head rubs.

"He likes you," I said.

"No. He knows the visit is over. There was no chip. What's this guy's story?"

I told her about the murder. "Can you check your records to see if Mr. Basset ever brought the cat into this office for an appointment?

"Back in a jiff." Tech Terri was gone for several minutes. "No appointment under that name. All I can suggest is that you keep searching the neighborhood. His owner might show up looking for the cat."

"I tried a few neighbors, but no one recognized him."

"Well, I guess you got yourself a cat. Be sure to stop at the desk and schedule a health appointment and shots for him."

He snuggled into the back of the carrier and gave me one of his "aren't I cute looks." "Just because you hustled back in there with no problem doesn't mean your behavior merits a treat when we get home." Home? Was my house now his home?

He yowled.

"Please don't start that again. I lied. I'll give you a treat."

As I handed the woman at the checkout desk my credit card—fifty dollars to run a wand over him looking for a chip—another vet tech, Heather—exited one of the examination rooms. My cat companion stopped his yowling and replaced it with a loud purr.

"Who you got in there? It sounds like Spike," Heather said.

"Spike? You know this cat?"

She peeked in the carrier. "Looks like Spike, and I'd never forget that purr. Loudest I've ever heard."

"Whose cat is it?"

"Well, I'm not sure. A young woman brought him in for an abscess on his ear. It looked as if he got into a fight with another cat. We took care of him. That was about four weeks ago."

I explained Spike's situation. "Can't you remember the woman's name?"

She shook her head. "I don't remember, but I should be able to find out by typing in Spike's name." She hit a few keys on her keyboard, then looked up from the screen. "Spike is in our system, but his owner's name isn't." She looked confused for a minute. "Oh, now I remember. That was the day our computers were giving us difficulty. The system was down for the afternoon, so everyone who came to the clinic had to fill out information on paper. We put Spike into our records. His name is here, no owner's name. I'm not surprised the information is incomplete. That day was crazy. We had several emergencies. We treated Spike but must have overlooked getting any contact information from the owner. Our records indicate payment was made in cash. I'm sorry I can't be of more help."

"It's a murder case."

Heather's eyes grew large with astonishment. "You don't mean Spike is a suspect."

"Of course not."

"I'll ask one of our vets if she can help."

Heather returned five minutes later in the company of a tall woman wearing her brown hair in a plait down her back.

"I'm Dr. Grady. I'm sorry our records aren't complete for Spike, but I don't think there's anything else we can do. You think finding the cat's owner is that important?"

Spike yowled.

"Shh. Your treat is coming. Be patient." I held up my finger. "Let me give you the name and number of the sheriff's office in case you think of anything else." I jotted the information on a notepad the tech handed to me.

I said thanks and started to leave. Spike upped the decibels of his howl.

"I'm hurrying. I'm hurrying. Don't get your floof in an uproar." What was wrong with me? Now I was talking with a cat, one I barely knew. I put the carrier in my car. Then I remembered something. "Back in a minute"

The howling intensified. I ran back into the office and caught Heather as she was about to go into one of the examining rooms.

"One more thing. Did the woman come in alone?"

She hesitated. "I think someone drove her to the clinic. I saw her get into the passenger's side of a car when she left."

"Do you remember the color or make of the car?"

Heather shook her head. "Sorry."

"If you remember anything else, you've got the number. Ask for Sheriff Montgomery."

I rushed back to my car expecting to hear the continued yowling protests from Spike. But all was silent when I opened the door.

I investigated the carrier sitting on the passenger's seat. "Did you die on me for spite?" I asked. The cat huddled in the rear of the carrier. Was he all right? I opened the door and poked my finger in to see if he was breathing. He moved so suddenly that I jumped backward. Spike shoved his way past my hand, jammed his body through the carrier door and jumped onto the top of the carrier. He didn't look happy.

"Treat at home, remember?" I cajoled.

He leaped into my lap. My hands flew to my face to protect it from what was coming, teeth and claws. But once in my lap he started to circle round and round, stopping every now and then to knead. He settled down on me with a kitty sigh followed by a rumble of purrs. He put one of his paws on the steering wheel and looked up at me with his "I adore you" look–round, wide eyes. He then shifted his gaze to the windshield.

"You want to drive, or should I?"

He made a mewing sound.

"Oh. No driver's license, is that it?"

I was losing it, all right. Talking to a cat and getting his okay for me to drive. Yikes.

CHAPTER 9

ONCE BACK HOME AND SEATED in front of his plate of tuna, Spike gobbled it down, washed his face and then curled up on the couch. The cat-to-the-vet ordeal was fatiguing, not just for my new buddy but with the lack of sleep last night, I was exhausted also. I didn't bounce back from strenuous emotional and physical events the way I had even ten years ago. Spike had the right idea. A nap, but first I knew I should call Geoffrey and Abigail to see how they were faring.

Abigail answered the phone. I asked her if Geoffrey was home or if he had gone into the office.

"No. He's here. Do you want to talk to him?"

"Sure, but how are you doing? Did you and Geoffrey work out everything last night? You know there was nothing between him and Tanya, don't you?"

"We didn't talk. He drank too much of your wine. He's still in bed."

I glanced at my watch. It was after eleven in the morning. I suspected it was not my wine that kept him in bed. He didn't drink that much of it. It was embarrassment that prevented him from talking to Abigail last night and dealing with her this morning.

"Who's tending the office today?" I doubted Tanya had volunteered.

"We closed it for the day. Neither of us are in any shape to do usual business."

"The word that Geoffrey was brought in for questioning must have gotten around the village by now. Don't you think not opening looks bad?"

"Of course, it does, but who do you suggest we get to take over for today?" Abigail knew better than to ask me to cover.

"How about you, Abigail? I know you've both had a blow with the murder, but someone should be in there to at least answer phones."

"I don't know if I can handle that."

"Oh, buck up, Abigail. Unless . . ."

"What?"

"You could call Tanya in to cover today."

"Are you out of your mind?"

"Have you called her to tell her not to come in today? If she had keys to the office, she might be in there right now. Have you checked?"

"You're making my head ache with all your questions. I've got a better idea. You call the office. You tell Tanya we're not coming in today. And if you're so worried about the business being open today, you go in and take care of it. Afterall, we did hire you the other day."

Well, I had pushed Abigail too far and she was unraveling. "I'm sorry, honey."

"Well, you should be," she sputtered. "This had all been such a strain on both of us. We could use your support, you know."

"You have it. You know that." I thought back on last night and hoped no one who knew our family had driven by the house and seen the sheriff's car out front so late. Being supportive of Geoffrey did not mean canoodling with the sheriff who had questioned him. Abigail was right when she said I was asking a lot of questions. I'd done the same at the vet's office. I was a writer, not a detective, yet I'd rather easily obtained information about Spike today, hadn't I?

All because I wanted to find Spike's owners? Not even close. I was worried about Geoffrey, worried he was the authorities' prime suspect. As I rolled these concerns around in my head, Abigail interrupted my thoughts.

"Hold on a minute, could you? There's someone at the door." I heard her open the door, gasp in surprise and say, "Dan! What are you doing here? I'll call you back, Maddie. It's Geoffrey's father."

I was so busted.

After last night's visit from Dan followed by Zack rescuing me from him, I knew Dan would be delighted to reveal the events of the evening to Abigail and Geoffrey. There was little I could do to stop Dan from talking. Abigail and Geoffrey would feel betrayed by Zack's presence at the house. Should I rush over to their place in hopes I could smooth over Zack's role in tossing Dan out of my house? That felt so defensive on my part. I had done nothing wrong, but I was certain with Dan's help in elaborating on the evening, I would look like a traitor to my children. I might be able to convince Abigail of my innocence, but Geoffrey was the person taken for questioning by Zack. Now my son would never forgive a friendship of any kind with Zack, and Dan would convince Geoffrey that we were more than friends. Well, I could pave the way to getting Abigail back on my side by doing what she suggested: I'd drop by the business and see what I could do. My curiosity about why Dan was back in this area could wait. Besides, I knew he'd be contacting me at some point. He seemed pretty determined last night to talk with me about something.

I could accomplish another goal today also. I took a couple of pictures of Spike with my phone thinking after I stopped at the office, I could show the picture around Basset's neighborhood.

When I arrived at Abigail and Geoffrey's business, Tanya was leaving.

"Oh, Mrs. Sparks. Where is everybody today? Usually, one of them comes in in the morning before I get here, but I was late today because I was detained by . . ."

I finished for her. ". . . the police. They wanted to question you about your father, Mr. Basset. Am I right?"

"How did you know?"

"I assumed the police would talk to you after they uncovered the relationship between you and Basset. You have to be one of their prime suspects."

She put her hand on her hip in a defensive posture. "You're wrong. I'm not a suspect in his murder. The police wanted to ask me some questions about him. I don't know how they found out about our relationship so soon, but . . ."

"Geoffrey told them. You didn't expect he would keep the secret about your father when someone had killed him, did you? You felt your father had abandoned you and despised him for his refusal to accept you into his life. That's a great motive for murder."

"Geoffrey told the cops about my father? How did you find out though?"

"Geoffrey is my son. He doesn't keep things from me." I didn't add that Geoffrey didn't keep anything from his lawyer either.

A flush worked its way up Tanya's neck and onto her face. "Here. Take the keys to the business and tell Geoffrey and Abigail I quit." She tossed me the keys, and before I could stop her ran out the door and down the sidewalk.

"Hey! Stop." I hurried after her and before she would open the door to her car parked at the curb, I grabbed her by the arm.

"Let go."

"If you're thinking of leaving, don't. The police will find you. Running also makes you look more guilty."

She tried to shrug off my hand, but I held tight to her arm. She looked frantic, her face red, tears coursing down her cheeks. "I'm not a killer. I'm not. My boyfriend . . ."

"You have a boyfriend? Did he know about your father? Did you tell him what your father had done to you?"

"He knew and thought my father was a jerk. I've got to run. I promised to meet him for an early lunch, and I'm late."

"So, how serious is this relationship?"

Tanya sighed and rolled her eyes. "We met one night at the bar my friends and I like to go to. That was early summer. We've been seeing a lot of each other since then, so yeah, I guess it's serious. He asked me to marry him."

Early summer? That was less than two months ago, He was a fast operator.

"Why don't we both meet him then? I'd very much like to talk with him, especially if the police haven't had that opportunity yet." I pulled her away from her car toward mine. "Where were you two meeting?"

"At the Billinghouse."

Where Zack and I had dined. This time the visit didn't promise to be as romantic as the other night had been.

"And don't quit. Abigail and Geoffrey need you." I gave the keys back to her. "Put the "Back After Lunch" sign on the business. We'll take my car."

WE ASKED FOR A TABLE IN THE BACK of the restaurant for privacy. As we made our way past tables already filled with diners, someone called my name. It was Zack. He stood up from where he sat with three uniformed deputies.

"Maddie."

Tanya turned her head in the direction of his voice. She must have recognized him from the police questioning this morning. She blanched and tried to pull away from me, her gaze traveling around the room as if she were looking for a table to crawl under or an exit she could run to. I held tight to her.

"He's not going to arrest you. Calm down."

Zack greeted both of us, the curiosity over why we were here together clear in his expression.

"We came from Geoffrey and Abigail's business. We're covering for them today and thought we'd grab a quick bite of lunch."

"I see. I won't keep you then." He leaned into me and said in my ear, "See you later?"

I nodded.

As I turned to follow the waitress to our table, out of the corner of my eye I caught sight of a man entering the restaurant and stopping to peruse the tables. The sun shining through the window into the darkened restaurant created a glare that prevented me from getting a good look at him before he turned and left, but there was something about him that made me think I'd seen him before.

"C'mon, Tanya. Let's sit down, order and get going."

But Tanya seemed frozen to the spot, her eyes glued to the front door.

"What's wrong?" I asked.

Her face turned pale, and she dropped to the floor in a faint.

I fell to my knees and patted Tanya's face to try to get a response. She moaned and began to regain consciousness. I punched 9-1-1 into my phone to call for the paramedics.

Zack rushed to my side. "What's happening?"

"She fainted."

"Odd," he said.

"Maybe not." I got up and ran to the door of the restaurant, flung it open and looked both ways down the street and into the parking lot out front, thinking I might catch a glimpse of the man who had come into the restaurant and left so suddenly. I heard the sirens down the street and saw flashing lights. Emergency personnel hopped out of the ambulance as soon as it stopped in front of the restaurant.

Zack joined me when I came back inside. I saw the EMTs examine Tanya and then place her on a stretcher.

"When was the last time she ate?" one of them asked me.

I shook my head. "I don't know."

"She's somewhat dehydrated." The EMT lifted the skin on the back of her hand and the peak it created took seconds to collapse. "See?"

I shrugged. "I don't know her well. We were here to get lunch."

Tanya's eyes opened and she gazed up at me. "Tell Robbie not to worry."

"Who?" I asked as the EMTs wheeled her out.

"Robbie."

"Who's Robbie?" asked Zack.

"I'm guessing it was her boyfriend. She was going to meet him here for lunch. I'll follow her to the hospital and check on her."

"She didn't tell me about a boyfriend when I questioned her this morning. What about this boyfriend? What should I know?"

In the brief time we'd known each other, Zack was already reading my mind. I wanted to tell him the truth, but would that be betraying Tanya's confidence? I reminded myself that in a murder confidence could mean the killer got off or someone else got killed or an innocent person like my son went to jail. I wrestled with what I was going to say. I went with the truth.

"I think her boyfriend didn't like Basset much."

"And you knew this?" He sounded irritated at me.

I shrugged. "She said something to me earlier."

"You ran after someone who came into the restaurant for only a moment and then left. You think it was him?"

"I don't know. Maybe."

Zack spun around on his heel in exasperation. "Did you get a look at him?"

"Not enough to describe him well, but there was something . . ."

"Tell me."

"It needs to percolate a bit. I'll figure it out, but not right now. Okay. This is what I do know. Someone, maybe her boyfriend, came into the office one day and had words with her. Geoffrey heard them together. He might know more." I stopped talking for a minute. "The problem is you'll have to question Geoffrey again and . . ."

"That bulldog of a lawyer . . . Sorry Maddie. I meant your son the lawyer will be there."

"Let me help. I'll talk to Geoffrey about Tanya's boyfriend."

"Throwing Tanya under the bus."

"Better than having you continue to harass Geoffrey."

"You know I don't harass people."

I shrugged. "Just me, trying to help the law." Suddenly I realized that wasn't entirely the truth. This was me trying to play detective, which was, I told myself, totally understandable since my son had been questioned about the murder. But did I have the chops to do the job and did Zack want my interference? Writing mysteries meant I created the clues that lead to the killer. In real life information came only if you were clever enough to ask the right questions or follow the right clues.

Zack stuck his hands in his pockets and stared into space for a minute. I gave him the time to decide whether he wanted me to talk with Tanya. "Go ahead. See what Tanya will tell you."

"Not now," I said.

"What? You changed your mind about helping me?"

"No, but I think right now Tanya could use a friend. Now isn't the time to press her. Let me see how she's doing. Maybe she'll tell me something. She did want me to tell 'Robbie' that she was alright."

"Fine." He said this with doubt in his voice.

"Wait," I touched his sleeve before he left. "What about Geoffrey? Are you going to talk with him about the guy with Tanya in the office?"

"No. I'm counting on you to get the story out of Tanya." He tipped his broad-brimmed hat to me and said, "Ma'am," that sexy, lop-sided smile on his face.

I'd deal with him later. Right now, I ran to my car to get to the hospital. Questioning suspects was a whole lot more physical than sitting in front of a computer. The pursuit of the killer was consuming my days. I wondered how I could fit writing into my schedule.

As I HEADED DOWN THE LONG HILL that led toward the nearby hospital in Stony Side, a few miles from the restaurant, I ran into a line of cars stopped by a state trooper.

I rolled down my window and yelled to the driver in the car stopped ahead of me. "What's going on?"

"An overloaded hay wagon overturned. There are bales strewn into both lanes. It'll take a while to clear."

There was no choice. I'd have to wait. I settled back into my seat and heard my stomach rumble. My watch told me it was after noon, and my early morning cup of coffee and piece of toast had long ago been digested. Ahead I spied the roadside stand selling hot dogs. I jumped out of my car and ran down the road to the stand. It was obvious the other drivers had the same idea as me. At least ten people stood in line. I'd have to keep my eye on the stopped cars to make certain the road blockage had cleared, and my car didn't impede other vehicles.

The guy ahead of me ordered several hot dogs and cans of soda. I groaned and waited for him to pay for his order and leave. As I stepped up to the window to order my dog and drink, I saw the stopped cars begin to proceed forward.

Hurry, hurry, I said to myself, unwilling to abandon my lunch and run back to my car.

I grabbed my order out of the vendor's hand, tossed a five dollar bill at him and dashed for the car. I opened the door with one hand, my soda can in the other and my hot dog clamped between my teeth. When I jumped in, I felt the mustard ooze its way out of the bun and drop on my blouse. I set the soda can in the beverage holder, put the car in gear and took a quick peek at my face in the rearview mirror. Oh no. Mustard leaked out of the bun, and the pickle relish was smeared over my chin. I took my foot off the gas for a moment and felt something jar the back of my car.

"Hey, lady." The driver in the car behind me was waving his hands and yelling. "Step on it. I'm late for an appointment."

"Not until I find out what damage you did to my car when you ran into my back bumper." I jumped out of the car and walked around the back. My bumper was fine, but his souped up, big tire pick-up truck had hit my taillight and bashed it in.

"I need your name and insurance information." I turned to get my license and insurance papers out of my car when I heard his engine rev up. He pulled around me into the other lane, floored the truck with a squeal of his giant tires and roared down the road. Other than him, there had been no one behind me, and I didn't get his license number.

Oh, darn. That taillight would cost me, but I was relieved the hit to the car hadn't caused whiplash. I slammed the car door, swiped at the mustard and relish on my face with the napkin wrapped around my hot dog holder and headed for the hospital. I gobbled down my hot dog as I drove. My stomach appreciated the food offering. For now. I burped and knew I'd be tasting hot dog the remainder of the afternoon.

There were no parking places nearer to the hospital's entrance, so I headed to the back of the lot. As I stepped out of the car, I peered at my face in the outside rear mirror. As clean as I could make it without soap and water. I slung my purse over my shoulder and sprinted as briskly as my old bones could carry me and entered the hospital through the emergency room doors. I rushed up to the desk.

"Tanya . . ." I drew a blank. What was her last name? "The young woman who was brought in by ambulance a short time ago. How is she doing? Can I see her?"

The attendant at the desk smiled at me and shook her head. "You know I can't tell you that. Privacy. Unless you're police or a relative and then you need her last name and date of birth."

Defeated, I turned and left. An older man and woman sat on the bench outside the emergency entrance. If Tanya had left, they might have noticed. On a whim I described her to them.

"I know she came in, but she might have left. Did you see her?"

They hesitated answering, so I quickly explained.

"The hospital has strict privacy rules so unless I'm a relative or official of some kind, they can't give me any information. She's a friend of mine." I was stretching the truth of our relationship a bit. "And besides, if you saw her leave then no one's violating any rules, are they?" I gave them my sweet, just-concerned-about-her smile.

The woman returned my smile. "You just missed her. A car with a young man in it pulled up and she ran out and jumped in."

"Did you see which way they went?"

"Can't tell you that. Didn't see, but you couldn't help but notice them," the man added. "He pulled out of here with a squeal of tires and then almost hit an ambulance pulling into the lot. Young people these days."

"Thanks so much." I headed toward my car and called Zack.

"I hate hay wagons and young men driving trucks with giant tires."

"Me, too, Maddie, but why is that important?" Zack sounded amused at my words.

I burped. "I also hate hot dogs."

CHAPTER 10

I TOLD ZACK WHY I COULDN'T TALK TO TANYA. "She left the hospital in a car, male driver. I don't know where they went."

"She'll turn up. I'll send an officer to her house. Maybe the man who picked her up from the hospital took her back to her place so she could get some rest. Sounds like her boyfriend."

"Meantime I'll stop by to see Geoffrey. I can ask him about the guy who came into the office and talked to Tanya. He's more likely to tell me than you since his lawyer has warned him about talking to the police." I paused, then added, "You know, there are too many men we don't know a thing about in Tanya's life—her boyfriend, her father, the guy who came into the office, the man at the restaurant, the man at the hospital. And I'm betting it was Tanya who brought Spike into the vet's and a man picked her up there. So many men, so little information. Tanya knows more than she's telling us, uh, you. We know the identity of her father, but who are the others and does their connection to Tanya make them suspects?"

"Maybe they're all the same man." I could hear the hopeful note in his voice.

"That would simplify things, wouldn't it?"

There was a pause at the other end of the connection.

"On a happier note, there's our dinner tonight." There was plea-sure in his voice.

I grinned at my phone, as if he could see my face.

NO ONE ANSWERED THE DOOR at Geoffrey and Abigail's house, so I got back in my and drove to their office. The "Back After Lunch" sign remained on the door. I cupped my hands around my face and peered through the front windows thinking Geoffrey and Abigail were in the back office. I didn't spot anyone.

Someone tapped me on the shoulder. "I caught them a few minutes ago leaving their house. They told me they were going to meet with the lawyer at his office."

Dan. Just the person I had no time for right now.

"We need to talk," he said.

"No, we do not. Everything there was to say between the two of us was said a longtime ago. I have errands to run. Leave me alone or . . ."

"Or what, Maddie? Will you tell your sheriff boyfriend?"

At that moment Pamela Applebottom emerged from the beauty salon two doors away. Next to Dan, Pamela was the last person in this town I wanted to chat with. I tried to hustle Dan off to my car in hopes she wouldn't spot us. There was nothing Pamela liked bet-ter than gossip, and seeing us together would make an otherwise boring day in this village exciting, even if what she told everyone would be closer to a lie than the truth. Too late. She spied us and dashed over, taking Dan's hand in hers and giving me one of her phony, toothy smiles.

"Well, well. Maddie and Dan. I didn't know the two of you were back together. I thought you were rid of Maddie years ago, Dan. How desperate are you to take up with your ex-wife again? Didn't you tell me she was a bore in bed?"

Before Dan left me, he had had affairs with several women in town, Pamela being one of them. She was a horsey-faced woman—my apologies to horses whose faces fit their bodies—with short legs, no ankles and a penchant for insulting most other women, me in particular.

"Oh, I'm sure he's desperate. He always was when it came to his infidelities." I returned her smile with my own insincere grin.

"Pamela." Dan used his sugared tone of voice. "How wonderful to run into you. We should have coffee now that I'd back in the area."

"You're back in the area? For how long?" I choked. "Since when? And what for?"

"I'd love to have coffee." Pamela's lips pursed in a look of sexual invitation.

"I'll call you, honey." Dan winked at her.

Pamela took a step closer as if she meant to lean in for a kiss.

I stepped between them. "Okay, Pamela. Now you've got your date. And your bit of gossip. Off you go." I gave her a little push to propel her down the sidewalk while I took Dan's arm and walked him toward my car. She gave a coy wave to Dan, then fished around in her bag and pulled out her cellphone. Oh, boy. Let the rumors begin.

"You insulted me by asking that horrid woman out, yet I got the feeling the other night you wanted something from me. You're trying to work both of us and in front of one another. You never change, do you?"

"I was trying to get rid of her so we could talk alone, Maddie. You aren't jealous, are you?"

Jealous? I thought about that. Was I? No, I'd gotten over Dan's women long ago. Now I found his presence wearied me and his flirty games as annoying as a mosquito in a wet summer.

"So, Maddie? Coffee?"

"That line is used. Try something new."

"A drink, then? At your place.?"

"Aren't you worried you'll get tossed out by my sheriff friend again?"

"Wouldn't you rather have me in your bed than him? Think

back. We had fun, didn't we?"

No. How wrong he was. "I've got important errands to run. If there's something you need to tell me, although I can't imagine what after all these years, call me tomorrow on the phone. I'd prefer to keep distance between us. By this afternoon, the rumor hotline will be in full force and people will think we're married and I'm pregnant again."

"But I need to talk to you now. It's important. It'll be all over town, and I want you to hear it first."

"Tell me."

"My wife threw me out and I've got no place to stay, no money."

"Old news. You told me before." I sighed. The man kept coming back and coming back. "And you want what?"

"Let me stay in one of your spare bedrooms. I swear I'll leave you alone. I'll be good."

I almost choked as laughter spilled from my mouth and erupted in such howls of glee that I worried my hot dog might work its way back up from my stomach to my mouth.

Dan looked insulted at first then his face reddened in anger. His hand curled into a fist, and I thought he might punch me. Instead, he hit the parking meter.

He howled in pain. "I think I've broken my hand."

Pamela who still stood a few feet down the street, dropped her cell phone into her purse and ran toward Dan. "Oh, you poor thing."

"Ice will take care of that, Pamela, and while you're nursing him, you can do it in your own home. Poor Dan needs a place to stay."

I LEFT HIM ON THE CURB, PAMELA COMFORTING HIM, and got into my car to head out to find Spike's owner. If, as Dan said, Geoffrey and Abigail were conferring with Richard, they didn't need me to interfere. Wait. I never interfered. As a mother it was my job to help my children whether they needed or wanted it. This time I was certain Richard could handle the situation, but I owed it to Spike to find his family.

The crime scene tape was still around Basset's place. Jane, the neighbor I'd had tea with just yesterday, wielded pruning shears on her runaway roses. She saw my car and waved. I pulled over to the curb in front of her house and got out. She might have information for me.

She swiped at the damp hair which fell into her eyes. "Did you find the cat's owner?"

I shook my head. "But I have made progress. His name is Spike."

"That seems an odd name for a cat, don't you think?" She hooked her shears on the garden fence. "I think I could use a cold glass of iced tea. How about you?"

"Sure. Why not?" I followed her onto her back porch where we'd had our tea before.

"Ooh. Lemon cookies," I said when she set the plate down in front of me and poured me a glass of tea.

Even if Jane had no information on Spike's family, my run-in with Dan and that horrible Pamela person made a tea break seem necessary. My aggravation over it must have shown on my face.

"Something's bothering you, Maddie. Can I help?"

I flapped my hand in the air as if I could chase away the memory of Dan's words. "My ex accosted me in front of Abigail and Geoffrey's business a few minutes ago. He said something I find disturbing."

She leaned forward. And widened her eyes in interest.

"He said he was back in the area like he was staying for more than a quick visit."

Jane took a gulp of her tea. "A physical assault?"

"No, but . . ." I saw his fist come back as if it was headed for me then hit the meter. Had Dan intended to hit me but stopped himself?

"No, of course not. He's all mouth. Always has been." However, the look of rage on his face and that fist unsettled me.

"Sometimes that can change in a second, but I'm sure you know that and know what to do about it. If the rumors around town are true . . ."

"About me and the sheriff? We're friends."

Jane chuckled. "But I can tell by the look in your eyes that you'd like to change that. I hear tell he's a real hunk."

"He is that."

We continued to sip our tea, both of us gazing across the lawn into the trees beyond as if fond memories and the promise of more good times in the future nestled there in Jane's garden.

She cleared her throat. "Sorry. My mind's wandering off to those danged roses. Well, sorry I can't help with the cat, but you might ask the Allen family down the street. Their kids are always dragging home any stray cat, dog, rabbit or chipmunk. Their daughter Sheila has a big heart for animals."

"Thanks. I'll do that now." I grabbed a last cookie. "One for the road. Still interested in coming to the historical society meeting with me?"

"You bet." She took final swig of her tea and accompanied me back to her pruning work.

I left my car parked in front of Jane's house and headed down the street in the direction she had indicated to the Allen's place. Three bicycles, a set of swings and a sandbox sat in the front yard of a large brick house two lots removed from Jane's. A picket fence enclosed the yard and ivy grew up the front façade of the house. I opened the gate, approached by two small dogs who barked, then changed their greeting to enthusiastic tail wagging.

"Roscoe, Penny. Don't lick that lady to death now." A dark-haired woman sat on the front porch shelling a pot of peas. At her call, the two dogs ran back to the porch.

"Do you like peas?" She held up a pod.

"Fresh out of the garden? Love them."

"Great. I've got too many for our dinner tonight."

"You could always freeze what you don't use."

"Not enough here to bother, but the right amount for someone else's dinner."

I stepped onto the porch and held out my hand. "Hi, I'm

Maddie. I talked to your neighbor, Jane, and she said you might help me with a stray cat."

"I'm Marsha Allen. Have a seat." She shook my hand and gestured to a wicker rocker. "The person you want to talk to would be my daughter Sheila. Sheila," she called. "Come out here and help this lady find a lost cat."

"Well, the cat isn't lost. I found it in the Basset house the other day. We don't think it was his cat, and we have no idea how the cat got into his bedroom."

"You're certain it wasn't Basset's cat?"

"I don't think so. The vet thinks his name is Spike but doesn't have information about the owner. It's complicated."

"It always is with cats. Dogs, now. That's a different story. They are loyal to their owners. Cats are loyal to whoever feeds them."

"That's not true, Mom." A girl of about twelve, curly brown hair cropped short and wearing a pair of khaki shorts and a blue tee-shirt, stepped out the front door. "Cats are dead loyal once they find you worthy of loyalty." She plopped down on the porch glider across from her mother and me. "I'm crazy about both cats and dogs."

"And every other animal that walks this earth. We now have a rule in this house. If you want to adopt another animal, you must find a home for one in the menagerie we now have. It's like we're running a zoo around here." Mrs. Allen swiped at a fly buzzing the pot of peas.

"What's the cat look like?" asked Sheila.

"He's big, orange and long-haired."

"I haven't seen him around the neighborhood, unless . . . I saw a young woman go into Mr. Basset's house one day with an animal carrier. You remember, Mom. It was when there was yelling and shouting coming from his place later that day."

"Do the police know this?" I asked.

"You mean about the animal carrier or about the noise?'

"Both."

Sheila shook her head.

"Tell me what happened and what else you heard and saw."

Marsha Allen answered. "There was such a ruckus there. I can't believe everyone in the neighborhood didn't hear what was going on. Angry voices shouting at one another."

"Male, female?"

Sheila's brow wrinkled in concentration. "I think I heard Mr. Basset's voice and that of another man. I heard the door slam and a car drive off."

"Did either of you see the man?"

Sheila looked at her mother who shook her head. "I heard voices, but I didn't see anyone. It must have been when I was busy doing the laundry. With this handful, there's always more than one load a day to do."

"And what day was all the noise?"

"A few days before Mr. Basset died," said Sheila. "I remember because it was the morning I found that baby bunny in the wood-pile out back."

Marsha Allen's head jerked up, and she leveled a serious gaze on her daughter. "What bunny? You never told me about any bunny."

"He's in my bedroom, Mom, in a cardboard box on the floor by my dresser. And quit giving me that look. I know, I know, and he goes to Jennie Martin's house tonight. She'll take care of him until he's able to be on his own."

Marsha's chest heaved in a relieved sigh. "I think that's all we remember about the day we heard the arguing from Mr. Basset's place. Should we call the authorities and tell them about it?"

"I'm friends with the county sheriff, and I'll see him tonight. I'll let him know. Sheila, you didn't happen to see the man's car, did you?"

"I don't remember. I went into the garage to get my bike. Is it important?"

"I'll see what the sheriff says. You've been very helpful. If he needs more information, he can contact you."

We all jumped at the sound of a loud bang from the side of the house.

"Oh, no. I think another bird flew into our picture window." Sheila jumped off the porch and ran around the side of the house.

"The birds do that from time to time. They don't see the window and fly right into it. Is he okay?" Mrs. Allen got out of her seat, ran over to the railing and looked toward the side yard. I followed her to see what was happening.

Sheila waved her arms. "Just dazed a bit. Oh, good. He flew off."

Marsha shook her head. "That's good. We don't need a bird to rehab."

"If you think of anything else you think might be important about Mr. Basset, call me or call the sheriff's office." I waved and headed down the sidewalk to my car.

"Wait. You forgot your peas." Sheila ran after me and handed me a paper bag of peas. "I hope you like them. You're doing us a favor. We have so many peas that we've been having them with every meal for weeks. We're tired of them"

"Thanks, Sheila." I waved back at her mother and continued toward my car.

Sheila started toward the house, then turned back. "Oh, gosh. I just remembered something else about that day. Before all the yelling started, I was sure I heard a cat yowling. I might have imagined it because the sound stopped."

"The cat howling stopped before or after the yelling?"

Sheila looked down at the ground, lost in thought. "Uh, at around the same time, I think. The cat sounded mad."

"Thanks again." I held up the bag of peas. "And tell your mom thanks for these, again."

Marsha yelled at me from the porch. "Stop by in a few days. We've got another batch of peas coming in."

Sheila looked at me with a pleading look. "Yeah, please stop by again. Soon, or we'll be eating peas until next Christmas."

I continued my tour of the neighborhood and contacted anyone who answered their door when I knocked. No one I talked to recognized Spike the cat when I showed them his picture. Most were surprised the cat had been found in Basset's bedroom. The consensus of the neighbors' feelings about Basset was that he was withdrawn, not neighborly. He never showed up when invited to stop by for barbeques at neighbor's houses or at the July fourth parties each summer. He had lived in the house for over two years and had few visitors. No one saw him as a cat person.

"Come back later," one neighbor told me. "The man who lived in the house that backed Basset's, Mr. Grenada, has been gone for several weeks visiting his daughter in California. I've seen him talking with Basset over the back fence. He might know more about the guy and that cat. Oh, wait. That's him now."

I spied a small red car pulling into the driveway of the house whose back yard abutted Basset's.

I thanked the neighbor, cut through the yard and walked over to the car.

"Hi, I'm Maddie Sparks. Your neighbor told me you're returning from seeing your daughter. I hate to bother you. It must have been a long trip, and I suspect you're tired, but . . ."

A man with a full head of salt and pepper hair, got out of the car. He was shorter than I, looked to be about my age and gave me a cheery smile.

"I slept on the plane all the way back. I feel great. What was your name again? And how can I help you? Well, let me get my suitcase out of the trunk. C'mon in and we can talk." He strode up his drive, continued to talk, unlocked his back door and gestured me into his house.

I repeated my name. "I'm here to talk about Mr. Basset."

"Basset, hmmm? Weird fellow. I heard someone killed him. Over the few years he's lived here he's come around a bit, at least with me, probably because I helped him get rid of the pesky Japanese knotweed growing on the bank of that little creek bordering the other side of his property. Nasty stuff, not easy to tame. Best thing for it is to cut it, stuff it in plastic bags and put it out for the garbage men. If you don't bag it, it'll grow where it's dumped. Sorry, I'm blathering on." He set his suitcase down and walked over to the stove, grabbed the kettle there and filled it with water. "You'll have tea, won't you? Sure you will."

He made the tea. I offered to help, but he shook his head. "You're a guest."

"Mr. Granada, you don't know me. I'm a stranger, yet you invited me into your house. That's brave of you."

"You don't look like a thief or a killer."

"Looks, as they say, can be deceiving."

"I'm not worried. Besides, I recognized your name. My daughter reads all your mysteries, so I saw your picture on the back of the books. You look younger in person, you know."

I swept a hand over my hair. "Do I? Well, I had my hair done last week."

We sat at his kitchen table, and he poured the tea.

"Sorry that I have nothing in the house to accompany our cuppa."

We chatted for several minutes about my writing and the neighborhood. I was about to ask him about Basset when he jumped up from the table and ran to his suitcase.

"While I've got you here. My daughter gave me one of your books for the plane. I'm sorry I didn't get around to reading it. I will though." He extracted the first cozy mystery I'd ever written. "Will you autograph it for me? Once I've read it, I'll send it back to my daughter. She'll be delighted to have an autographed copy and excited I met you."

"I'd love to sign it."

I pulled a pen from my purse, signed the book and handed it back to him.

He looked at the signature. "Oh, my. You personalized it to me."

"Of course. I'll sign another copy and send it off to your daughter."

His deep brown eyes widened in delight. "That is so kind. But you didn't come here to sign a book. You came about Mr. Basset. Did you know him?"

"No, I didn't. No one seems to know much about him. You knew him better than anyone in the area since the two of you talked."

"Well," he said, raising his gaze to me shyly, "I did most of the talking, as you'd guess."

"Anything you know about him would be helpful."

He raised a finger to his lips and stared across the kitchen. "Let's see. I know he wasn't married now, but he could have been in the past. He told me a woman claiming to be his daughter had sent him annoying letters."

"Annoying how?"

Mr. Granada shook his head. "'Annoying' was the word he used. I do know he worked in the tech business. I'm sorry. As I said, I did most of the talking. We chatted now and then about our gardens, the problem with weeds, the noise from the kids around here. I don't mind them, but he found them 'annoying.'"

"That seems to have been his favorite word."

Mr. Granada smiled. "That's the way some people are. I don't think he was ever happy. He mentioned a love affair that didn't work out. 'Can't trust women' is what he said."

"Did he mention family?"

"He told me he had a brother, younger than him. Got into trouble and was sent to prison."

"Were they in touch?"

Mr. Granada shrugged. "They exchanged letters sometimes. He told me his brother was being paroled this summer and intended to visit him. I don't think he was eager to see him."

Hmmm. His brother a convict, but it sounded like he was due to get out of prison soon. It was a lead Zack could track down.

I turned down a second cup of tea. I'd had enough caffeine this afternoon that if I didn't leave soon, I'd have to ask him for the use of his bathroom.

As with the Allens, I asked Mr. Granada to call me or the sheriff's office if he remembered anything more about Basset.

He walked me to his front door. "I just remembered something, but maybe it's not important. You're gonna think I'm trying to get you to stay so I can continue to talk your ear off."

I smiled at him. "Of course not." I tipped my head to one side and looked at him with curiosity.

"Basset told me he and his business partner never got along. I didn't think much of it because, as you've gathered, he didn't get along with anyone much."

I continued to smile and leaned forward to indicate my interest in what he was saying.

"Something about a lawsuit. He said his partner or his ex-partner was suing him for something."

CHAPTER 11

That evening, Zack came over for dinner. I may not bake, but I make a mean meatloaf and Zack gobbled down two large pieces in appreciation, and then sat back in his chair a smile of satisfaction on his face.

"I'll make coffee," I said. "We'll have it in the living room."

"You've been immensely helpful, Maddie, discovering Basset had a brother in prison. We've not had much luck finding out about Basset's life or his family. We traced his parents, but they're both deceased. There was no record of a brother, only an older sister who lives in Portland, Oregon. I talked with her on the phone. She said they haven't had contact since he left the family home when she was still a kid. She remembers him as withdrawn."

We sat on my sofa drinking our after-dinner coffee, Spike lying between us, purring, as Zack and I took turns petting him.

"He's a sweet cat," I said.

"And you're getting attached to him. What happens when you find his parents? Or are you hoping you never do?"

"I must continue my search. It wouldn't be fair to Spike or his family if I didn't try to get him back home."

Spike opened his eyes, looked up at me and gave a short "meow."

"I don't know if he's agreeing with me or not. He seems happy here." I sighed. "Poor thing. To have witnessed a murder. What a trauma for him."

"Maddie, he's a cat."

"He's very sensitive."

Zack gave Spike another long stroke down his back. "I know. I wish he wouldn't plop himself on the couch between us. It would be nice to be closer to you then a whole cat's length."

Spike gave another "meow" got up and stretched, then jumped off the couch.

"Do you think he understood what I said?" asked Zack.

"I'm wondering about Basset's brother. Did his sister say anything about a brother?" I slid closer to Zack as he slipped his arm around my shoulders.

"She said nothing about another sibling, and we can't find any record of one. Among the documents we found in the house were several pertaining to his business and the name of his ex-business partner, Hiram Barley. The partner lives in Syracuse, so I'll be making a trip there to talk with him. I wonder if Granada heard Basset correctly about the lawsuit. No information about a will, however. Great work, Maddie. You are one fine partner when it comes to getting information about Basset." Zack pulled me even closer to him and brushed his lips across my hair.

"Keep that up and this conversation will come to an end."

"That's fine with me." Zack took my chin between his thumb and finger and raised my mouth to his. I expected his lips to be warm and soft. I leaned in for the kiss, but instead of Zack's lips I got a mouthful of Spike's fur when he jumped back onto the couch and pushed his head between the two of us.

"Too soon?" Zack reached up and picked a cat hair off his lips.

"Well, he thinks so."

"It's getting late, and I need to get up early tomorrow anyway. We can take this up another time." Zack got off the sofa and headed for the door. I followed while Spike remained on the couch with what could be described as a smile of catisfaction on his feline face.

At the door, I stood on tiptoes and gave Zack a peck on the cheek.

"Oh, you can do better than that, Maddie." He grabbed me around the waist, and we kissed. This one was what I expected from Zack. A long, slow kiss that intensified until our lips were so locked together, I couldn't tell where my mouth ended and his began.

"Wow, wow, wow." I felt my heart thump in my chest. "Do you think the cat should be watching this?"

"Next time, you can put him in another room." Zack gave me a slow smile, lifted my fingers to his lips, kissed them and left.

Oh goody. There was going to be a next time.

I crawled into bed and fell asleep in minutes. My dreams were X-Rated.

WHEN A RINGING PHONE AWOKE ME THE NEXT MORNING in the middle of yet another Zack dream, I considered not answering it so I could finish what he and I had started, but I reconsidered. It might be Zack, the real thing, instead of a product of REM sleep.

"It's Dan."

What a horrible way to wake up. I hung up and pulled the pillow over my head when the phone rang again.

I knew I'd have to answer or risk having him appear on my doorstep.

"What do you want?"

"You can do better than that."

Zack had said that to me last night, and with him, I could do better. With Dan, no.

"Not with you, I can't." I put as much growl in my voice as I could muster in my state of half-sleep. "It's early. I haven't had coffee, and I have no interest in talking with you. Call back in another fifty years or so."

"Don't hang up on me. I have some valuable information for you. It's about Basset, that guy who was killed. Your boyfriend the sheriff might find what I have to say interesting."

"Tell him then."

"Oh, no. I'm not going to deal with that guy again. Since you haven't had coffee yet, I'll buy. Meet me at Sloan's Bar."

"Isn't it a little early for a bar?"

"Sloan's has great coffee. Trust me."

Years ago, Dan had told me to trust him. I had and that had proved to be a big mistake.

"Not on your life, buddy. We'll meet downtown at Mary's Café. I don't want anyone to see me in a bar with you. I have a reputation to protect."

"Oh, that's right. You're the oh-so prim lady who writes those silly mysteries."

I hung up. I should have reminded him that this lady's mysteries put his kids through college when he failed to come through with any financial help for their college educations.

MARY'S WAS PACKED WITH THE MORNING COFFEE CROWD, but Dan had snagged a table in the back corner. He waved me over.

He got up and pulled out my chair, then leaned in as if he was going to kiss me. I shoved him away.

"We used to be married, Maddie. We did more than just kiss then. What's your problem?"

"My problem is our marriage is long over, and I don't consider us friends after what you did to our family."

He resumed his seat and ran his fingers through his hair. "You're right, Maddie. You always were."

"Don't try to sweet talk me. Now get on with what you know about Basset."

"Okay, but first I need to tell you Belinda threw me out."

"You're repeating yourself. You've already told me that two times before. I didn't have any sympathy the first two times I heard it, and I don't now." However, the thought of it made the corners of my lips lift in a smile, which grew wider and wider. I knew it was petty of me, but I broke out in laughter and followed it by clapping my hands. Everyone in the restaurant turned their heads to look at us.

I decided the breakfast crowd should share in my celebration. "Sorry to interrupt your breakfast, folks, but I got good news. Want to hear it?"

Dan reached across the table and grabbed my hands. "They don't need to know my business."

"Well, they all knew your business every time you abandoned your kids and me. I thought they might like an update."

"You are a hard woman, Maddie. That's why I tried to find comfort in other, softer, more understanding women."

His words surprised me. Was I that hard? I prided myself on my reasonable approach to life, Maybe I needed to reexamine that. I had a second chance to open myself up to love with Zack. "Maybe it was more than old-fashioned lust I was feeling." I didn't realize I'd said that aloud.

Dan smiled. "Lust is never old-fashioned, Maddie. And whatever you're feeling, Maddie, I'm right here. Let's give it another chance."

"What?"

Dan's smile faded. "Oh. I guess you didn't mean me. That sheriff guy, huh?"

"None of your business. Now what's this about Basset?"

"It's not about him. It's about his brother."

"How do you know he has a brother?"

"I know, that's all. The brother has a different last name."

"What is it?"

"Polander."

Not a common name, and I thought I'd heard it before, but I couldn't put my finger on where. I shook my head as if that would jiggle the memory loose and into my consciousness, but no luck. The incident remained shrouded in brain cobwebs.

Dan interrupted my thoughts with a warning. "You can't tell the sheriff you got the information from me."

"Why would I cover for you?" And why would Dan tell me this? "Are you involved in Basset's murder somehow?"

"No."

"But if the sheriff finds out I learned information from you, then you're implicated somehow, and you want me to keep your name out of it."

He nodded.

"Do you think your connection whatever that might be, however innocent, won't be uncovered in this investigation?"

"Bring my name into this, Maddie, and it will give the authorities more reason to suspect Geoffrey."

"What? How?"

"I won't tell you that. I'm trying to protect our son."

Was he trying to protect Geoffrey? He looked concerned, but knowing Dan all these years, I wondered if he was only trying to save his own butt somehow. Or lying. I didn't know where this information would lead us, away from Geoffrey was my prayer. I couldn't take a chance that bringing Dan's name into this would make Geoffrey vulnerable.

"Fine. I'll pass the name on to Zack." I needed a cover story, and I needed it quick. Zack had entered the restaurant. And he saw Dan and me together. He didn't look happy. I had to tell him without jeopardizing Geoffrey, and I knew I shouldn't withhold information that might crack the case.

"Zack," I called. "Join us."

Zack smiled at me, frowned at Dan. He came over to the table. "Early morning coffee?"

In an attitude of nonchalance, Dan slumped back in his chair. "This little gal was always up at dawn and made certain the rest of us were also. It's a habit she still keeps." He made it sound as if he and I had spent the night together and rolled out of bed for coffee.

I ground my teeth together at the "little gal" phrase. "You were the one who called me to come meet you. But now the company has much improved. Didn't you say you had business to attend to and were leaving, Dan?"

Dan wrinkled his forehead in annoyance but left his chair and headed toward the door.

"Nice seeing you, Maddie. Sheriff."

Zack moved his lips in the direction of a smile, but never quite completed it. "I'm surprised the two of you are still speaking after the encounter at your house."

"I'm being the bigger person." I grinned.

"I suspect you always were. Rumor has it around town that his present wife showed him the door."

"That's what he said. At least three times. I must remember to stop by the drugstore and pick up a congratulations card to send her."

Zack laughed. "Can we start this morning over again?"

I gestured at the chair Dan had vacated. "Of course."

We talked but my attention was not quite on his presence as my mind chewed on how I would share what I had learned about Basset's brother with Zack.

"Have you located Basset's brother? I mean, if he has a brother?" I asked.

"Not yet. No Basset in the prison system in New York."

"You said Basset's sister never mentioned a brother, I'm assuming the brother is from another marriage and has a different last name."

"Your mentioning that before got me thinking it's the most probable explanation, but I need a name. I talked to Basset's sister earlier this morning and she's unaware of her mother marrying someone other than Basset's father, and I've not be able to track any other marriage."

"People have children without being married, you know."

"I do, and that complicates my search."

"You could look for an inmate being paroled sometime in the near future."

"I've got my staff working on it, but that's a lot of tracking to do."

"A name would help, huh?"

I wanted to blurt out the name, but without a reasonable story about how I got it, would he believe me? And Dan warned me bringing his name into it would somehow make things difficult for Geoffrey. I didn't get how, but I wasn't going to risk it. I would tell Zack and soon. My dilemma was I didn't know what story I could use about how I got it.

"What?" I said when I realized Zack was talking to me and I hadn't heard a word he said.

"I got a lead on Basset's business partner. I thought he was in Syracuse, but it turns out he works here at the garden center outside of town. I'd love to stay and talk with you, but I should get over there to talk with him."

"Interesting. Mr. Granada told me the business partner was suing him. Did I also tell you the Allen family heard an argument at Basset's house?"

"Yes, and I talked with the family yesterday. Interesting information about a lawsuit." Zack slid back in his chair and crossed his arms over his chest. "Nothing like legal wrangling to make for a motive for murder."

"Glad to help." I tipped my head to one side and gave him my best sexy smile.

"You know I can't have you along on official business."

I changed my provocative smile to a pout. "Fine then. I can't sit here and chit chat. I'm a busy woman." I grabbed my purse off the table and stalked out, leaving Zack shaking his head in exasperation.

I FOLLOWED ZACK TO THE GARDEN CENTER. I watched him park, get out and approach a male worker at the center. They talked for a few moments, and then the man signaled him into one of the greenhouses. I followed, making certain they didn't notice me. The worker and Zack walked to the back of the greenhouse where they met another worker, this one older, short, chubby and balding. The first worker left, and Zack pulled his credentials from his pocket and showed them to the short man. I couldn't hear what was being said, so I grabbed a large potted begonia and held it in front of me while I moved closer to the two men.

"... expecting you'd want to talk with me," said the short man.

I moved even closer to them so I could hear their exchange.

"Mr. Barley, I understand you were Basset's business partner, and now you're working for a gardening concern? Why the career change?"

I could see the short man's face. A red flush worked its way up his cheeks. Anger, and a lot of it. "The man cheated me out of my rights in the company. The majority of the ideas were mine, but he took all the credit, filed all the patents without my name on them, then bought me out for pennies. So now I'm taking him to court. I've got nothing to show for my work. He made me look like I had no hand in developing our software. No tech company would hire me. Working here made it possible for me to keep an eye on him to make certain he wouldn't skip out on the suit."

"And now he's dead."

"You think I had something to do with that?" Barley picked up a watering hose and directed it toward the plants nearest him.

"Well," Zack said, "you had reason to hate him."

"I did hate him, and I'll still get back at him for what he did to me. My lawyer says we can file suit against his estate." Barley turned off the water and began deadheading the plants.

"If that's true then killing him may make little difference in the outcome for you one way or the other. If you win your suit, that is, but, here's a thought. Could he have left something to you in his will, out of guilt, perhaps?" Zack gave Barley one of his slow, confident smiles.

"Guilt? I doubt it. That's not an emotion he ever experienced."

Zack said the authorities hadn't located a will among Basset's papers. Who inherited was important. Was it his brother? Tanya who claimed to be his daughter? And what of his company? The dispensation of Basset's estate could be messy and take months or even years especially if no will was located. If Barley killed him, he must have done so in a fit of anger. A knife in the chest indicated rage.

The pot I was holding was getting heavy and began to slip from my hands. I tried to shift it up to maintain its position in front of my face, but the pot tilted to one side and then tipped forward, falling to the ground in front of me. My grunt as it fell caught the two men's attention, and they broke off their conversation to glance my way. Barley watched the plant drop to the ground and spill dirt all over my feet. He shook his head. "Stupid woman."

Zack recognized me and rolled his eyes at my foolish attempt to eavesdrop on his questioning of Barley.

I reached for one of the packages on the shelves near me, grabbed it, ran for the cashier and skedaddled back home.

I wasn't surprised when Zack knocked on my door minutes later.

"Before you say anything," I pointed to the package on my coffee table, "I realized I needed slug bait for my garden. The buggers are eating everything in sight."

"I have no doubt of that, Maddie. It has been a rainy summer, but you don't have much of a vegetable garden."

I gave him a weak smile. "Never too late to plant."

"Maddie, Maddie, Maddie. What am I going to do about you? "

I had an idea, but I decided not to push our developing affection for each other.

"Is it too early for lunch? I've got tuna salad in the fridge."

"Trying to take my mind off what you did by engaging my stomach?" He tossed his sheriff's hat onto the coffee table and followed me into the kitchen. "I'll toast some bread."

I sighed in relief. If we were going to have a showdown about my snooping, it wasn't going to be now, thank goodness.

We avoided any shop talk during lunch. Instead, we chatted about village life.

"How long have you lived here?" He bit into his sandwich, chewed and then took a sip of his lemonade.

"Dan and I lived here right after we married, that's over forty years ago. We started our family right off. Dan worked for the local paper then as a reporter. The village had a paper, a weekly at that time. It went out of business only a few years after Dan wrote for it. He then worked at a real estate office, and I became assistant librarian at our local library. I loved the job. Being around books is my passion, all books, but my favorites are mysteries."

"It makes sense that's what you'd write."

I laughed. "Like Agatha Christie."

He reached across the table and took my hand. "Now. I guess you heard everything Barley and I talked about."

"Unless you said something more when I fled from the greenhouse."

"We did."

"Okay."

"And I'm not going to tell you what was said."

"Oh."

There was silence between us for a minute.

"Let's forget about earlier. It's a wonderful day. How about we take a hike in the state park when I get off work? About five. We can take a snack, hike up to the falls and stop for the view.

"A hike sounds like what I need."

Zack took my hand and helped me up from my chair. "I'll bring a blanket."

"Right." What's a picnic without a blanket? He was such a naughty man. And I loved it.

CHAPTER 12

I TRIED WRITING BUT SPENT MOST OF THE TIME in front of my laptop daydreaming about Zack and our afternoon picnic. When I tried to bring my attention back to my manuscript, my thoughts wandered instead to Basset's murder and what part Tanya might have played in it. I closed my laptop and decided I should have a talk with her. Although Zack told me the authorities hadn't located her after she left the hospital, I decided I'd take a shot at finding her.

I stopped at the real estate office, but a sign on the door indicated it was closed and would reopen tomorrow. I used my key to enter and went through the personnel files in Geoffrey's office to find Tanya's address. It was fortunate there weren't many files because I didn't know Tanya's last name, but thumbing through them, I located her file under "T" for Tanya. Interesting filing system. I wondered whose idea it was to file by first names, or was Tanya's file an anomaly in the system? Curious, I looked under "S" for Sparks for my file. Nothing there. "M" for Maddie produced the same. I found the application for property management I'd filled out under "M" for Mom. That had to be Geoffrey's idea of keeping track of employees.

The address Tanya had given led me to a modest neighborhood west of town. There was no car in the driveway or in front of the tiny yellow clapboard house. No one answered my knock at the door. Was she staying with her boyfriend? That was a dead end and one I couldn't get around. I had no idea of his last name or where he worked. I'd not seen him or met him. Tanya's friends might know him, but I didn't know who they were.

I called Geoffrey and Abigail's house.

Abigail answered. "Mom? What's happening?"

"Do you know where Tanya is today?"

"She asked to take off today because of her fainting episode yesterday. Geoffrey is out of the office meeting with potential clients about property listings. We need the business. Word has gotten around town about the murder and that Geoffrey was brought in for questioning. Five clients cancelled their property management arrangements with us."

"So you won't be needing my services, at least not now."

"Right. Did you call for a reason?"

"No. I'm just checking to see how the both of you are faring. I'm surprised Tanya is still working for you."

"Geoffrey is insistent she needs direction, something she tried to get from Basset. Geoffrey told me she insists he came around to believe her assertion that she was his daughter but too late. And her biological mother? Geoffrey says she was a drug addict who left Tanya alone for days at a time. Tanya came to the notice of social services and spent her teenage years in foster care."

Tanya's background had earned her Abigail's sympathy as well as Geoffrey's. If Tanya had experienced the kind of life Geoffrey had told Abigail about, it was no surprise the young woman wanted to connect with her biological father. She had no one else. Taking up with a boyfriend also made sense. She was needy for love and acceptance. But living with an addicted parent and traversing the foster care system also meant she could be more resilient and more damaged than we thought.

"I tried to visit her when she was in the hospital yesterday, but I got there too late. She'd already checked out. I believe her boyfriend picked her up. I thought I'd see how she was doing today, but she's not home. Do you know any of her friends?"

"No, we don't."

"How about her boyfriend Robbie's last name?"

"Nope to that also." A note of suspicion crept into Abigail's voice. "Why so interested in Tanya?"

"I think I misjudged her, and like Geoffrey, I'm not convinced she isn't in some danger especially if a man came into the office and threatened her as Geoffrey attested to when he told us about Tanya's story."

"I'm afraid I can't help you. She sounded tired when she called in this morning, and she said she had a headache. I thought she'd be home resting. Should we be worried?"

"She might be with her boyfriend. She appeared very attached to him. If she doesn't show up tomorrow or call in sick, let me know. Meanwhile, get some rest yourself. You and Geoffrey are going through tough times."

"Why, Maddie, that's very kind of you to say."

"You're family and I love you."

I checked my watch and realized I had only a few hours before Zack and I would leave for our hike. I didn't feel like being alone. Spike was at home, but his conversational skills were limited when he was awake and nonexistent during his afternoon snooze. I'd visit my new friend Jane.

WHEN I PULLED UP IN FRONT OF HER HOUSE, Jane was standing out front with her back to the road gazing with a fixed stare at her rose bushes. I ambled up the walk, but she didn't turn around. I cleared my throat and she jumped.

"Sorry. I didn't mean to scare you."

"Maddie. Good to see you. Come on out back. I want to get away from those roses. They're driving me crazy. Too much sun, too little sun, too much rain, and not enough mulch, but grubs, beetles, other annoying insects in abundance. I feel like giving up this gardening fancy I have. Maybe I'm too old to garden well anymore."

"I'm glad I stopped by. It sounds like you could use a break."

I glanced over at Basset's house on our way to Jane's back porch. I had noticed a car parked in front of his place when I pulled up to Jane's. The crime scene tape had been pulled from around the house, so I knew the authorities had finished examining the premises. I noticed a lone figure standing in the middle of the backyard.

"One second, Jane. I'll be right back."

I crossed the back lawn, realizing as I got closer that it was a woman, one I recognized.

"Tanya. How are you feeling?"

She jumped at the sound of my voice and turned to face me. "What are you doing here?"

"I'm visiting my friend Jane next door. What are you doing in Basset's backyard?"

The surprise on Tanya's face turned to a look of anger. She clenched her fists in defiance. "I have a right to be here. This is my father's house."

"I'm not certain the authorities would want you here, at least not until there is evidence to support your claim that Basset was your father. Until then the sheriff's department might see you as a trespasser and wonder what you're doing on the property of a homicide victim."

Tanya put her hands on her hips and stuck out her chin. "Then you're a trespasser also."

"Maybe, but I don't have a motive for killing Mr. Basset."

"And you think I do? Robbie told me everyone would be suspicious of me because of all the fights we had. But that was in the past. We worked everything out. He accepted me as his daughter."

"Do you have proof of that?" I intended to badger her because I wanted to see what losing control might bring out. Sometimes getting someone riled up weakened their defenses and the truth tumbled out of their mouth.

Tanya looked for a moment as if she was about to blurt out something, but the lines of anger smoothed into a friendlier expression, one that was tinged with sadness.

"I shouldn't be so annoyed at you, Mrs. Sparks. Your son and his wife have been so kind to me. And I know you were trying to help me yesterday when I had my fainting spell in the restaurant. I saw . . . Well, never mind about that. Robbie says I shouldn't trust anyone around here. He says everyone thinks I harassed Mr. Basset, uh, my father to try to convince him I was his daughter when I wasn't because I wanted all his money and killed him for it. But that's not true. He knew I was his daughter. We were about to begin a new relationship together as soon as he returned from his trip. I wouldn't kill the person I most wanted to love and who I knew could love me." At this point Tanya's voice broke and tears welled up in her eyes. "You do believe me, don't you?"

I wanted to believe her but her lighting fast shift of moods from suspicion to anger to desperation left me wondering if I was being played for a fool, but before I could sort out how I felt, I heard a footfall behind me.

"Well, well, what a touching display, and on the dead man's property also. My two favorite suspects in Basset's murder." Deputy Stevens strode across the lawn toward us, his fingers linked in his belt, face contorted in an ugly look of disgust. "Now I'm beginning to wonder if the two of you were in it together."

"What are you doing here?" I asked.

"That's what I'd like to know about the two of you. Revisiting your recent triumph, the successful murder of the man who lived here?"

"Oh, for heaven's sake, you idiot. Neither of us had anything to do with the murder." I didn't, and I knew of no evidence to accuse Tanya. I glanced at Tanya's face. What was written there now? All evidence of those unshed tears were gone. She glanced at Stevens, then back to me. Without warning she grabbed my arm, shoved me into Stevens and made a dash for her car out front. As I fell, my elbow hit Stevens right below his belt and he yelped in pain.

"She's trying to kill me" he yelled.

I didn't know if he meant I was trying to kill him or instead he meant Tanya was. Either way, Stevens was down and appeared unable to catch his breath or find his feet. I got up, undamaged, and ran to intercept Tanya. Instead of running around her car to the driver's side, she opened the passenger's door and the car drove off. Someone was waiting for her. Robbie, I wondered?

Stevens picked himself up from the grass. "Did you get the license number of that car?"

I shook my head. I figured the car was Tanya's and that her boyfriend Robbie was driving it. I shared my suspicions with Stevens.

He was anything but grateful at my insight. "Might as well arrest you, then. I can get her later."

"Me? What for?"

He smiled his weasley smile. "Let's try trespassing."

Jane had witnessed everything and approached Stevens and me, overhearing his intention to charge me with trespassing.

"Don't make a fool of yourself, deputy. Maddie was comforting Mr. Basset's daughter who seemed distraught. Now I'm standing on his property. Are you going to arrest me also?"

Stevens's face grew redder and redder until I thought he might explode in rage. He opened his mouth, but no sound came out, then he brushed off the front of his uniform and marched away toward his cruiser.

"Thanks for intervening, Jane."

"Stevens and I have had our run-ins before. He tries to find anything he can to issue a ticket or a citation. He stops and tells the kids on the block to stop yelling when they're playing. He had no sense of humor or perspective. He wanted to arrest me for a noise violation."

"What were you doing?"

"I was mowing the lawn. He said my mower was too loud. It's a lawn mower. They make noise, and besides no one in the neighborhood complained about it. On Sundays when all of us around here mow our lawns, it's so loud no one can think. Let's go." She grabbed my hand and led me toward her back porch.

"Lemonade?" I asked.

"Yes, with a bit of this. We need it after dealing with Stevens." She pulled a bottle from a cabinet on the porch and poured a healthy tot of vodka into my glass.

I took a sip. "Just right." My thoughts, however, were not focused on the drink, tasty as it was. "From her reaction, Tanya believed Stevens thought she was guilty of her father's murder."

"He's all bluff." Jane sat back in her chair and took a long pull on her drink.

"Annoying though, isn't he? And he frightened her."

Tanya's moods were all over the place. From grief at Basset's death to paranoia that people thought she was a killer. But she had said her boyfriend was the person who told her everyone thought she was guilty. The more I heard about the guy, the less I liked him. Instead of being a comfort to her, he was reinforcing what Stevens thought, and I found Stevens an idiot but a dangerous one if he could convince his superiors of Tanya's guilt. Or of mine. But I discarded that idea. Steven's superior officer was Zack who was level-headed and reasonable in his execution of the law. I trusted Zack. Was it trust or lust? I giggled.

Jane shot me a look of concern. "Too much vodka?" she asked.

"Ah, no. My mind wandered off to my tea date later this afternoon."

"Date?"

"Yup. With the sheriff. We're getting to know each other a bit."

"From what I hear, he's someone worth knowing." Jane winked at me. "If you know what I mean."

I did. I downed the last of my lemonade. "I'd better get moving. I have to dig my hiking boots out of my closet for my date."

"I thought you said you were having tea."

"Hiking to tea."

Jane lifted one eyebrow in puzzlement.

"I'll let you know how it goes." I hurried off Jane's porch and headed toward my car. It was nice having another woman to talk to. Most of my friends had left the area when they retired and relocated to a warmer climate. Winters were long and cold here. I smiled to myself. Maybe this coming winter I'd have a friend to chat with over a cuppa and a man to curl up with in front of a warm fire.

One of our state parks was a brief half hour drive from the village. Zack called me around five to say he was running late. At six, he arrived, apologized for the delay, and we left for the park.

"We'll hike to the waterfall, stop for our snack and bask in the early evening sunlight." Zack was bursting with energy. I was looking forward to our outing also, but I worried I wouldn't be able to keep up with him on the trail.

"It's been years since I've been here. I almost forgot about the falls. It's uphill, isn't it? Not too steep?"

Zack grabbed me around the shoulders and hugged me. "You'll do fine. We can take a break whenever you feel like it."

"That doesn't answer my concerns."

"There are some steep sections, but your hiking boots will handle it, and I'll help you if you need it." He hefted the day pack with our snack and the thermos onto his back, and we set out.

Whenever I was huffing and puffing and began to lag behind, we used one of the benches along the trail to sit. The views on the way up were breathtaking: the small stream meandering down the hill next to the trail and the lake beyond it, calm, blue and serene. The sun nestled at the top of the trees at the other side of the lake.

"The weather station predicts rain later. I wouldn't want to get stuck on this trail after the sun sets. It would be treacherous going in the dark especially if it's raining."

Zack gave my hand a reassuring squeeze "Don't worry. We have time to get back to our car."

The waterfall at the top was small, a drop of less than thirty feet, but on its way down, it crashed onto the boulders below and created a spray of water that made the rocks along the trail slippery and wet.

"Watch your step here." Zack took my hand and helped me over a cluster of moss-covered rocks and onto a small shelf that stood halfway up the falls. We moved back from the spray and continued to the top to a dry spot. Zack opened the pack, took out our cookies, the thermos and a small blanket which he placed on the ground.

We finished our snack and laid back, our arms propping up our heads so we could look across the lake at the shoreline beyond where the sun bathed the water in a golden glow. Soon the shadows from the trees grew longer, and the sun slid down into their branches, creating undulating light and dark on the water's surface. Zack rolled toward me, slipped one arm behind my back, and we kissed. The kiss went on and deepened. I sank back onto the blanket and Zack rolled nearer to me, the length of his body touching mine. I could stay here forever, I thought. I lost track of time enveloped in Zack's warmth.

Thunder rumbled in the distance. In minutes the wind picked up, lashing the tree branches in a frenzied dance. Clouds rolled in, blackening the sky overhead. We ignored it, our focus on each other. I felt safe in his arms, a warmth penetrating my body.

"Are you sure this is what you want, Maddie?"

I answered him by pulling him closer to me. Wow, wow, wow. He leaned on one shoulder over me, lifting his head to gaze into my eyes. There was a crack from behind us. Had the thunder gotten closer? Or was a tree falling on us?

He shoved me away from him, grabbing his shoulder with his hand. Another crack, and I was certain an entire tree was coming down on us.

I rolled back toward him, his body still.

"Zack! Are you okay?" I began to rise to my knees, but Zack pulled me back down onto the ground. He slumped next to me.

"Stay where you are and don't move." His voice sounded raspy and weak. His eyes were closed, and there was blood on his shoulder.

"Zack." I shook him, and his eyes fluttered open.

"I'm sorry about this, Maddie."

"Not your fault. Can you move?"

"I can move, but I don't think I should. I'm losing too much blood from my shoulder."

I pulled the blanket from under me where it had become lodged when Zack had pulled me to him. I pressed it into the wound to staunch the flow of blood. "Can you put pressure on this with your hand while I call for help?"

He nodded.

I held up my cellphone. No service. Not up here in nowhere. I grabbed Zack's phone out of the pack. No bars for him either. No, no, no. Our perfect paradise had become a nightmare.

Zack gave me a tiny smile. "I'll be fine here for now, but you need to go for help."

I looked at the sky overhead. The wind blew harder and howled, accompanied by rumbles of thunder and lightning flashing from cloud to cloud and from the roiling sky to the earth. Between flashes darkness obscured the setting sun. A raindrop hit my cheek, then another. Soon the drops became a sheet of water, sometimes coming straight down, at others blown sideways by wind gusts.

"There's a flashlight in my day pack. It will help you pick your way down the trail." Zack's voice was no louder than a whisper.

I grabbed the flashlight and gave Zack a look of encouragement before I turned my back on him to begin the dark, slippery trek down.

"And Maddie."

"Yes?"

"When you get service and call 9-1-1. Tell them I've been hit by a bullet, not a tree."

I PICKED MY WAY AROUND THE ROCK-STREWN TRAIL, but the rain came down in heavy sheets making the trail slick with mud. So far, I could see where I was planting my feet, but as the skies continued to blacken, I had to flick on the flashlight. Its powerful beam made me feel more assured, and I increased my pace checking my phone and Zack's to see if I had picked up service yet. With my attention diverted from the path and onto the phones, I didn't see the stream of muddy water coursing down the trail ahead. When I stepped into it, I jerked my attention back to my path, but too late. I slipped and fell into the dark water and knocked the flashlight out of my hand. It tumbled down the steep drop off to my right and I heard it clatter against the rocks and tree roots. Down, down and into the stream of water until the sound of its falling faded into the thrashing of trees overhead and the deafening sound of thunder.

I wanted to sit down in the mud and cry, but Zack was lying wounded behind me. I had to get help for him. Well, I thought to myself, I'm already on my fanny. I might as well stay here, and butt walk my way down the rest of the way. I tried that mode of locomotion until my feet dropped off into thin air. It was as if the trail had ended. I waved my foot around to see if I could feel firm ground anywhere below me, but I encountered nothing but air. The pounding rain must have washed away the trail. I'd have to veer off, grab tree roots and anything else that might hold me and work my way up the side of the hill perpendicular to the established route, then head back down and hope I could feel where the trail began again. The flashes of lightening overhead might provide some light for my climb. I waited for one to strike, and then followed the image of what I remembered it lit up ahead. Waiting for a bolt to provide illumination was slow going.

I crept up, grabbing anything that afforded me a hold on the hill—roots, rocks, bushes. After working my way upward for thirty feet or so, I paused to catch my breath, patting the pocket of my shorts to find the cell phones. And then it hit me. If I could check for cellphone service and see if I had any, I also should be able to find either my or Zack's flashlight app on the phone. What a dummy I was. I was even more of a dummy when I realized I'd never used the light on the phone and had no idea how to find it. I leaned back against a small tree and tried to turn on my phone. The face of the cell lit up, and I began punching all the apps I could, hoping I'd find one with enough light to get me out of here. The dim light from one of my social media apps lit up and I held the phone aloft to look around me. Not enough illumination to see beyond the tree I clung to for support. I punched all the apps on Zack's phone, hoping I'd have better luck, but I couldn't find the flashlight there either. Lightning struck somewhere near me, and I jumped, but the bolt also brought enough brightness to spot below me one of the benches we'd rested on while climbing to the waterfall. I tried to turn on my phone to spot the bench again, but nothing happened. My battery was dead.

I used the light from the face of Zack's cellphone to lead me to the bench. Was this the first bench we encountered coming up or the second one? I hoped it was the first one because that meant I was over halfway down. I was safe here, but Zack was not. I began to stumble my way down the trail once more. I didn't want to run the battery down on Zack's phone because I needed to use it to make my call for help when I got someplace where I had service. I trod with care, testing each step to make certain I didn't step into another place where the trail had been washed out. I was making progress, stepping where I felt the ground firm underneath me and could use a tree along the trail to hold onto, butt walking when my tree handholds disappeared. I stepped forward onto a rock that seemed firm, but with no warning it rolled from beneath my foot, and I fell forward down the trail, landing on a patch of moss. Not only did it feel like moss, I realized, but I could see its dark green surface. I could see it. I could. A light from a building up ahead shone onto where I fell. It came from the outside light on the consignment shop building next to the beach area of the lake. I'd made it down! I checked Zack's phone for service. Two bars. It would do.

I made the 9-1-1 call, told them my location and Zack's situation and was told they would be there in less than half an hour.

"Hurry." Exhausted, I pressed the side of my face into the wet ground.

CHAPTER 13

S OMEONE SHOOK ME.

"He's up there." I pointed behind me and tried to get up. "I'll show you."

A hand pressed me backwards not onto the muddy pillow I remembered but into a crisp fabric one. I could still hear rain, but the thunder had stopped. My nose detected a chemical smell, not at all like the odors of mud, trees, and dirt.

My granddaughter stood next to me while someone else reached toward a bag of fluid hanging nearby and adjusted it.

"Hi, Gram. Don't try to get up. Lie back and the nurse will take care of you." Sara's face was gray with concern.

"But what about Zack? Is he . . .?"

"He's in surgery right now, Gram, but he's doing fine. You both were suffering from hypothermia when the rescue squad found you. You're in the hospital. Mom and Dad are on their way in."

A noise at the door caught Sara's attention.

"Mom, Mom." Geoffrey rushed to my bed and grasped me in his arms.

"Watch the IV." The nurse pulled Geoffrey away from me. "You can stay for a few minutes, but she's exhausted and needs to sleep."

Abigail approached the bed and planted a kiss on my cheek.

And that's all I remembered until I woke up again. The room was dark, and everyone had gone. There were no sounds from the hallway. It had to be near morning. I could see a weak light pierce through the gap in my window curtains.

Zack! I had to see Zack.

I'd been in this hospital earlier in the summer visiting one of my friends who had broken his leg crawling up a ladder to clean his gutters. I told him he was an utter fool at his age, more than eighty, to be doing that job, but eighty-year-old men never listen to anyone. I assumed Zack would be in ICU after his surgery, and that was where I'd visited my friend, so I knew its location. All I had to do was follow the hall toward the elevator and push the button for the second floor. I maneuvered myself out of bed, careful not to tangle my drip line, grabbed the pole the bag was attached to and rolled it to the door. The nurse's station was abandoned. It always was in my cozy mysteries. Here, too. I was a lucky old bat. I rolled the portable drip past the desk and toward the elevators, pushed "Down" and, when the doors opened, stepped in and punched the second-floor button.

My luck continued. The nurse in ICU got up from her chair and headed down the hallway away from me. I looked through the ICU glass partition. There was one patient there. My sweet Zack. I couldn't see his face in the dim lighting. The rise and fall of his chest told me he was alive, but asleep. I didn't want to wake him, but I did want to assure myself he was okay. I pushed the door open and shuffled over to the bed. His eyes popped open.

"Who the hell are you?" The man stared at me with muddy brown eyes, not the blue of Zack's.

I drew back from the bed in shock. "Where did they put Zack?"

A hand touched my shoulder. "You need to get back to your room." I recognized the nurse from ICU.

"Where's Zack Montgomery?"

The nurse took my arm and led me to her desk. "And you are?" she asked.

"Maddie Sparks. Where have you put Zack?"

The ICU nurse picked up her phone and made a call. "You're not supposed to be here."

The door to the elevator opened and a security guard and the nurse from my floor got off.

"Ms. Sparks," said my nurse, "you can't go wandering around the hospital. You need to go back to your room."

"I was looking for Zack Montgomery. He had surgery earlier, so I assumed he would be here."

The nurse accompanied by the security guard steered me to the elevator.

"I strolled through half this hospital with my butt showing. These hospital gowns are a disgrace, you know that, don't you?"

"Yes ma'am, but they aren't meant for taking walks. Or for invading other patients' privacy." The nurse pushed the button for my floor.

As we stepped out of the elevator, I shoved the pole toward her.

"Here, you push the pole. I need to use both hands to pull this flimsy nightgown around my backside."

The push I gave the apparatus was strong enough that it rolled past the nurse and down the hallway faster than I could keep up with it. Before it pulled the IV out of my arm, I rushed after it as it veered to the left and bumped into the entrance of a patient's room, quivered there for a moment, then rolled into the room.

"Is that you, Maddie?" Zack's voice came from inside the room.

I grabbed the IV line and followed the pole into the room.

"Hiya, Zack. It took me a while to find you, but here I am. Is it too early for visitors?"

Zack, his arm and chest swaddled in bandages and hooked up to several drip lines, gave me a tiny smile, enough for me to know he was going to be okay. His eyelids fluttered. I knew he was tired.

"Back to your room. Now." With a firm grip on my arm, the nurse directed me toward the hallway.

"I'll be back soon." My drip and I turned to leave the room.

"I like your nightgown, Maddie. Very appealing," Zack gave a chuckle of appreciation.

This was not the way I wanted that lovely, sexy man to be introduced to my private assets.

THE HOSPITAL RELEASED ME LATER THAT MORNING, but before I left, I asked the floor nurse if I could visit Zack. She signaled me to wait while she checked to see if he wanted to see me. He did. He was sitting up in bed having a cup of warm liquid. It was too dark to be tea and too light to be coffee.

I leaned over to give him a quick kiss and sniffed his drink.

"What are you drinking?"

"It doesn't taste like anything I recognize."

"It's beef broth to build up your strength." The nurse plumped his pillows.

Zack rolled his eyes at me in a look of despair. Once the nurse left the room, he looked up at me with pleading in his eyes. "Can you help me out here? Get me cup of coffee, strong and black."

"I'll see what I can rummage up downstairs in the cafeteria."

"I'm happy to see you're okay, Maddy."

"I'm fine. I lost a few pounds, and I'm as anxious for real food and drink as you are. I'm going home to check on my, er, the cat, then I'll come back here with anything you'd like."

"I'd like a few minutes alone with you to finish what we started before this happened." He nodded at his bandaged shoulder.

"I think you need a little time before we try anything athletic." I caressed his hand.

The smile on his face faded. "There were two shots, Maddie. The shooter could have wanted to hit both of us."

"You get your strength back, and we'll find out who's behind this. Until then, you'll have to track down clues from your bed."

"I may not be tracking down anything."

"That's not the Zack Montgomery I've come to know. What are you saying?"

"I was appointed sheriff on an interim basis."

"So, you take two or three weeks leave of absence or whatever time you need. Until then I'll be right by your side helping you out. Unless you think I can't be of service."

"It's not that. The county is not going to want to leave this case in the hands of an interim appointee who's now laid up with a bum shoulder."

"You mean you think they'll fire you?"

"Not fire. Let me go back to retirement."

"But you're the best man to do this job."

"The county won't see it that way."

"I suppose they'll put Deputy Sourpuss in your position."

"Maybe."

A dark-haired woman wearing a white lab coat knocked on the doorframe. "How's my patient this morning? I see you already have company." She stuck out her hand. "Hi. I'm Doctor Gonzalez."

"This is the surgeon who operated on me. My friend, Maddie Sparks. You have my permission, Doctor Gonzalez, to say anything about my case in front of her."

"Doctor Gonzalez, you did a durn good job. He's trying to get me into the broom closet for a little fun and games."

Doctor Gonzalez laughed. A sense of humor and great medical skills. I liked her.

She leaned over Zack's bed for a closer look at him. "You're doing great. I'm willing to release you as soon as tomorrow, but you'll need home care for at least a week."

Back home to his place in Madison County?

"Where are you living now? I never did ask you, Zack."

"I'm staying at a B and B outside of town, but if the county does what I expect, let me go, then I'll go back home."

"I'd recommend you hire a health care worker to come in a few hours a day, and then you'll be going to physical therapy," Dr. Gonzalez said.

"Was there any brain damage?" I asked.

Dr. Gonzalez looked puzzled.

"I'm asking because Zack is staying with me. I guess he forgot."

Zack opened his mouth to protest. I held up my hand to stop him from speaking. "Shut up, or you can forget the broom closet or a blanket on a hillside."

He clamped his mouth shut.

"Good. You can take orders then. And you'll be doing that for the next few weeks." I held out my hand and shook the doctor's. "Is there any reason he can't have a cup of coffee, real coffee? He'll be less grouchy. The nurses will bless you for agreeing."

"He can have anything he wants," said Dr. Gonzalez.

"Not anything. Not yet." I waved good-bye to Zack. "I'll be back as soon as I can."

The breakfast the hospital served me before I was released did nothing to reduce my hunger. Although it would take more time, I wanted to go home and make decent coffee rather than offer Zack the weak hospital cafeteria fare. Since my cell had no charge, I borrowed one from a nurse and called Sara to come pick me up and take me home. She pulled up at the hospital entrance taking advantage of the overhang to avoid the rain which continued as heavy as yesterday. My stomach grumbled on the way home in Sara's car. I bounced out of the car and into the house.

"Gram. Wait for me. I've got an umbrella."

I didn't care if I got wet. I was so happy to be home.

"I hate hospitals because they're places for sick people and they're always so cold. I still can't get warm." I shivered.

Spike circled my feet and rubbed against my legs the minute I entered the house. I leaned down and petted him.

"He's glad to see you."

"I'll feed him. He must be starved."

"I came over earlier and gave him some food."

"Oh, Sara. You are so wonderful." I hugged her.

"You're wearing the clothes you had on for your hike. They're still damp. I should have thought to bring you a change of clothes.

Here. Get this off." Sara helped me remove my shirt and wrapped the Afghan from the couch around my shoulders.

"That's better." I smiled and patted her hand.

"Coffee?"

I nodded, and she steered me into the kitchen. Sara grabbed the coffee pot and got a brew going.

"Thanks, sweetie. I'm starved. How about scrambled eggs?"

"Why don't you sit down, and I'll make them for you." Sara pushed me into a kitchen chair and opened the fridge.

"But I feel fine."

"I know you think you do, but you've been through an ordeal, and, if I heard right, when the hospital released you, the nurse who wheeled you out said something about you're being Zack's caregiver for a few weeks?"

"Don't tell your mother and father. I'll talk to them when I've got Zack settled in here."

Sara pulled a skillet out of the drawer, cracked four eggs into a bowl and beat them. "Toast?"

"You're not saying a thing about Zack, but I sense you have reservations."

"No. That's your business, but I think you're in for a lot of trouble."

I wiggled my butt around on the chair and realized I was sore all over from the falls and tumbles I took last night getting down the hill. "You mean your mother and father won't approve."

"Well, yes, them, but Grandpops is back in town, and his wife tossed him out. Mom and Dad said he visited them, begging for their support."

"Financial support, no doubt."

Sara turned to me with a troubled look on her face. "Well, that goes without saying. Grandpops never was good with money, was he?"

"Honey, let's be honest. He contributed little support, financial or otherwise. 'Not good with money' is your father's polite way of putting it."

"Yeah, I know." She poured the egg mixture into the heated pan.

"But Dad told me Grandpops wants you back, and he's willing to fight for you."

I snorted. "What he wants is this house, the money from my book career and bragging rights that I took him back."

Sara grabbed two plates out of the cupboard, put slices of toast in the toaster, and ladled eggs onto the plates.

When she sat down to the table, she looked up at me shyly and asked, "Are you still in love with Grandpops?"

"No. That ended for me years ago when I tossed him out"

"Good. I love my grandfather, but I can understand how he made a bad husband." She paused and took a bite of her egg. "I'll bet Zack would make a great partner."

I merely smiled and bit into my toast.

We wolfed down our food. Sara left after breakfast. I promised her I'd call her if I needed help with anything.

I hugged her at the door. "I'm so glad you like Zack."

She waved and drove off. I filled a thermos with the remainder of the coffee to take to Zack at the hospital. I'd stop at the bakery in town and pick up half a dozen cinnamon buns. If he was hungry for something more substantial, I could drive to the diner in town and get him a full meal.

I grabbed a quick shower and changed into a pair of jeans and a figure-hugging cotton sweater to show the man what was waiting for him once he recovered. I was tired, but I wanted to get back to Zack as soon possible. After that I'd consider a nap.

I was about to leave the house when I saw Geoffrey's car pull up in front. Oh, dear. I didn't want to take the time to talk with him now. I'd promised Zack real coffee, and I was late getting it to him. I opened the door and stepped out onto the porch, but it wasn't Geoffrey who got out of the car and ran up the walk.

The man was as persistent as a bear after honey.

"I can't talk now, Dan." I tried to push past him to my car, but he blocked my way off the porch by placing his hand around my arm. I shrugged it off.

"I just came from the hospital. I stopped there after hearing about what happened to you yesterday, but they wouldn't give out any information about you. Maddie, baby, are you okay?"

"I'm fine. The one you should ask about is Zack. Someone shot him."

"Yes, I heard." Dan sounded so dismissive.

"He could be dead, you know."

"You could be dead, Maddie. That's what concerns me. I still love you, you know. I've never stopped loving you." He stepped closer to me. His breath smelled like whiskey and his body gave off the odor of sweat, the kind a person produced when anxious, a sure sign this encounter was stressful for him.

"Does your wife, Belinda know this is how you feel, how you've felt all these years?" I didn't believe Dan's declaration of love for me for a minute.

"Belinda isn't important right now. You are. We are." Dan pulled me to him and began to kiss me. I struggled with him, but he wouldn't let me go. He moved his hands over my body and pressed himself against me. "You know you want me. We were so good together."

His cliched declaration of love and lust weren't winning me over. They infuriated me. How dare this man think I would take him back? I pushed at him, but still he held onto me, so I pretended I liked his embraces and went limp in his arms.

"Oh, Maddie." He breathed into my ear, and thinking I was giving in to his passion, he loosened his hold a bit.

"Oh, Dan." I moved a half step backward then shoved him hard. Taken off guard, he fell backwards down the porch steps hitting his head on the cement. He lay still.

"What have I done?" Had I killed him? Would I go to prison for this?

I stooped down and felt his throat for a pulse. It was there, but faint.

CHAPTER 14

I CALLED FOR AN AMBULANCE and then the sheriff's office. There was no sense putting off an encounter with the authorities. I had to be up front with what I had done.

The ambulance arrived, and moments after it a county sheriff's car pulled up and Deputy I-Don't-Care-For-Animals got out.

I groaned in dismay. I had hoped for the woman deputy sheriff or any officer other than him.

Two other county cars pulled up behind him.

"What have we got here? Looks like you killed someone. Isn't that your husband?" Deputy Smug—now I remembered, Deputy Stevens—walked over to where the medics were examining Dan.

"It was an accident. I pushed him away from me, he slipped on the wet cement, and he hit his head."

"From what I hear about the two of you, you have history together and it's not that of a loving wife and husband. Turn around." He spun me around and snapped cuffs on me, then walked me through the pouring rain to one of the county cars. "Take her to the jail."

"Wait!" I was frantic to know whether Dan was dead or how serious his condition was. "I need to go with him to the hospital." I hoped the hospital was where they were taking him and not the morgue.

"He's got a concussion, but he'll live," said one of the techs.

"And that's why you're not accompanying him to the hospital. We're not going to give you another chance to kill him." Deputy Stevens looked pleased at my helplessness.

The other deputy pushed me into the back of the car, and I struggled to find a position where my arms and back didn't ache from the cuffs. I was soaking wet from talking to Deputy Stevens explaining what happened between Dan and me.

The female deputy approached the car and looked in.

I yelled at her from inside. "Tell Zack what happened."

She leaned over. "It won't do any good. He's not acting sheriff any longer. They removed him from the position an hour ago."

"Who did the county appoint in his place?"

She glanced at my nemesis deputy.

"Oh, no." I slumped back on the seat. "Do I get a phone call?"

She nodded. "Once you get to the jail."

I hated to do it, but I knew who I had to call. My son Richard would be getting a lot of family business this month.

"YOU DO INSPIRE PASSION IN MEN, MOM. Lucky for you one of your neighbors saw the confrontation between you and Dad and told the sheriff's deputies what happened." Richard must have broken the speed limit to get to the county jail so fast.

I rubbed my wrists to restore a decent blood flow in them.

Deputy Stevens stood in the hallway and scowled at us as we left the jail.

Richard opened his umbrella and walked me to his car. "What did you ever do to that guy, anyway? He dislikes you."

"I rescued a cat he deemed unworthy to continue living. The cat scratched him."

"You mean Spike? He seems like such a gentle soul."

"He is unless you're the kind of sad excuse for a human the deputy is."

"Maybe he's a dog person." Richard started the car. "Where to?"

"The hospital, of course."

"You want to check on Dad. I understand."

"No. I want to check on Zack. The county removed him as the acting sheriff. Your father is alive. That's better than he deserves."

"Mom!"

"Don't act so shocked. Your father mistreated me and you kids. You remember that, don't you?"

"I know. I wondered if after all these years you had forgiven him."

"I have not."

"And neither have I. You deserved better."

"We all did."

Richard was silent for a minute. "Geoffrey still has a soft spot for Dad. What do you think that is all about?"

"Geoffrey is a kind-hearted man. Take Tanya, for example. She may not be the sweet gal he thinks she is, I'll bet, but he believed her story. There's more to her relationship with her father than she's telling us."

"She told you she has a boyfriend. Do you think he played a part in Basset's death?" Richard pulled into a parking slot at the hospital.

"If I could get that little piece of work alone, I'd find out."

Richard laughed. "I'd rather be interrogated by the police than questioned by you, Mom."

Well, good. I guess I did have some skills that transferred to sleuthing.

We dashed through the downpour to the hospital entrance and got permission at the information desk for Richard to accompany me to see Zack. I fluffed my hair out to remove the raindrops. If I had to deal with this rain any longer, I'd mildew.

Zack was wide awake and happy to see me.

"I'm so sorry about your coffee. I had to take a detour." I didn't explain what it was. Zack had enough to worry about right now. "I heard about your replacement. How could the county be so stupid?"

He took my hand and stroked the back of it. "Calm down, Maddie. There's nothing that can be done about their decision to remove me."

"Maybe not, but they should know better than to replace you with Stevens." I sat on the side of Zack's hospital bed with Richard sitting in the chair across the room.

"It was an emergency appointment, but he seems to have pull with the head of the county commission." Zack gave a rueful smile.

Richard scowled. "It's family. Stevens is the county commissioner's nephew."

"How do you know that?" I was surprised my son knew so much about the doings in this county.

"I've followed county politics around here for years. And Zack is right, Mom. Stevens occupies the position on a contingency basis because there weren't enough county reps at the meeting to make his appointment final."

"I like the blonde woman deputy. She seems smart and competent." I straightened Zack's blanket and tucket it in around his legs, mindless fidgeting on my part, the kind of thing I always did when the kids were young and sick in bed.

"I like her, too." Richard smiled. "We went to high school together."

"Oh, right. I thought I recognized her. Anita Burroughs, right?"

"She was also in my law school class in Albany, but she dropped out after a year to get married. The marriage didn't work out." Richard smoothed the crease in his pants and then looked up at me, his gaze trying for innocent, but he couldn't fool me.

"Richard, you sly fox. You have a crush on the woman, don't you?"

"Maybe. All I'm saying is that she would make a better sheriff for this county than Deputy Stevens."

"I suppose you know him, too."

"No. I hear rumors, however."

"Tell me."

Richard cleared his throat. "I shouldn't spread tales when I don't know the truth."

"I won't tell anyone."

Richard guffawed. "What I could tell you might color your interactions with him, and he's now in a position to make life difficult for Dad."

Zack followed our discussion with his full attention, his gaze traveling between Richard and me. "I might be interested in hearing whatever you've heard about Deputy Stevens. And I promise I won't spread rumors. My observations of the man indicate he's lazy and prejudiced against women and nonwhites. Does that match what you've heard?"

"Here's a better idea that we all can get behind. Why don't we let other people who know Stevens and work with him tell us about him?" I gave Richard a pointed look.

"What are you suggesting, Mom?"

"As if you don't know. Ask Deputy Sheriff Anita for coffee or dinner. Then let the evening evolve as it may."

Zack nodded. "Great idea, Maddie. She looks neglected to me. Richard may be what she needs."

"Conflict of interest," said Richard.

I clucked my tongue. "It's dinner, Richard. People talk over dinner."

Richard got up out of his chair and paced the small room. "I'll think about it. Now, here's my concern. Who shot at you? And was my mother in danger also?"

Zack didn't reply to my son's question about whether I was also a target of the shooter. "You could help there, Richard. Check on Basset's brother's parole date. I couldn't find the guy in the system, but I understand he might have a different name from Basset's."

"Give me the name."

"We don't have it, but we're thinking one of your bright young law clerks might be able to track him down somehow."

"That would require a magic wand, and that isn't something even the brightest law clerks come equipped with. I need a name."

Zack shrugged his good shoulder, flinching when he moved his damaged shoulder. "I can't give you one."

I listened to their conversation and thought, oh what the hey. "Polander. His name is Polander."

They both looked at me their eyes widened in surprise.

"Don't push me for how I know. Look it up."

Richard picked up his briefcase. "I've got to go. Since I drove you here, Mom, you'll have to do your goodbye kisses quick."

"I can find my own way home. Besides, you may want to rethink your leaving here without visiting your father, Richard."

"What?" Zack sat forward in his bed. "Dan Sparks is in the hospital? Here? What happened?"

"My mother tried to kill him." Richard winked at Zack and gently removed me from Zack's bed.

"I can explain." I tried to resist Richard's walking me out of the room.

"Never mind. I'm sure you had your reasons. You can tell me when you drop by with my dinner tonight." Zack blew me a kiss.

WE CHECKED WITH ONE OF THE NURSES on the floor and got permission to visit Dan.

When Richard and I entered his room, Dan pulled himself up in bed and pointed at me. "I'm pressing charges, Maddie."

"So am I, Dan."

"You pushed me."

"You molested me, and I've got witnesses. Interesting how quickly your eternal love turns to a lawsuit. I brought my lawyer with me in case you want to confess."

"Dad." Richard gave a curt head nod.

"Richard." Dan tried to return the nod but grabbed the side of his head. "Yowie that hurts."

I turned at the sound of a tap on the doorframe.

"What are you doing here. Maddie?" Belinda. Dan's soon-to-be ex. We would be in the same club together. She never liked me much, and I felt the same way about her although over the years I gave her points for tolerating Dan for as long as she did.

"I hear you came to your senses and threw him out." I gave her a snarky smile.

"I should never have taken him in. He's incapable of fidelity." Belinda took a tissue out of her purse and blew her nose.

"Didn't I warn you?"

"You did, but I thought you were jealous that despite the divorce you still loved him." Her eyes filled with tears, and she gave her nose another loud blow.

"I don't get it, Belinda. If I were in your shoes, I'd be madder than hell at him, not sad."

"I'm not sad. Summer allergies."

"Hey, you two harridans. Have a little sympathy, would you? I'm lying here in a hospital bed with a head injury. I could have died."

Belinda and I rolled our eyes in unison. "Unlikely." We chimed in together.

"I hope you're not here to take him back." Belinda wiped her eyes and gave one more honk on her nose. "You know he'd come back to you if he can't land another, younger woman with the money to support him. It's a pattern with him."

I did know. "You're done with him?"

"Hey, like I said. I can hear you. I'm right here. And I'm not some used up guy you both can toss out into the trash."

She and I exchanged knowing looks. "I'm filing for divorce." She tossed a sheaf of papers at Dan and stalked out of the room.

I almost grabbed her before she left to give her a hug.

CHAPTER 15

RICHARD AND I BOTH WATCHED BELINDA'S retreating figure. Richard was too good a son and too much a gentleman to do a celebration dance with me, and the sounds of sobs from Dan's bed made a jubilation jig appear insensitive on my part.

"I loved that woman," he said.

"Yeah. Me, too. I didn't realize what a service she did for me all these years taking you in." I did a short celebratory two-step.

Richard cleared his throat. "Let's finish this up, Mom. You had a couple of questions you wanted to ask Dad."

I did. The name Polander had been ricocheting around in my brain since Dan had mentioned it in connection with Basset's brother.

I grabbed the box of tissues off the windowsill, tossed it to Dan and then took a seat at the foot of Dan's bed. "Get hold of yourself. We need to talk."

"You still love me, don't you, Maddie? We were so good together. Don't you remember . . ."

"I seem to have developed complete amnesia about any of the good times we might have had together. Your son is in trouble, and you need to help him. You said Basset had a brother with the last name of Polander and that he was in prison. I wanted to give that name to Zack, but you told me if I did, it would somehow connect the murder to Geoffrey."

Dan's glance bounced between Richard and me. His Adam's apple rose and fell in this throat as he nervously gulped. I could tell he was bargaining for time to make up a story to cover his lie about Geoffrey, but I cut in before he could begin his fabrication.

"How could Geoffrey be connected to a man like Leon Polander, I asked myself. And he wasn't. Not directly. The connection had to be through you. Once I made that association, I remembered that about ten years ago—you were no longer living here—a man appeared at our house asking for you. He was a seedy-looking dude who claimed you owed him money. I'll never forget his eyes, the color of gun metal, flat, no depth to them. If eyes are the window to the soul, then this guy had none. I sent him away, telling him you and I were no longer together, and I didn't know where you were. But the guy knew your son was a businessman in town, so he went to Geoffrey and tracked you down through Geoffrey. I'm sure you didn't have the money to pay the guy, but you knew Geoffrey did and so did the dude. You told Geoffrey the guy would hurt you if you didn't give him the money."

"So what? How does that tie into Basset's murder?" Dan reached for a glass of water and sipped it, trying for a look of nonchalance.

"When that guy came to the house looking for you, he introduced himself as Leon Polander. I'd forgotten all about him because it happened so long ago, but when you mentioned the name the other day, something in my brain clicked. 'I should know that name,' I told myself. And I do."

"Not smart, Maddie. You've put Geoffrey in danger as I told you would happen." Dan sounded smug, but his face registered something else. A trickle of sweat rolled down the side of his face.

I leaned forward. "What do you mean?"

"Leon Polander is not a nice person."

"I figured that out for myself, but he's in prison. And will remain there for several more months."

"Wrong again, my dear."

Something about the certainty in Dan's voice chilled me.

Richard stepped over to the bed. "You'd better tell us what's up, Dad. Is Geoffrey's life in danger?" Richard's eyes were dark with anger.

"Well, you see, dear boy, your mother is right. I was a little short of money when Polander found me, but I told him I could borrow it from my son. Before I could get the money and pay Polander he was arrested and sent to prison. He never received the money he was owed, and I kind of led him to believe it was Geoffrey's fault. Polander expected his money regardless of being behind bars."

"But the truth was that you took the money Geoffrey gave you to pay Polander and you were the one who didn't pay him off." Could I be any more disgusted with this man?

Dan fidgeted with his bed sheet, rolling the edge it up and down in his fingers. "Polander got an early release. He hit the streets weeks ago. He might have contacted Geoffrey for money already. And he told me before he went to prison that he had a brother, even told me his last name. Basset. He hated the guy."

"And you were going to keep this from me, from all of us? And put your son in danger? What kind of a father are you, Dan?" I made a fist of my hand and stepped toward Dan. Before my fist could connect, Richard pulled me off as a nurse came into the room.

"She's trying to finish the job. The woman is trying to kill me. Again." Dan fell back into his pillows, looking pale, his hands shaking.

Richard set me on my feet and gave me a gentle push toward the door. "Let's get you out of here, Mom."

Before I let Richard direct me out of the room, I spun around. "And how do you know Polander is out of prison? You've had contact with him, haven't you?"

Dan blanched and pulled the covers over his face.

"Coward." I let Richard walk me to the door as the nurse reached for a buzzer to call for security.

Richard interceded with the nurse. "No need to call anyone. She's a little upset. He said things he shouldn't have. And I'll bet you've seen cases like this, head injuries and all."

Richard's reassuring smile and words might get us out of the hospital, but I was certain Dan would accuse me of accosting him in his hospital room. Deputy Stevens would pay me another visit and soon.

Out in the hallway, I tried to calm myself, but I still wanted to hurt Dan and hurt him bad. A head injury wasn't good enough.

"I can hear your brain plotting, Mom. Let it go for now." Richard and I found a waiting room where he settled me onto a couch and got me a cup of water.

As soon as he seated himself beside me, his cell rang. "I've got to take this. I'll only be a minute." He walked away to the other side of the room but was back at my side in a matter of a minute. His lips were drawn tight to the corners of his mouth and his eyes told me something awful was happening.

I sprang off the couch. "What is it?"

"Deputy Stevens strikes again. That was my office. He arrested Geoffrey for Basset's murder five minutes ago, Abigail tried to reach me at the office. I've got to get over to the jail."

"I'll come with you."

"No, Mother. You will not. You will go see Zack and tell him what's happened. Dan is the least of our worries now." He put his arms around me. "Find your tough, Mom. I'll take care of Geoffrey, but since Stevens thinks he's got his man, I doubt he'll look for another suspect. I could use Zack's expertise if he's well enough to help me."

I gave Richard a hurt look.

"Oh, and of course, your expertise as a mystery writer, too, Mom."

"Don't patronize me, Richard." I spun on my heel and headed back to Zack's room as Richard strode down the hall the other way toward the exit doors. "I'll grab a taxi home,"

I burst through the door to Zack's room to find him dressed in the civilian clothes one of the deputies from the department had brought him earlier in the day. He sat in a wheelchair.

"Surprise. We're going home." He saw the pain in my eyes, and he started to get out of the chair.

"Don't." I held out my hand to prevent him from rising. I had to find my tough, as Richard had said. "Stevens arrested Geoffrey for Basset's murder. We need to get home and lay plans for how we prevent my son from going to jail. Richard's with Geoffrey now. He wouldn't let me go with him. I'll explain everything on the way down the elevator."

Once in the hallway, I turned to Zack. "Polander. The name is Polander."

"What? Zack asked.

The nurse punched the "Down" button, and Zack and I got in with her pushing his chair.

"Leon Polander is Basset's brother," I said. "And he was paroled early." Zack knew me well enough not to ask questions that might impede my forward motion, but once we were ensconced in the taxi, he put his arm around me and hugged me the entire ride.

It continued to rain. The windshield wipers made annoying slapping noises against the glass.

"RICHARD'S RIGHT." ZACK AND I SAT on my couch and sipped tea. "Stevens isn't going to look for another suspect, although there are plenty of them almost begging to be questioned. Including Mr. Polander, wherever he is now. I'll work on Stevens and see if he can track the guy down."

"Closer to home, although you've already talked to Tanya, I think she needs to be questioned again, don't you?" I poured us another cup of tea and urged a cookie on him.

Zack nodded in agreement and nabbed a cookie. "Both of us have been more than reasonable with her. No one tried to arrest her for the murder."

I told Zack about my encounter with her at Basset's house before we had gone off to the park. I had listened more than plied her with questions, but that was about to change.

I laughed. "The kind, motherly approach isn't working with her. You're getting to know me better, but you haven't witnessed me in stern mother mode."

"I've seen a bit of it."

"You're about to see a lot more." I sank back into the sofa cushions with a sigh. "Right now, I think we all could use a little nap."

"Nap? Don't you want to get right on applying your version of bad cop routine to Tanya?"

"Later. We need rest to get our strength back. Then we concoct an excuse to get Tanya out of her house so I can look around."

"No way, Maddie. If she's implicated in this murder, it's dangerous for you to snoop through her house. Remember, someone shot at us. And it's illegal for you to break into her house."

"I don't think she was the person who shot at you, at us. Tanya's not the hiking in the rain kind of gal. The only chance she might take would be buying clothes in consignment shops." I got off the couch and held out my hand. "Now, let's get you upstairs."

Zack's eyes grew wide. "That sounds like fun."

"Zack, if you're not going to take this mission seriously, I'll farm you out to a rehab facility, and they can take care of you."

"I'll be good." He gave me a hug and then we climbed the stairs.

"You're in the spare bedroom." I pointed toward the first door on the right. "There's a guest bathroom down the hall."

"In my condition I think I need an around the clock nurse, one who stays in the same room with me."

"I thought you were going to behave yourself."

Zack reached out and put his good arm around me. "It might be a promise I'll find hard to keep."

A few minutes later, when I tiptoed past the bedroom and looked in, I saw Spike cuddled against him, making biscuits with his paws and putting forth his usual loud purr. Zack's chest rose and fell with his even, deep breathing. No sense in waking him.

I left a note on the kitchen table saying I'd gone out to get groceries. That was a lie, of course. No sense in alarming him.

I'M NOT A FOOL. I'D NEVER PUT MYSELF IN DANGER by going alone to a suspect's house. I wrote and read enough mysteries to know how stupid that was. I called on Jane.

"How would you feel about being a lookout?"

"Me? Do something illegal? Let me get my shotgun." She sounded more excited than horrified at my question.

"No weapons necessary. A bit of snooping. I want to take a quick peek into someone's house while they're away. All you have to do is sit in the car and make certain no one comes along while I'm inside."

I had called Tanya before I contacted Jane and was surprised to find her at home. I explained what had happened to Geoffrey. "Abigail is at the jail now, so they need someone at the office. I'm taking care of a sick friend, so I can't tend to the business. Can you help?"

"You'd trust me to do that?"

"Well, of course, dear. We all trust you." I crossed my fingers when I said it.

I dropped by Jane's to pick her up, then we parked down the street from Tanya's house, arriving in time to see her jump into her car and leave.

"The coast is clear. You stay put in the car and honk three times if anyone comes along."

"Take your umbrella." Jane handed it to me.

While snooping in all this rain was unpleasant, it also meant anyone driving past would find it hard to see me on the porch, and they would be concentrating on the road, not rubbernecking the neighborhood houses.

I walked up Tanya's front walk with a clipboard in one hand. If anyone saw me at her door, they'd think I was there soliciting names on a petition or soliciting for a charity. Who would suspect an older, well-dressed woman of doing something illegal in the middle of a rainy afternoon?

I rang the doorbell, then reached under the front mat where Tanya had told Geoffrey she'd hidden a spare key. He'd offered to check her house earlier this summer when it rained for over a week. She had gone to Albany and worried her basement might flood while she was absent.

What was I looking for? I had only a vague idea but thought I might begin with her mail and then look for household and personal paperwork. I propped my umbrella against the porch rail, opened the door with the key and stuck my head inside for a quick look before entering. This would be easier than I expected. The house was one story, a living room/kitchen combination, one bath off to the left, and beyond that a bedroom. Even better for my search, the house was neatly kept. Tanya had put today's mail on the kitchen table—two bills, one from the electric company, the other from a local appliance store, neither of interest to me. I opened all the drawers in her kitchen and found the usual—flatware, pots and pans and a junk drawer with miscellaneous items such as twist ties, rubber bands and a small bottle of glue. The cabinet under the sink held a garbage bin. What looked like a brand-new toaster oven sat on the kitchen counter next to an electric coffee pot. The counter-top oven could account for the bill from the appliance store where Tanya must have made the purchase and charged it to a store card. A guess, but a good one.

Two bowls sat in the drainer. One for her morning cereal? What about the other one? Perhaps the boyfriend had stayed overnight. I moved on to her bedroom where I hoped to find any important papers.

I peeked in the bathroom as I passed, sparkling clean, towel hung on the towel bar, still damp. Only Tanya showered this morning? Or hadn't the boyfriend slept over? Or wasn't he into bathing daily?

The door to the bedroom was closed. I turned the knob and pushed open the door to yet another tidy room, bed made, no clothing strewn around. The closet door stood ajar and a quick look in revealed a clothing bar jammed tight with hanging clothes. Lingerie, nightgowns and pajamas along with tee-shirts, jeans and shorts filled the dresser sitting next to the closet.

There was one drawer in the bedside table filled with paper-work. At last, something interesting. At the bottom of the drawer was the treasure I had hoped to find, Tanya's birth certificate. Interesting. Basset was not listed as her father, and I didn't rec-ognize the name there. A good reason for Basset to have resisted Tanya's claim he was her father. I took out my cell and snapped a photo of the birth certificate.

Overall, Tanya's house yielded little of interest except for the birth certificate. I had no intention of taking anything from the house. That would be theft. What I was doing was exploring, and what I discovered about Tanya was meager. While I was here, I should look at the basement. The sound of a horn honking three times made me scurry from the bedroom and rush to the front window. A county sheriff's car pulled up in front of the house. I was worried about Tanya returning, but I hadn't counted on this. I dashed back into the kitchen, opened the cabinet under the sink, grabbed the garbage bag—a potential treasure trove of information—out of the kitchen waste can, tossed a new bag in and dumped the coffee grounds and vegetable peels from the old can into the replacement, leaving any interesting material like papers and mail in the old bag which I took with me.

I had to change my escape route. I took another quick peek out the window. Dang! If it had been the female deputy, I might have concocted a story about why I was in Tanya's house, dropping off papers from the office, but Deputy Stevens got out of the car, hiked up his pants and headed for the door. Back door here I come. I hit the back steps when I heard Steven's knock on the front door and his announcement that the sheriff's department had arrived. Had someone seen me on the front steps when I entered, thought my presence suspicious and called the sheriff or was Stevens here to question Tanya?

The horn honked three more times. No time to figure out why he was here. I sprinted through Tanya's back yard, across her neighbor's yards and down the street in time to see Jane speed off past Tanya's house and turn the corner at the end of the street. I had told her to stay put in the car. Where was she going? I hid myself near the edge of the street behind a row of bushes where Stevens couldn't see me from Tanya's house. I peered around the shrubbery and saw he was still on her porch. I heard him knock again and shout "Sheriff's Office."

Jane had circled the block and headed back up the street. A break in the downpour allowed her to see me waving my hand and pointing to the cross street. She turned down it, and I sighed in relief. The last thing I wanted was for Stevens to spot me in the neighborhood. I watched him step off the front porch and circle around to the back of Tanya's house. I sprinted to the cross street to meet Jane, but I didn't see the car. That was when I heard the noise and saw my car backing out of a driveway with a garbage can hooked to the front bumper. If I heard it, Stevens would too, but I was closer. I dashed for the car.

"Are you hurt? What happened?" I was breathless from running.

Jane sat behind the wheel, her face red with anxiety. "I'm fine. I oversteered, I guess. I don't drive."

"You don't drive?"

Jane gave me a sheepish look. "I don't have a license."

I wanted to ask her how she managed to run her errands, but we didn't have the time to discuss transportation needs now. Stevens would have jumped into his car to see what the ruckus was about. I had to get Jane out of here. I looked up and down the street but saw no one had come out of their house to see what was happening.

"Do you know anyone around here?" I wanted Jane away from

the car, gone so that Stevens didn't know of her involvement in this escapade. I was at fault for getting her mixed up in my scheme, and I wanted to make certain Stevens didn't know about it.

"A cousin lives right around the corner." Jane pointed in the direction away from Tanya's house.

"Go visit her."

"But . . ."

"Run. That deputy will be here in a few minutes. I don't want him to know you were with me and that you were driving." And especially that I had talked Jane into my snooping scheme. If he knew my car was around here, he'd figure I was up to something, something that had to do with Tanya. The guy wasn't brilliant but even he could figure out that connection. And he didn't need to find Jane in my car.

"Go, go, go." I made shooing gestures with my hands. Jane turned up her coat collar against the rain, started off down the street and turned the corner as Stevens drove up.

He got out of his car and gave me his beady-eyed stare.

"What are you doing here?"

"Here? Where here?" Despite the rain pouring down my face and the feeling I was drowning, I tried for my most innocent, beguiling look.

Stevens didn't fall for it.

"Why would you drive into someone's driveway, hit their trash-cans and then try to drive off with them hooked to your bumper? Unless . . . Oh, I get it. You were up to something shady at a house around here." He looked around the neighborhood. "Doesn't Tanya live over there?"

"Yes. The direction you arrived from. I assume you were talking to her."

"I wanted to talk to her, but she's not home, and I'll bet you know that. Did you break into her house looking for something that would help get your son off?"

"No, I did not break into Tanya's house."

"What is that in your hand." Stevens pointed to the garbage bag which I had taken from her house.

"Garbage."

Stevens looked at the garbage cans lodged under my bumper. "You were stealing garbage from this house and tried to drive off with the cans?"

"Something like that." I always try to tell the truth or at least make up an interesting lie.

CHAPTER 16

STEVENS, HAND GRIPPING MY ARM, WALKED ME into the sheriff's department. He held the garbage bag in his other hand.

"It's garbage." I nodded in a disinterested manner at the bag. "It must have popped out of the can and into my car when I hit the cans."

"It's evidence."

"It's going to get smelly if you keep it in here." Whatever was in that bag was now the property of the department. I'd never know if my snooping was worth getting arrested. Again.

I heard him order one of the deputies to remove the trash cans which he had loaded into the trunk of his cruiser. They were also evidence.

"I assume you'll want legal representation." Stevens pointed to the phone on the wall in front of me.

"I don't know my lawyer's number. It's on my cell phone, in my purse." I nodded to the purse he also held. "Can't I use my own phone?"

I had directed my request to the deputy sitting behind the counter in the front cubicle.

Stevens slammed my purse on the counter. "Let her use her phone but keep an eye on her. She's shifty."

I'd never thought of myself as shifty. Snoopy, yes, but shifty? I decided not to argue the point with him. He slammed through the door to the back offices and disappeared.

"Richard? Hi, honey. Sorry to bother you, but . . ."

"I just returned from the sheriff's department. Did something happen to Geoffrey?"

"Not Geoffrey. Me."

"Oh. I'll be right there."

"Thank you dear. It's so wonderful having a son who puts his family before his law practice."

"Mom, my family is becoming my law practice." He hung up.

Richard must have been midway between his office and the sheriff's department when I called because it took him only fifteen minutes to come bounding through the door.

I was sitting on the bench chewing my lips in worry. I got up and gave him a hug. "That was fast."

"Tell me what happened."

We walked down the hall for privacy, and I told him everything. If you're going to hire someone as your lawyer, you owe them honesty particularly if you're guilty and especially if they're family.

"So have you been arrested or not?"

"I don't know. Stevens said I might want legal representation. That's all I know."

"We'll make everything right." Richard took out his cell phone and made some calls. "Done. And now." His gaze swung toward the door leading to Stevens' office.

Stevens banged through the office door, two beaten up garbage cans in his hands. He tossed them into the entry, gave Richard a dirty look and slammed back through the door.

I banged on the door and shouted in hopes Stevens could hear me. "Where is the garbage bag?"

A few minutes later the door opened, and a garbage bag came sailing through. Stevens stuck his head around the door. "You think those people want their garbage back?"

I shrugged. "I took it, and my lawyer said we would make it right."

Stevens hesitated a moment, anger reddening his face. I was sure I saw his hand move toward the gun on his hip. I was certain he was considering whether shooting me could be construed as self-defense. He raised his arms over his head in a gesture of frustration and then slammed the door.

"Let's go, Mom." Richard took my arm and walked me out.

I got into Richard's car a little shaky from yet another brush with incarceration, and with a sigh of gratitude settled into the seat, thinking of a nice cup of tea with Zack. Then I remembered Richard had warned me my get out of jail free card came with a condition: I had to return the trash cans.

"I think we owe the people whose cans you demolished a new set of cans." Richard drove around the back of the sheriff's department, parked and hopped out of the car next to the department's dumpsters.

I followed him. "Get rid of the cans, dear, but we need to keep the garbage bag. It might have important items in it. I haven't had the time to check it." Or it could hold nothing more than garbage.

"Fine, Mom, but I don't want the smelly thing in my trunk any longer than necessary."

"If that's the case, then we should toss the bag in my trunk."

"Your car is drivable?"

"Yes, but the problem is I don't know where it is. Would the department have towed it?"

Richard ran his fingers through his hair. "I'd guess it's been impounded."

Now we had three errands to run before I could have my tea and a snuggle with Zack: impound lot to pick up my car, hardware store to purchase new trash cans, and a visit to the family whose cans Jane had ruined.

On our way I called Zack, explained my afternoon encounter with the law and told him I would be "a little late."

"From what you've told me 'A little late' could be days." He didn't sound happy.

"Don't be silly. They didn't arrest me. I called Richard. We have a few stops we need to make and then it's teatime." I hung up before I had to explain myself any further. I hated long explanations on the phone with Zack. The longer my tale, the more I backed myself into a corner. In person I would take his mind off my misbehaving with cuddles, kisses and promises. Nothing too passionate, mind you. The man was on the mend. I didn't want to impede his healing.

I owed Jane a phone call to apologize for bringing her into this situation. She could have been standing next to me at the sheriff's department if things had been worse.

"Jane. It's Maddie. I . . ."

"Are you okay? I saw the sheriff put you in his car and drive off. Are you calling from jail?"

"No. I'm with Richard, my son, the lawyer. He did his usual magic, and I'm free. Deputy Stevens' face was so red when I left the department that I thought he could have a heart attack and the county might have to get another person to fill the sheriff's slot."

"Nasty little man."

I could almost hear acid dripping from her tongue. "You've had a run-in with him, have you?"

"Word gets around town. He's a by-the-book guy unless he thinks it's to his advantage to break the rules. Stupid guy thought he could arrest the little Allen girl down the block for poaching animals on state land. She was rescuing a turtle off the side of the road. I saw what was happening, and I intervened. Told the little toad I'd call him in for speeding through the neighborhood. He must have been going over sixty miles an hour on our street."

"Did you complain yet?"

"Nope, too busy trying to get the Japanese beetles off my roses and the slugs out of my vegetable garden."

"Well, keep your grievance in your back pocket for the time being. We might be able to use it later." I cleared my throat.

"Listen, my dear. I called because I owe you an apology. I should never have asked you to accompany me today. You could have been arrested."

Jane guffawed into the phone. "No apology needed. In fact, I haven't had so much fun since, well, since I can't remember when. It was thrilling. I hope you're not mad that I disobeyed you when I drove off in the car. I had to do something more than honk. I hope you'll consider me when you have another caper in mind."

I returned her laugh. "Getting older shouldn't be boring. We'll think of something thrilling to do next week."

"I hope it's more than attending a historical society meeting."

"I'll work on it."

"Before you go, Maddie, I hope this isn't going to be a problem, and I meant to mention it earlier, but when you came back to the car you didn't have your umbrella."

Oh, no. I remembered propping it on the railing outside of Tanya's house when I entered. Had Stevens seen it there? If I was lucky, it didn't register as important. But Tanya would see it. I made a mental note to retrieve the umbrella, somehow. I mentally kicked myself for being so bad at searching a house.

"And what about the clipboard?" Jane asked.

The clipboard I'd left on Tanya's kitchen table. Wow was I bad at this.

"I'll take care of it, too. Talk to you soon, Jane." I hung up.

"Something wrong, Mom?" Richard gave me a sly look.

"I left a few items behind this afternoon." I told Richard about the umbrella and the clipboard.

He said nothing for a minute, then pulled over to the curb and turned to face me. "And that's why you shouldn't be doing things against the law. Criminals get caught."

"But I'm smarter than most criminals. And I've got you to help me. We'll go back and retrieve the items. No one will know."

"I am not going to be party to illegal entry. I could lose my license to practice law."

"Okay then. You grab the umbrella off the porch, and I'll enter and grab the clipboard." At least I could be proud of myself for putting the key back in its hiding place after I unlocked the door.

"That is wrong in so many ways, Mom."

We stared at each other for several minutes, then I slid down into the seat. "I know."

"We'll leave them where they are. Don't say anything about them now. Let me think about this."

"The umbrella matches my rain parka. It's got yellow ducks and white clouds on it."

Richard continued to stare at me, then he shifted the car into drive and pulled back onto the road. "Like I said, I'll think about it."

"I'll think, too."

"No, Mom! Absolutely no thinking on your part."

I sat back in my seat, reflecting there was at least one good thing that came out of today—the feeling of profound satisfaction I received at jazzing up another senior citizen's life. The sense of fulfillment and the need to find a caper equally exciting for Jane and me must have showed on my face because Richard gave me a puzzled look.

"What are you plotting now, Mom?"

I shook my head and reached over to give his arm a reassuring pat. "How much money will it take to get my car out of impound, do you think?"

"Enough for you to reconsider engaging in illegal activity again, I hope."

I crossed my fingers. "Of course, dear. I've learned my lesson." I was laying it on a little thick.

"Don't lie to me, Mom. I know you better." Richard grabbed his cell. "I have to call the sheriff's department to find out where they take impounded cars. This county is too small to have their own lot, so they must haul them off to one of the local garages that has a fenced in area. I also want to make certain you have permission to take the car."

"It's my car."

"True, but it's now under the county's jurisdiction."

"For hitting a bunch of garbage cans? Stupid." I sat back in my seat, arms crossed over my chest.

"Don't pout. It won't help." Richard called the sheriff's office and was given the address of the garage that was holding my car hostage.

The man at the garage informed me I had to pay him a hundred dollars holding fee, but that he couldn't let me take the car until I had paperwork from the county indicating I had permission to remove it.

"Back to the sheriff's department, I guess." I started to get back into Richard's car, a sense of frustration overwhelming me. Bureaucracy, I muttered to myself.

The garage owner shook his head. "Nope. You get the paperwork at the county clerk's office."

"That's at the county seat, twenty miles from here." Durn the inconvenience of being a lousy crook. I pounded my fist against my leg.

"Don't worry. I'll take you there right after we grab two new trashcans, drop them off and apologize to their owners." Richard massaged my shoulder to calm me.

"I wasn't even the one who ran over them. It was Jane."

"But it was your idea." Richard shook his finger at me.

"Hey, who's the parent here? Don't treat me like a misbehaving kid."

"Aren't you? And by the way, do you have your checkbook with you?" Richard buckled himself into his seat.

"Oh, rats. My checkbook is in my glovebox." I jumped out of the car and ran over to the garage owner. "I need to get into my car."

"No can do until you get the county papers."

"But I can't pay the fee unless I get my checkbook. It's in the car. Could you get it for me then?"

"No can do. I can't move that car without those papers."

I strode back to Richard's car mumbling under my breath.

When I told him about the catch twenty-two, he chuckled. "County rules and regs. Don't worry about it. I'll pay the fee and you can pay me back."

"You seem pretty sanguine about all this. I guess you're used to all these legal ins and outs."

Richard's lip twitched as if he was suppressing laughter. "What I figure is that a brush with spending time in the county jail doesn't upset you as much as all these hoops—the trash cans, the impounding of your car, the need to drive to the county clerk's office to get the papers and pay a fee . . ."

"What's really frustrating is I suspect Stevens has a big smile on his face because of the inconvenience he's caused me."

SHINY NEW TRASHCANS STASHED IN RICHARD'S TRUNK, we drove to the Longworth's house, the people whose garbage cans suffered the damage from my car. Although they were delighted to receive the new garbage cans, I sensed Mr. Longworth had something on his mind.

"What did you do with the old ones?" asked Mr. Longworth.

"They were too battered to use."

He gave a dissatisfied grunt.

"I think one of those cans went flying in the impact and crushed several of my rose bushes." Mrs. Longworth pointed to a flower that seemed healthy to me. "Those were my prize roses. I was hoping to take them to the county fair this summer to show."

"Mrs. Longworth, that rose looks . . ." I was willing to argue with her, but Richard stepped between us.

"How much for the rosebush?" he asked.

"Rosebushes," Mrs. Longworth said. "There were two of them. Mature roses worth, let's see . . ."

"How about the garbage cans and fifty dollars for each damaged rose bush and you sign a paper saying that's all my mother owes you." Richard was a sharp negotiator.

"Seventy-five each." Mr. Longworth stepped forward ready to argue if Richard said no.

"Fine. And I'll draw up the paper and drop it by tomorrow."

"I'll need the money now." Mr. Longworth held out his hand.

"You're getting the durn trashcans now. Back off." I'd had enough for one day. My patience, of which I never had much, was a thin as pond ice in April. I shoved the trashcans at the Longworths and spun on my heel.

"I think, since we have to wait for our money and sign that paper, the amount should be a hundred for each bush." Mrs. Longworth nodded her head in agreement with her husband's demand.

"Fine, but I'm holding these hostage until then." I grabbed the trashcans and tossed them back into Richard's car. Richard and I drove off before the Longworth's could demand something else.

He and I rode in silence until we left the village.

"Do you know anything about roses?" asked Richard.

"Not much. I know Jane is battling Japanese beetles on hers. Why do you ask?" I'd never known Richard to take any interest in gardening.

Richard put on his blinker, and we turned north onto the highway heading toward the county seat. "I don't know a thing about growing flowers, but the tag on Mrs. Longworth's said they were from the big box store."

"Hmmm. I wouldn't think that was where you'd buy "Prize" roses."

I turned in my seat to stare at Richard. "I don't feel right about giving them the money to replace the roses. The bushes didn't look damaged to me. It takes loving care and time to produce those blooms. I think we should stop at Jane's and ask her if she'd be willing to part with two of her roses. The Longworths will be thrilled to receive two of Jane's bushes since she's won first prize for hers at the county fair the last three years."

"But I thought you said her plants have some kind of beetles on them." Richard's forehead wrinkled in puzzlement for a moment.

"Right you are."

Richard's gaze met mine, and we broke into laughter.

"Mrs. Longworth is expecting money, but she'll be getting so much more." I reached into my purse and extracted a hanky to wipe away the tears of laughter that spilled down my cheeks.

CHAPTER 17

Traffic was light on the road to the county seat. We made it to the courthouse in less than a half hour, much of the time punctuated by continuing peals of laughter at the Longworths' attempts to extract money from my car's run-in with their trash cans and the untouched "prize" roses. It made no sense to be mad at them. It had been an exhausting day and I was tired. All I could do was laugh at the situation.

Richard paid the fee to get my paperwork from the county, and we headed back to the garage. The garage owner made a big deal about examining the permit, but then agreed everything was in order.

Richard started to make out a check for the hundred dollar holding fee when the owner stopped him.

"The charge is now one hundred fifty dollars."

"What? You told us one hundred a short time ago." Despite my fatigue, anger pumped adrenalin into my system. I ground my teeth together and pumped my fists up and down.

"Mother. Please." Richard tried to calm me by grabbing my shoulders and holding onto me.

I stopped with my fists, but I continued to vibrate with fury. Richard wrote out the check.

"I should ask you for ID." The garage owner shot me a wary glance. "Or not. She looks as if you should get her home. She shouldn't drive in her condition."

"I could leave my car in your hands for another hundred dollars or so, couldn't I?" I tried to control the anger in my voice, but there was enough of an edge to it that the garage owner appeared eager to get me off his property. He threw me the keys, ran back into the building and slammed the door behind him. As if that would save him. I could drive my car through the front of his shop and . . .

"Don't even think it, Mom." Richard grabbed me by the arm and walked me over to my car. "Are you okay to drive?"

"I'm fine," I said through gritted teeth.

Richard followed me home. I knew he was worried I'd pull a U-turn to the garage and seek revenge on the owner.

At the house, Richard jumped out of his car and opened my door for me. "Feel better, Mom?"

"I'm over my mad at the garage owner if that's what you're concerned about. I'm placing the blame for this entire mess at the feet of the person who's responsible." I trudged up my front steps, opened the front door and tossed my keys toward the table inside. I missed and they slid to the floor.

Richard picked up the keys and put them into the bowl on the table. "And who do you feel is responsible for this day?"

"If you thought I'd take the blame for it, you're wrong. Deputy Stevens. I owe him one."

Zack sat at the kitchen table reading the evening paper.

"You're up. Don't you think you should still be in bed?" I ran over to him and threw my arms around him.

He planted a kiss on my cheek. "And nice to see you, Richard, but what brings you here?"

Richard hesitated. "I think I should let Mom tell you all about it."

"You're no son of mine if you chicken out and leave me to tell the story. I'll put on the kettle for tea." I went into the kitchen and pulled a bottle of white wine out of the fridge.

"That bad, huh?" Zack folded the paper and laid it on the table.

I shared a scrubbed version of the day's events with Zack while Spike, having awakened from his nap on the couch, rubbed his body against my legs.

"Guess who your mother thinks should be held responsible for her bad day?" Richard uncorked the wine.

"Jane, for her poor driving ability?" Zack was joking. He knew I'd never blame Jane.

"Your deputy friend, Stevens." Richard took three wine goblets from the cabinet.

I put one glass back. "Zack's not drinking. He's still on pain medication."

Zack looked with longing at the wine bottle. "Well, my dear, you can blame him for one more thing. The sheriff's department called this afternoon indicating they wanted to interview both of us about the shooting, and I asked what took them so long. The deputy said the new sheriff felt the initial statements from us indicated the shots were stray bullets from a hunter. I pointed out there was no game season at this time of the year and, even if there was, hunting after dark was illegal. He acknowledged that but said Sheriff Stevens thought the case didn't merit more investigation. I've got a call in to talk with Stevens."

"He's busy trying to find innocent people to harass." I drained my wine glass and held it out to Richard to refill.

"You don't agree with Stevens' take on the shooting, do you?" Richard arched one eyebrow inquisitively at Zack and poured me more wine.

"I don't. The deputies haven't even been able to walk the area because of the rains. The state closed the park, all the trails including the one your mother and I hiked have been washed out, but if the rain lets up, I'd like to look at the scene. Maybe I can convince our new sheriff that I can be helpful to him."

"You should tell him you'll take a look at the area and find evidence that will make his assessment that it was a hunter look like what it is, pure laziness on his part." That was what I would say to Stevens, but Zack was smart, people smart, even if the person involved was a complete idiot.

The phone rang and I popped up to answer it. Speak of the devil.

"It's for you." I screwed up my face in a look of disgust and held the receiver out to Zack. "Take it out on the back deck if you need privacy."

Zack talked with Stevens for more than ten minutes, then reentered the house.

"Fancy a stroll through the park again, Maddie?"

"You talked Stevens into investigating the shooting?""

"I'm nudging him in that direction. I told him the investigation of this incident would look good on his resume when he went for the permanent sheriff's position." Zack grabbed my glass and took a sip of wine.

I grabbed the wine glass from him and gave his hand a bit of a smack. "Naughty boy."

He winked at me. "I wish."

Richard cleared his throat as if we needed a reminder he was still in the room. "I better get going. I'll be back here tomorrow to see the Longworths and for Geoffrey's appearance."

"When can I see Geoffrey?"

"At the arraignment tomorrow. Around ten. I'll pick you up."

"Pick up Abigail instead. She'll need your support. I'll drive myself."

I walked him to the door and gave him a hug. "I'll call Jane about those roses."

Richard grinned. "You want to do that, Mom?"

"What do you think?" I closed the door and took a seat on the couch, but before I could settle in next to Zack, Richard stuck his head back in the door. "Here's your treasure trove, Mom." He held the garbage bag out to me.

"What's that, Maddie?" asked Zack.

"Evidence."

Zack and Richard looked over my shoulder as I explored the contents of the bag and found nothing but trash, old newspapers, advertising flyers, and an apple core but nothing of any interest to the case.

"Garbage," Richard said and headed back to his car.

Gathering evidence was proving more difficult in real life than it was when I wrote my mysteries. I plopped onto the couch, feeling defeated in my findings.

Zack tossed the garbage bag into my trashcan in the kitchen, then joined me, pulling me close to him. "I think there's more to the story of the Longworths than you shared with me."

"Being the kind person I am, I thought Mrs. Longworth might appreciate a pair of Jane's lovely roses rather than a check for new bushes. People know Jane's roses have won first prize several years in a row at the county fair."

Zack tipped his head back and let out a loud guffaw. "I understand this is a bad year for Japanese beetles."

"Where did you hear that?"

"From Jane. She called a few minutes before you got back. We had a chat."

"She told you what happened, didn't she? And you made me tell you the whole story again."

"Overall, the stories were close, although some aspects differed. What are you going to do about the clipboard and your umbrella?"

I gasped. Jane had spilled the entire event, detail by embarrassing detail. "I'll deal with that later. Right now, I need to call Jane. Jane doesn't know she's about to gift rose bushes to the Longworths yet."

"Will she agree?"

"Of course. Jane has a terrific sense of humor."

I called Jane and I was right: she was delighted to share her prize roses, beetles and all. "I'm not showing them at the fair this year because of the infestation."

"Fine. I'll take them over tomorrow with your best wishes."

"What are you going to do about your umbrella and clipboard?"

Out of Zack's earshot, I said, "Zack asked me that. And I might need a pal to help me out."

"Dark of night. I get it. A better time to work Tanya's house." Jane giggled. "Talk to you later."

I didn't hear Zack come up behind me. He tapped me on my shoulder, and I jumped about a foot.

"You sacred the living stuffing out of me. Don't sneak up on a gal that way."

"Don't hatch plots behind my back."

"Okay then, you help me work out how I'm going to handle the items I left at Tanya's."

"I may not be in law enforcement anymore, but what you have in mind is illegal."

"Figure out something legal then." I leaned into him and batted my eyelashes provocatively.

"Woman, you are incorrigible."

"I can be more than that if you'd like." I did a flirty tap of my finger on his chin.

"Call Jane and cancel tonight's event."

"She'll be so disappointed."

"I'm certain you can find some other way to entertain her."

I called Jane, and I was right. She was sad to hear I'd backed out.

"This sounds like Zack's doing. He doesn't want you to get in trouble with the law, does he? Are you allowing him to take all the fun out of your life? And mine?" Jane's voice quavered with disappointment.

"I don't let any man run my life. I came up with an alternative plan for questioning Tanya and explaining the umbrella and the clipboard."

"I'm intrigued. Tell me."

"Confront Tanya. Put her in the hot seat."

"Can I watch?" Jane's voice had regained its usual enthusiasm.

I hesitated.

"Oh, no. You're not going to take Zack with you when you see Tanya, are you?"

I caught Zack's glance across the room. "Of course not. You're still on for riding shotgun. But no driving this time or no more capers together."

I disconnected and gave Zack an embarrassed look.

"I told you, Maddie. Tanya may be the killer and she also may have been the person who shot at us. This is dangerous, not something two ladies of a certain age . . ."

"Careful what you say." I held up my finger in warning.

"You know what I'm going to say."

"I do, but you know I won't get a thing out of her if you're in the room. She's not going to pull anything if Jane is with me. Look, I'll tell you what. You can ride along in the car. I'll carry my cell phone and connect to your cell while I talk with Tanya. If anything goes wrong, you'll be right there to call the police."

"Or dash in and intervene."

My glance dropped from his face to his bandaged shoulder.

"Don't treat me like an invalid, Maddie." His tone was sharp. I had offended his masculinity.

"I'm sorry." I walked over to him and stood on tiptoe. My lips touched his cheek.

"WHAT'S HE DOING HERE?" Jane got off her porch swing when I drove up.

"Nice to see you, too, Jane." Zach held the car door open for her and extended his arm to help her in.

She grabbed her skirt and pulled it into the car with a "humph." "As if women can't take care of themselves."

"Maddie didn't want to leave me home alone because of my injury."

Wow, I thought. That was so smooth of Zack. But it didn't work.

"She left you alone this afternoon." Jane settled back into the seat with another "humph."

We drove in silence to Tanya's.

Jane and I went to the door while Zack, as we had discussed, remained slumped down in the backseat of the car, our cells connected so Zack could hear what was happening inside the house.

My umbrella no longer leaned against the porch railing.

Tanya opened the door at my knock, her eyes wide with surprise. "Mrs. Sparks, is there something wrong at the office?"

"No, dear. I thought we should have a little chat about everything." I pushed past Tanya into her living room. "This is my friend Jane." I didn't explain why Jane was with me. On the couch sat a man in his mid-twenties.

I held out my hand. "You must be the young man Tanya mentioned."

He had brown eyes and sun-streaked brown hair that came down to his shoulders. He wore a dirty tee-shirt and a ripped pair of jeans. Fashion statement or slob? It was hard to know nowadays.

He didn't get off the couch but looked at me through half-closed, heavily lidded eyes. Another unknown: drunk, on drugs or was that his usual demeanor?

He ignored my hand, slunk further down into the couch and plopped his feet on the coffee table. "And who are you?"

"A friend." I took the chair across from him.

Tanya gave us a nervous smile. Jane sat on the other end of the couch from the young man. Tanya perched on the end of the couch nearest him.

"Tanya thinks someone was in her house today. I'm betting it was you." The young man pushed forward, confronting me with eyes now wide open and dark with dislike.

"Is that so?" I ignored his gaze and focused on Tanya. "You should have reported it to the police. Did you?"

She shook her head.

"I came to talk about Mr. Basset, the man you claimed was your biological father, but his name isn't on your birth certificate, is it? Were you trying to blackmail Basset, thinking he'd cave to your accusations because he had been in your mother's life around the time you were born? I'm right, aren't I?" Talk about flying by the seat of my pants.

"I think you need to leave." The young man got off the couch and hovered over me. "Or we will call the police."

I continued to ignore him, although his aggressive posture was beginning to make me uncomfortable.

Tanya moved between the two of us. "Robbie, stay out of this."

I smiled to myself. The gal had gumption if she could talk down a man who had six inches of height on her and a body full of muscle.

She turned and faced me. "I have proof Basset was my biological father."

"What proof?" I asked.

Tanya crossed her arms over her chest and locked eyes with me. This was a different Tanya from the one I'd talked with the other day at Basset's house. She'd lost or buried the longing and sadness she's expressed that day. Who was the real Tanya? The lonely woman looking for a family or this one, confrontational and angry? Or did having her boyfriend at her side bring out a more negative side of her?

"Robbie is right. You need to leave. I'm sorry your son has been arrested for my father's murder. I don't think he's responsible."

"Of course he is." Robbie jumped up and grabbed Tanya by the arm. "The man was a lech, tried to get in her pants all the time."

I knew my son, and that wasn't in Geoffrey's nature. Would Tanya defend him or support her boyfriend's claim?

For a moment Tanya seemed to weigh the odds: alienate the boyfriend or lie about my son's behavior toward her.

"Geoffrey was always a perfect gentleman. The reason he was at Basset's house the morning of his death is that he knew I'd gone there, and he wanted to support me. He believed Basset was my father and he wanted to tell him so. I went to my father's because I'd left my cat with him. I couldn't keep Spike here. Robbie hates cats.

I was stopping by to take Spike to be boarded while Dad was away, but we couldn't find him. Dad said he'd look and call me before he left on his trip." She shot Robbie an angry look.

"You and Basset had resolved your differences?"

Tanya nodded. "He was coming around."

Robbie guffawed. "She had the old guy wrapped around her fingers."

Tanya whirled to face him, sparks of fury in her eyes. "That 'old guy' was my father."

"Yeah, well, he owed you. I told him that."

"You met with Basset?" Somehow, I wasn't surprised. Robbie believed Basset was Tanya's father. Maybe he also thought he could push Basset enough to make him settle money on Tanya and then Robbie could cash in on the windfall.

Tanya's mouth dropped open in shock. "You didn't tell me you visited him. Did you threaten him? You didn't hurt him, did you?" She pushed Robbie toward the door. "Get out of my house!"

He whirled around and grabbed both her arms. "I'm not a guy you should mess with." He shook her and drew his hand back to slap her, but the front door burst open, and Zack stood in the opening.

Zack grabbed Robbie and pulled him off Tanya, then shoved him out the open door. "Time for you to leave." Zack slammed the door after him. "You should consider pressing charges against your boyfriend. He could come back and attack you again."

I watched Tanya's face when Zack warned her about Robbie and could see Robbie's violent behavior toward her was something she had experienced before. Alarm that her boyfriend might have turned his aggression against Basset made Tanya's face turn ashen. She couldn't help but worry Robbie was the person responsible for her father's death. I shared her concern.

She opened her mouth, but I held up my hand. "Please don't tell me he loves you or you love him. There are far better men in this world, ones who will treat you well."

Tanya rubbed her wrists where Robbie had grabbed her. "He'll be back. He left his things here."

"Gather them together. Now." I stabbed my finger at her. She seemed reluctant to obey, but then she shook her head and with eyes lowered she went into the bedroom and returned with a backpack. I took it from her, opened the front door and tossed it out into the yard.

"Now he has no reason to bother you." I dusted my hands together as if I'd disposed of unwanted garbage, but I had a feeling Robbie wouldn't leave her alone. If Tanya could prove Basset was her father, she stood to inherit a substantial amount of money, and I had Robbie pegged for a man who would do anything for money.

CHAPTER 18

"**I** KNOW YOU." TANYA STARED across the room at Zack. "I thought you had been hurt and weren't sheriff anymore."

"I'm not."

"Well, then I'd like all of you to leave. You have no right to be here." Tanya opened the door.

"How ungrateful." Jane arose from the couch and pushed her way around Tanya. "That young man could have killed you."

I didn't move because I had unfinished business with Tanya. "Where's my umbrella?"

Tanya's face turned red with anger. "Go. Go."

Dang. That umbrella matched my yellow duck boots. I shrugged and followed Zack and Jane out the door. As we were walking toward the car, I heard the front door open again. Something landed behind me. I turned to look and saw Tanya had thrown my umbrella and clipboard out the door. I picked up the umbrella to find that three of the ribs were bent.

"Well, I guess that's fair." I bent for the clipboard and examined the umbrella wondering if it could be repaired.

"What's fair?" asked Zack.

"Tanya doesn't know why I was at her house, and we don't know what kind of proof she has that Basset was her father. Her birth certificate names someone else as her father." I showed Zack the picture I had taken of the document.

He scanned the photo. "I thought you were guessing about the birth record, but you knew."

"What proof does she have? She seemed pretty confident of it." I settled myself in the driver's seat.

Zack leaned forward from the back seat. "It has to be DNA."

"There were no records of that in the house when I was, uh, visiting."

"She keeps it in her purse, maybe?" said Jane, fastening her seat belt.

"No, I don't think so. Not secure enough. Someone has it or it could be in Geoffrey and Abigail's office in Tanya's desk there. Let's look."

Zack chuckled. "Well, at least that's one place you can enter legally, assuming your son and daughter-in-law will loan you a key."

"No need. I'm an employee. I have a key." I stomped on the accelerator, and we sped off for the office.

"And she thinks I'm a bad driver." Jane grabbed her seat belt and gave it another tug to tighten it around her.

The search of the office including Tanya's desk and those of Abigail and Geoffrey yielded nothing.

I plopped down on Tanya's desk chair in defeat.

Zack gave my shoulder a comforting rub. "She could have lied about 'proof.' Or she gave it to someone she trusted to keep it safe for her."

"Someone she used to trust until tonight. Robbie." I punched Tanya's connection into my cell.

"What do you want?" Tanya's voice sounded filled with anger.

"Level with me. It could mean your safety and my son's freedom. Did you give your so-called proof about Basset being your father to Robbie for safe keeping?"

There was silence on the other end of the phone.

After some hesitation Tanya's voice came through again. "Yes. There was no one else I could trust."

"What lab did you use to get the DNA match? Tell me, we can retrieve a copy of the results there and the authorities will know you're Basset's daughter."

"Look, Robbie came off tonight looking bad, but he's a nice guy, a little mixed up, but a good person." Now Tanya sounded defensive.

"You need to stay away from Robbie. He's violent. You cannot trust him."

"I can't. Robbie and I are married."

Now that complicated things.

WE DROPPED JANE BACK AT HER HOUSE, and I thanked her for her help.

"Any time." She jumped out of the car and waved goodbye to us.

Zack got into the passenger's seat. "Jane's life has become more exciting since capers with you have replaced her search for pests on her roses." He ran his finger across my chin. "Let's go home."

Zack and I sat at my kitchen table drinking tea. I would have preferred a healthy shot of whiskey, and I knew Zack would have also, but he was still on pain killers, and it was best not to mix drugs.

"If you were still sheriff, you might have been able to pull some strings with what we suspect and talk to the labs in this area doing DNA testing. If she's Basset's daughter, she would inherit. That's motive for murder." I shook my head. "But there's no way we could convince the idiot Stevens to do that." I slumped back in my chair, feeling defeated. As I was about to suggest we turn in for the night, an idea struck me. "But the labs don't know you're not still sheriff, do they?"

Zack shook his finger at me. "At present I may not be a member of law enforcement, but what you're suggesting isn't legal. And any lab would require a search warrant."

"I know." I sighed a bone deep sigh. My days of breaking laws were behind me. At least for now. Spike, having polished off the last of his dry cat food, jumped into my lap and stared at me.

"He's hungry." Zak reached out and chucked his chin.

"He's always hungry." I got out of my chair and went to the pantry. Spike followed me.

"Looks to me as if you've got yourself a cat. There's no way Robbie will allow Tanya to keep him."

"He's good company."

"Am I?" Zack gave me a come-hither look.

"Not yet, but soon I hope you'll be."

We went to bed in our separate bedrooms. I assumed he felt as eager for the future as I was.

ZACK GOT UP EARLY THE NEXT MORNING, made coffee and left me a note on the kitchen table. "Off to talk with my replacement." Stevens probably needed more nudging to follow up investigating the site where Zack was shot, but I wish he had awakened me before he left. Ah, well. We'd run into each other at Geoffrey's arraignment today.

I fed Spike, gave him pets and snuggles and hopped into my car. My first stop was Geoffrey and Abigail's business. I didn't think Tanya would feel compelled to baby sit it while Geoffrey was being held in county lock-up and Abigail was there trying to support him. If I was wrong and Tanya was at the office, I had additional questions I wanted to ask her.

The office was open, and Tanya sat at her desk. When she heard the front door, she looked up with a pleasant smile until she saw it was me.

"Hi. Feeling better today?" I grabbed the chair opposite her desk, sat and tossed my bag on the floor at my feet.

"What are you doing here?"

"Not only am I Geoffrey's mother, but you forget I'm also an employee. Any house visits scheduled for today? I can fit them in before I go to Geoffrey's arraignment." Without pausing for a breath, I continued, "Did Robbie return last night?"

"No. You and your boyfriend chased him off."

"Tanya, you were the one who threw him out."

She waved my words away. "He knows I didn't mean it."

"I wish you did. Why did you marry him?"

"He loves me, and I love him. We're going to be a family."

I thought the man was bad news, but I suspected Tanya didn't want to hear the truth. "Well, I'm sure he's keeping your 'proof' safe."

Tanya had to have caught the sarcasm in my voice. "He is."

I sighed. There was no sense in battling with Tanya. The woman was so needy for love and connection that she couldn't see what a loser Robbie was. "Listen, I appreciate you coming in to take care of the business today. I'm sure Geoffrey and Abigail do, too. They'll thank you when this mess is cleared up."

"I know Geoffrey had nothing to do with my father's murder. He's a decent man. His mother, however . . ." She frowned at me.

"I don't get why this so-called proof of your relationship with Basset had to be such a secret. You're either his daughter or you're not. If you are, then you're his next of kin and stand to inherit his estate. You know that, don't you?"

Tanya stared at me. "That's what Robbie said."

"Do you know where Basset, uh, your father was going right before his murder?"

"He told me he needed to get away and think about some things."

"What things? It sounded like Robbie might have talked with him. Would he know?"

She shrugged. "I don't know."

Fed up with Tanya's passive attitude when it came to dealing with Robbie, I wanted to yell at her, but I knew that would get me nowhere. I checked the schedule of property management visits, but as Abigail and Geoffrey told me the day after the murder, several customers backed out of their management contracts.

There was nothing on for the next few days. I hoped Geoffrey and Abigail's business wouldn't be permanently damaged by Geoffrey's arrest.

"Thank you for helping out during this tough time and for believing in Geoffrey's innocence, Tanya."

She looked up at me and nodded as I left the office.

IN THE COURTROOM GEOFFREY WAS CHARGED with second degree murder and forced to wear an ankle bracelet because the court deemed him a flight risk. Anyone who knew him knew that was not going to happen. Geoffrey was a homebody. He and Abigail rarely vacationed. My son was a kind man and one who liked his home and family. I don't think he even had a passport, nor had he ever gone far beyond the borders of the state.

The ersatz sheriff, Stevens, smiled when he heard the judge's words. He clapped his hat against his thigh and strode out of the courtroom, a look of arrogance on his weasley face. He got what he wanted, I thought to myself, and considered sticking out my foot to trip him as he passed me in the hallway of the courthouse.

Richard tapped me on the shoulder. "I've arranged for Geoffrey to be fitted with the ankle bracelet now, but I'd like to take him out the back way because there's a crowd of reporters on the court-house steps. We'll meet you at your place in half an hour or so. Less chance the press will follow him there. They'll be surrounding his house and business instead."

Zack joined us. A crowd of reporters had swarmed Stevens and the DA. "Let's get out of here. I know a side exit." He grabbed my arm and led me toward the bathrooms and then down a flight of stairs.

Instead of picking up either his car or mine, we decided to walk to the nearby park and wait for the crowd to disperse.

We sat on a bench and Zack put his arm around me.

"Now what do we do?" I felt like crying, but I knew that would not help.

"He's got the best lawyer, you know." Zack pulled me toward him. "And I've got some good news."

"About Geoffrey? So soon?"

"Not about Geoffrey. About us. About the person who shot at us."

"You know who it was? Who?"

Zack chuckled. "I'm not that much of a miracle worker, but I made a deal with Sheriff Stevens."

"How can you call him that? He's a lazy, bumbling idiot."

"And he's now sheriff, so he has the authority to investigate crimes. I finally convinced him he should look into the shooting. I told him I could put in a good word for him in the fall election for sheriff."

"You're out of your mind. Why would you back that piece of . . ."

"He has to be nominated for sheriff, run for the position and win. No one is going to nominate him to run."

"You're certain?"

"His uncle, the board member who convinced the board to put him in as temporary sheriff, is having trouble retaining his membership on the board. He may have to resign." Zack grinned.

"Oh, ho. You know something. What is it?"

"A few of the women who work for the county are considering talking to the press about the uncle's lack of physical boundaries with female employees. If the uncle resigns, Stevens will have difficulty getting the party nod to run."

"Ha, ha. And the story hasn't hit the newspapers yet, so Stevens doesn't know his one supporter at the county level won't be around to vouch for him. I'd like to be in the same room when Stevens discovers how short his career as sheriff will be." I clapped my hands together like a kid with free run of the candy aisle.

"Until then, we have work to do. In return for my support, Stevens has agreed to examine the place in the state park where someone shot at us. I had my conversation with him in front of the DA who supported my point of view that whether the shooting was intentional, it was done after dark and outside hunting season, all crimes that the DA was eager to have investigated."

"How clever of you to present this plan when the DA was present. I'm assuming that was intentional on your part?" I gave Zack a playful punch on the shoulder and followed it with a kiss.

As we walked back to get our cars, Zack stopped me, spun me around to face him and put his hands on my shoulders. "How do you feel about returning to the park to walk the crime scene with me tomorrow? Stevens and at least three deputies will be with us."

I trembled at the thought of returning to the place where I had almost lost Zack. I tried to get ahold of the fear that made my knees weaken and my hands tremble.

"I'm clear about what happened before I got shot. You can help with the aftermath." Zack looked deep into my eyes.

"I thought you were kidding when you mentioned a walk in the park again, but what's the point of my going along? There's not much I could help with. I ran down the trail, stumbled much of the way and then help arrived."

"There's more than that, Maddie. If you walk through the scene again, you'll remember more, things you might think aren't important, but that might be."

I wanted to find out who had tried to kill Zack. And had tried for me but missed. Whoever that was could come at us again. How could we defend against another attack when we didn't know the motive behind the shooting nor the shooter's identity?

"I know you're scared, Maddie, but I'll be there with you."

"What if the shooter isn't finished with us? What if there's another attempt?"

"All the more reason for us to revisit the scene to see what's there." Zack took my shaking hands and looked into my eyes. The confidence I saw there was reassuring. He was a cop and a good one. I trusted him, yet I hesitated.

"What's there has been washed away by the rain and by Steven's refusal to believe an attempt was made on your life and on mine." I wanted to help, but also wanted to believe nothing remained of the evidence of the shooting so I wouldn't have to relive that night.

"We couldn't have gotten in to look at remaining evidence until now anyway. The park and the trails have been closed."

I sighed and nodded my agreement. Zack was right. This would be the first opportunity to return to the park. "If we don't find anything, I still want to hold Stevens responsible, the lazy, incompetent troll."

Zack hugged me to him. "That's my gal."

CHAPTER 19

W HEN WE STARTED TO CLIMB the trail to the falls the next day, the sky was blue, not a sign of a cloud and no rain in the forecast, yet I still felt almost paralyzed by fear remembering the last time I had hiked here. I plodded up the trail, Zack first, me, Stevens, Deputy Burroughs and two other officers following. The route didn't look familiar. There was little evidence of the trail. What remained was a barren path of cement-hardened mud, strewn with rocks, branches and leaves. In many places, the days of rain had washed trees downhill over the trail, and we were forced to climb over them. I worried about Zack being up to the climb. I was using both my hands and arms to pull myself over the fallen trunks. Zack used his one good arm to help him climb, but he had the advantage of his long legs while I struggled to get my short ones over the large trees blocking the path. More than once, Zack reached back to help pull me onto the top of a trunk fallen over our path and ease me down beyond it. I could hear Stevens' heavy breathing behind me, but I cared little for whether he found the trek difficult. Where the mud had hardened, it was smooth as granite and gave little traction. Maybe Stevens would slide down the hill, and we'd be rid of him. I hoped.

When we reached the top, the view of the lake opened below

us. The evening we had picnicked here, trees obscured part of the panorama, but they had either been blown away by the winds or washed down the hillside by the heavy rains. Left in their place was a bare plateau marked by the trees behind us and the falls, full from the rains, roaring downhill into the lake far below.

"The shot came from that direction." Zack pointed uphill to the right of where we stood. "The direction from the second one, I'm unsure of, but unless there were two shooters, it must have come from the same location, perhaps a short distance away." He turned to me. "You probably remember it in better detail than I do."

I closed my eyes to try to visualize that evening. I heard the shot which had sounded like thunder to me followed by what I thought was another loud clap. "I think it came from the same area. Since I thought it was thunder, I thought it was odd it came so soon after the first."

"You two stay here. We'll spread out and search the area." Stevens started uphill, slipped on the bare rock and swore. Deputy Burroughs headed to the right of Stevens and the other officers began to walk the area nearer the drop off. "And be careful. There's no reason to take chances on this wild goose chase." Stevens words punctuated the attitude he displayed the entire climb—a waste of time.

"Sit for a minute, Maddie." Zack led me to a large boulder. "I'll take a look around this area." He walked toward the edge, looked over and stepped forward, then disappeared.

"Zack! What are you doing?" I jumped up and rushed over to where I'd seen him vanish. When I looked over the edge, I spotted him below me on a small ledge.

"Look what I found?" He held up the thermos that had held the tea for our picnic. "It's intact." He unscrewed the top. "There's still tea in it. Cold, however."

"Get up here. You scared me half to death. I thought you'd gone over."

He handed the thermos to me and scurried back up the

embankment, using his good arm for purchase. Back on top and away from the drop off, he brushed off his pants legs. From behind us came a sound that filled the forest. It was low and grating, like a dog's bark, but louder and more feral sounding.

Shouting and waving his arms over his head, Stevens burst through the trees. "Bigfoot. It's Bigfoot. Did you hear that? I think he's after me. Run!" Stevens took off downhill and was soon out of sight, but we could hear him stumbling, falling on the uneven surface and swearing while he continued to yell in fear.

Deputy Burroughs and the other officers ran out of the woods. "Did you hear that?" asked Burroughs. We all nodded

"Sounded like a coyote," said one deputy.

"Or maybe a dog, a big one." said the other.

"Where's Sheriff Stevens?" Burroughs scanned the hillside.

I pointed down the hill where Steven's voice still echoed from the trail.

"Help me. Help me." Stevens followed his cries with a final yelp and then all was silent.

I chuckled.

"We should see if he's okay. If it was a wild animal, he may be in danger." Burroughs started toward the trail.

"I'm sure he'll need rescuing, but not from an attack." I smiled.

"What's up with that grin, Maddie?" asked Zack.

"That sound was a barred owl. Sounds creepy, I know, but I doubt it pursued Stevens. Likely it was a male calling for a mate."

"Sheriff Stevens thought it was Big Foot," said Zack.

We all looked at one another and then broke into laughter.

"I think we should check on Stevens." Zack followed Burroughs as she started down the trail.

We picked our way downhill to meet Zack and the deputy. They stood over Stevens who lay groaning in pain at the side of a tree trunk that had fallen over the trail.

"I think his leg is broken." Zack took my arm. "And there's no cell service here."

"I'll head toward the concession stand to pick up service," said Deputy Burroughs. She headed downhill to make the call.

"Let's get you back to the car, Maddie. The deputies can stay with Stevens until the EMTs arrive."

"Don't tell me I should be sorry about Stevens." I spoke between gasps of breath as we descended the trail.

"I won't." Zack helped me avoid a large rock that stood in the middle of the path.

"I'll bet the county replaces him with Deputy Burroughs." I could hardly keep the delight out of my voice.

Zack nodded, but said nothing, his face devoid of expression.

"Aren't you happy that you'll be replaced by someone competent?"

"Of course, but that doesn't mean your son will be in any better a position than he is now. The charges aren't going to be dropped because there's a new sheriff."

He was right, of course. My joy was short-lived.

We waited at the park office until the ambulance arrived. Zack explained the situation to the EMTs, then walked me to the car.

"Can you drive home by yourself?"

"You're staying here? Why?"

"I want to walk the area Stevens was in when the owl scared him. I think I can convince Deputy Burroughs to walk it with me. If there's any evidence there, the two of us will find it."

"I'll be home. I'll put the kettle on."

"I'm off my pain meds. How about something a little stronger?"

I nodded. Zack leaned in for a kiss. "And I'm feeling much better." He cocked one eyebrow at me.

I watched Zack walk off to join Burroughs. As frightened as I was to come back here, I was more aggravated that they left me out of the search for evidence. It had been years since my family and I had used the park for picnicking and swimming, but my guess was that the old service roads that connected to the county highway still existed. When Dan and I first moved here, money was tight so outings in the park were our entertainment on weekends. We often bypassed the main gate and entered the park through these service roads.

I pulled out of the park entrance and headed right, down the hill and then up the steep grade to the far edge of the park's boundary. Sure enough, not half a mile at the top of the hill, a large log barricaded the entrance to a dirt road with a sign to "Keep Out." across the entrance. I parked my car off the shoulder and proceeded up the unused service road. If my memory was correct, the road would lead to a path that ended up at the falls overlook point. I also suspected that whoever shot at us used this way into the park. If there was any evidence to recover, it might be here. I had no idea what I was looking for, but at least this way I felt part of the search. Not far down the road, a path meandered off to the right and uphill. That had to be the trail to the falls. I huffed and puffed my way up the path, stepping over rocks and tree branches. The going here was much easier than on the trail Zack and I used to access the falls. The area was more protected and showed less wind and rain damage from the recent storms.

I kept my eyes downward to see if there was any sign of someone coming here in the past week. In the thunderstorm and the pelting rain on the night of the shooting, the shooter would have wanted to do his deed and get out quickly, no time for him, or her, to see if they had left anything indicating their presence here. I suspected Zack and the deputy were looking for shell casings that the shooter might have neglected to pick up. But three pairs of eyes were better than two, so I looked for the casings also. The path narrowed ahead, and I had to ease by two trees which leaned into the trail. The bark of one of the firs brushed against my arm.

"Ouch." I rubbed my sleeve where the bark had bitten into it and noticed something darker green against the gray of the bark. A scrap of cloth, its color bleached by the elements, but still clinging to the tree. I reached out and snagged the cloth off the tree. As I brought it closer to my eyes, the snap of a twig startled me.

"Put up your hands and move out here into the sunlight so I can see you better."

"Or what? You'll shoot me?"

"Maddie. What are you doing here? I sent you home."

"No one sends Maddie Sparks home. I'm not a child, Zack."

"I could have shot you sneaking around here, not knowing it was you."

"No, you couldn't. You don't carry a gun anymore."

"Well, you're right, but if it had been Deputy Burroughs and not me, she does carry a weapon and knows how to use it."

"And when not to. Do you think she would shoot someone hiking in a state park? Don't try to fool me. She's trained better than that."

"Okay, Maddie. What the heck are you doing here?"

"Finding evidence." I held up the scrap of cloth. "Here it is. It was caught on that tree over there."

Zack took the cloth from me and examined it. "So?"

"I know who it belongs too, I'm sorry to say."

"Who?"

"Your rival for my affections. My ex."

"How can you know that?"

"I bought this jacket for him years ago. I doubt there's another like it. It's waterproof. He liked to wear it when he was hunting small game. Kept the rain off him."

"And I suppose he owns a rifle, one that might fire a round like these." Zack held up two rifle casings. "I found them over there." He nodded his head toward a tree ahead. "There's a rub mark on one of the branches, the right height to steady a rifle to get a good shot."

"I can't believe Dan would do this."

"He's still crazy about you, Maddie."

I stared into the distance. Was my ex so enamored with me that he'd tried to kill any other man who wanted me? I didn't think so. Dan's real passion ran in another direction. Money.

"There's something wrong with this whole scene. Despite his recent declarations of interest, Dan's interested in something else, not me."

"His present wife threw him out and he wants to return to his first love, the mother of his children. You're not a woman easily forgotten, Maddie. Don't forget the two times at your house, once when I hit him, the other when you shoved him. On both occasions he declared his love for you."

"That was all for show."

"You don't want to believe him capable of trying to kill me, do you?" Zack sounded disappointed in me.

"Of course not. Dan was a bad husband, unfaithful, and he liked younger women. But this is attempted murder." Could I have been so wrong about the man I married? Was he a killer? Did he try to kill Zack? Could he somehow be linked to another murder? Basset's? The two couldn't be connected. Separate incidents. Two killers in our tiny village. How possible was that? The questions swirled in my head, making me feel confused as well as dizzy.

Zack's thoughts were still on Dan as the individual responsible for shooting him. "Assuming she becomes the acting sheriff of this county, I need to tell Deputy Burroughs about this evidence."

We both turned in the direction of the footsteps we heard coming from behind us.

"I thought you went home, Maddie." Deputy Burroughs' words belied the expression on her face. She didn't look surprised to see me. She figured me out the moment we met and surmised my curiosity would get in the way of Zack's reasonable desire to keep me safe. "What's up?"

Zack showed her the shell casings and the spot where someone had propped a rifle.

She smiled when she looked at the casings. "I got a bullet to match. I found it in a tree, the last one left standing on the hill beyond where you and Maddie were when you were shot at. I think it must have been the bullet that hit you and it lodged in the trunk.

As for the other one, chances are it went beyond the drop off and is somewhere in the lake."

Zack nodded. "Now we need to match them to a rifle, and I bet I can find the person who owns the rifle. Right, Maddie?"

I nodded and looked away. I wasn't happy about what the evidence pointed to, but I had to admit we had identified someone for the deputy to question.

"Are you in any shape to come back as sheriff?" asked the deputy.

"I'm not interested in re-assuming the role, but Maddie and I bet you'll be appointed." Zack turned to me. "Where is Dan staying?"

"I don't know, but maybe his about-to-be ex-wife knows.'"

It TOOK ONLY AN HOUR IN EMERGENCY SESSION for the county board to appoint Deputy Burroughs as acting sheriff.

Later that evening Zack and I were finishing a dinner of his favorite, pot roast. I heard a car pull up out front followed by a knock on the door. It was Deputy Burroughs.

"Congratulations. We heard about your appointment. Come in and sit a spell. Coffee? Cookies?" I gave her a hug and headed for the kitchen.

Zack also congratulated her and shook her hand. "This investigation is in good hands now."

She sat on the couch, fatigue lining her face. "I made a deal with the county board. I'm hoping you won't mind, either of you."

"What kind of deal?" asked Zack.

"The county is now down two people with you and Stevens gone. I think you'll agree I need more help. I've got the day-to-day issues to handle as well as the murder of Basset and the shooting."

Zack held up his hand. "I think I know where you're going with this, but I'm not interested in coming back as a deputy of any kind whether I work under you or resume the sheriff's duties."

Anita gave him a knowing smile. "I knew you'd say that, so I have a proposition for you. I've seen how restless you've been during your recuperation, so here's what I'm thinking: return as a consultant. Salary isn't great, but it's something."

"I don't care about the pay."

"I also suspected you'd say that. What do you think? You make your own hours. You don't report to anyone but keep me up to date on what you're doing."

Zack shot me a look.

This man had become important to me, and I didn't want him to put himself in any more danger. I also knew that he loved his work. "Don't ask me for permission to do what I'd find it difficult to prevent you from doing."

"We can iron out the details later. What do you say?" Anita's eyes filled with concern as well as eagerness to hear Zack's answer.

He gave me another glance as if okaying what he knew I would support.

I nodded.

"Okay then. Now all you have to do is get the board's okay."

"Like I said, I made a deal with them. I already ran this by them, my taking over as sheriff contingent upon you stepping in as a consultant."

"That's pretty bold of you, assuming I'd agree."

I high-fived Anita. "You're my kind of woman. She read you, didn't she, Zack?" I sank back into the couch, tired and worried but also satisfied Zack could continue the investigation he had begun and become an intimate part of.

The deputy let out a sigh of relief. "And I hope you can help also, Maggie, unofficially, of course."

I nodded, eager to be part of the team of Burroughs, Montgomery and Sparks, unofficially, of course.

Those details settled, Anita turned her attention to our prime suspect. "I checked. The present Mrs. Dan has no idea where her husband is now. She thought perhaps you knew."

"Why would I know?" I set a cup on the coffee table along with a plate of cookies.

"Thanks." The deputy took a long sip of the coffee and murmured a groan of satisfaction. "Just what I needed after this day. As to Mrs. Dan's recommendation I talk to you, she said Dan told her he was planning to stay with family once he got out of the hospital. I understand you punched him in the nose, Maddie, so that leaves you out of his plans." There was an appreciative twinkle in her eyes.

"Staying with family? Uh, oh." I dropped my forehead into my hand. "That means Dan managed to wheedle his way into Geoffrey and Abigail's house."

"Wouldn't they tell you he was staying there?" asked Zack.

I shook my head. "Geoffrey was always protective of his father, tried to see the good in him. Abigail would have followed what Geoffrey wanted."

"I guess that's my next stop then." The new sheriff swallowed the last drop in her cup and got off the couch.

I stopped her departure. "Let me go first. Abigail and Geoffrey have had enough trouble what with Geoffrey's arrest. The sheriff rapping on their door will create more anxiety for them. I'll stop by like a good mother should. I might be able to get more information out of them than a county officer would."

"I'll come with you then." Zack got off the couch to accompany me.

I held out my hand to stop him. "No. Geoffrey and Abigail think of you as a cop, and, if Dan is there with them, your presence will create problems. Dan doesn't care much for you."

"I don't like him, either and especially if he tried to shoot me. You're not trying to protect him, are you, Maddie?"

I was shocked Zack could believe that of me. I said nothing but gave him a steely look and brushed by him.

"Keep him here until I get back," I said to Anita.

ALL THE LIGHTS WERE ON AT their house, not unexpected because Geoffrey wore the ankle bracelet and where else could he go other than his house, his office or my place without alerting the authorities?

I rapped on the door, heard voices from within, and a door close. Geoffrey pulled back the curtain covering the window at the side of the front door and looked out.

"It's me. Let me in." I turned the knob and was surprised to find the door locked.

The lock clicked and Geoffrey opened the door. "Sorry, Mom. I locked it because we've had reporters surround the house this afternoon."

Abigail stood at the kitchen sink wiping her hands on a dish towel. "I was cleaning up after dinner."

"I guess you had company for dinner." I noticed three plates and three glasses in the dish drainer.

"No. Why would you say that? I'm making coffee. Would you like a cup?"

"You're as bad a liar as your husband, Abigail. I assumed Dan came here after he got out of the hospital, and I'm also guessing the door I heard close right before you let me in was him exiting out the back. If you can get a message to him, you might tell him to turn himself in because the cops want him for attempted murder."

"Dad? Attempted Murder? Whose?" Geoffrey, bless his naïve self never believed anything bad about his father.

"Zack's. And maybe mine. He missed me, not a surprise. He never was a good shot. I'm assuming you put him up in the spare room. Can I look at it?" I started down the hallway toward the stairs to the second floor.

"I don't think you should be snooping around his things, Mom." Geoffrey stepped in front of me.

"Look, love, I know you want to think the best of your father, but either I look around the room, or the police do it. There's enough evidence against him for a judge to grant a search warrant."

Geoffrey's face turned gray with misery. He stepped to one side, and I mounted the stairs.

In the spare room, I found a suitcase, the same one he had carried when he left our house all those years ago. When I opened the closet door, I spied two pairs of pants and three shirts on hangers inside. The twenty-two rifle the kids has given him for his birthday one year stood propped in the back corner of the closet. I knew better than to touch it. I left it for the authorities to confiscate and use for testing.

Geoffrey met me at the bottom of the stairs. "There was a man who came to see Dad right after he got out of the hospital."

"What man?"

Geoffrey shook his head. "I didn't get a good look at him. Dad answered the door and stepped outside to talk with him. They talked briefly, then the guy left. Dad said he was an old friend who needed his help. I didn't push it."

"You didn't hear their conversation?"

"No, but whatever was said upset Dad. He was sweating after he came back inside and there was fear in his eyes."

"Don't touch anything in his room. The sheriff should be here sometime later tonight or tomorrow. She'll want to look around. I suggest you don't stand in her way. If you do, she'll get a warrant."

"What if Dad comes back?" asked Geoffrey.

"Tell him what I said earlier, to turn himself in." I reached out and gave Geoffrey's arm a pat. "Stay out of this, Geoffrey. You've got enough trouble. Don't try to own your father's too." I was certain my advice would fall on deaf ears, both Dan's and Geoffrey's, Dan's because he was scum, Geoffrey's because he was such a caring and naïve son.

CHAPTER 20

I COULDN'T HAVE BEEN GONE MORE THAN fifteen minutes at Geoffrey's place. When I returned to my house Deputy Burroughs was getting ready to leave.

"That didn't take long." Zack's voice sounded relieved I was back so soon.

I hung my handbag on the hook inside the front door and plopped myself on the couch next to Zack. "Any word on the idiot Stevens, not that I care? Big Foot. What a jerk."

"He's in surgery. He should be out in an hour or so. I'll look in on him later." Anita's tone of voice made it clear she was doing her duty, but that didn't extend to feeling sorry for the man.

"You're so kind."

"Any luck talking to your son and daughter-in-law?" she asked. "I need to locate Dan Sparks. You know that, don't you, Maddie?" She was trying to spare my feelings about the man I used to be married to.

"I owe nothing to that cad. In fact, I can help you with that." I told her she could find him at Geoffrey and Abigail's, assuming he would return there. Where else could he go? "There's something interesting in his closet upstairs."

"I'll get a warrant to make it official." The deputy left without asking me more. She was a bright gal and so was I. I knew I shouldn't be more specific about what she might find. Her discovery. Not mine.

I got right back to the conversation where Zack had ended it when I left for Geoffrey and Abigail's. "As you can see, I'm not trying to protect Dan as you seemed to think."

"I didn't say that, but Dan is the father of your children, and you once loved him."

"Water under the bridge. I think I've found myself someone who is more honorable."

Zack enveloped me in a hug. Our bodies molded themselves to each other, and he kissed me in a kiss that grew in intensity and passion.

We broke off our contact with difficulty. I was breathless, but managed to add, "More honorable and a lot sexier."

"Should we . . . ?" Zack lifted his gaze to the steps leading upstairs.

At last, the time was right. "Oh, yes." I grabbed his hand and pulled him toward the stairway.

The phone rang.

"Leave it," Zack said.

"I had no intention of letting it interfere." Nothing was going to intrude upon this long-awaited moment. On the way up the stairs, my answering machine kicked in. It was Abigail.

"Geoffrey didn't want me to call you, but I told him it's the right thing to do. Dan came back here, ran up the stairs, grabbed his belongings and left."

I raced back down the stairs and grabbed the phone. "All his belongings?"

"Yes. Everything."

Executing the search warrant now would reveal nothing of interest to the authorities. Now where did my cur of an ex-husband go?

Zack watched as I slammed the receiver into the cradle. "Where would he run to?"

I picked up the phone and dialed his wife, soon to be ex-wife."

"Is Dan there?"

"That you, Maddie? I tossed his lazy butt out, remember? I have no idea where the man went if not back to you or to Geoffrey's house."

"He was at Geoffrey's, but he left. And he's not with me. Lock your doors in case he tries to get in. The authorities are looking at him for the attempted murder of Zack and me."

"Dan? You've got to be kidding. He doesn't have the nerve to take that kind of action. Look, Maddie, I'm busy here entertaining. I've got to go."

Well, well. Entertaining, was she? The woman didn't let any grass grow under her ample derriere. She'd moved on. Dan wouldn't find her willing to take him in. So where would he go?

As if reading my mind, Zack said, "Maybe to a girlfriend's place."

I threw myself onto the couch to think. Two ideas popped into my mind. "Not a new girlfriend. Who would have that broken down wreck? But there is one woman who might take him in." The other thought came from ex-wife's comments about Dan not having the gumption to do his own dirty work.

"We don't know Dan's rifle was used in the shooting. I don't think Dan would put himself in the position of shooting either me or you. Me, because he might find a way to use me in the future and you because if he missed, he'd be terrified you'd come after him."

"The law would come after him, Maddie."

"Dan doesn't think in those terms. That's too logical."

"Are you suggesting he would have had someone do the job for him?"

"Maybe. But what's bothering me is Basset's death and then the attempt on you, events that appear unrelated."

"It would appear so." Zack sounded as uncertain as I felt.

"Two killers running around this tiny village. I can't see it." I tapped my fingertip on the arm of the couch.

Zack sat beside me putting his arm around me and pulling me to him. I pushed myself away from him and sat up. "Let's think this through step by step."

He groaned. "I can see I've lost your undivided attention."

"Later. We have plenty of time to do the bedroom thing. Right now, my son has been charged with Basset's murder, and we've been targeted by someone. What's the connection between Basset and the shooting?"

We both stared across the room where the pictures of my family sat on the end of the cabinet holding liquor and glasses for drinks and snifters. One of the pictures was of all of us, the children, Dan and me taken right before Dan left the family. Times past when we were together. That's what Tanya wanted. A family, and she thought she'd found one, but now her father was dead. All she had was Robbie, as poor a choice for a partner as Dan had been for me. I sighed and slid forward, elbow on my knee. I couldn't tie Basset's murder and the shooting of Zack together, yet a thin cobweb of connection dangled out of reach, and I knew it had something to do with family.

"Geoffrey." I said.

"What?"

"I don't know. Something Dan said about danger to Geoffrey and Basset's half-brother who is out of prison and somewhere, perhaps around here someplace."

"I think we're right back where we started. There's no connection between the murder and the shooting. We're too tired to fit the pieces together tonight. Let's sleep on it." Zack cocked one eyebrow at me.

"You do mean sleep, don't you? Nothing more?"

With resignation in his eyes, Zack walked me up the stairs to my bedroom and with a peck on my cheek left me at my bedroom door. We didn't dare sleep together in the same bed or, you know, we wouldn't get any sleep. And right now, we both needed brains that worked at top efficiency.

OVER COFFEE THE NEXT MORNING, Zack and I felt better rested than we had been the night before, but still no clearer about who was responsible for the murder or the shooting or if the two crimes were related.

"When I'm at this point in an investigation, I go back to the beginning." Zack dropped two pieces of toast into the toaster and got the butter out of the fridge.

"You're suggesting we need to interview everyone again." I yawned, heard the toaster pop up and grabbed the toast.

"You're still tired," said Zack. "Maybe we should go back to bed."

I gave him a steely look. "I should take you upstairs and ravish you so you can concentrate."

He waggled his eyebrows at me and smiled.

"Not gonna happen, buddy." I bit into my toast and chewed. "So where do you want to start?"

"Let's meet with Sheriff Burroughs and work out a plan." He seemed excited about that.

I sighed. Much as I wanted to get to the root of these crimes, I also had to acknowledge that being able to replace Zack's enthusiasm for me with eagerness to execute a work strategy made me wonder if murder and attempted murder would remain more attractive to him in the future. I hoped having me in his bed would be enough to turn his head away from crime fighting for a while. Not permanently, of course. Who wanted a man as a lover who had no other meaningful interests in life?

Later that morning in Anita's office, the three of us talked over the best approach for using all our talents to crack this case.

Anita started off the discussion. "I'd prefer the two of you focus on the Basset murder while I take on your shooting. We want to avoid the perception of a conflict of interest."

"I still think the two crimes are connected somehow," I said.

"I'm certain these two lines of inquiry will converge," said Zack, "but until they do, I'm happy to reconsider the Basset case."

I reached over and grabbed his arm. "Me, too."

Anita threw me a troubled look.

"You know we need to include her because if we don't, she'll find a way to intervene. I'd rather have her at my side where I can protect her than to have her sneaking around." Zack's look was a warning for me to stay out of other people's houses without an invitation to enter.

"And where will you begin?" asked Anita.

"I'm going to reinterview Robbie, Tanya, and Basset's old business partner and try to locate Polander. We know he was out of prison at the time of Basset's death, so he had the opportunity to kill him and the motive. Anita, you checked with Polander's parole officer and discovered he hadn't checked in after he was released. Not unusual for a parolee to disappear, but we need to follow up. He could be in this area, but in hiding. My inquiries revealed no will, so Basset's estate goes to relatives."

Anita got up from her desk chair. "I've executed the search warrant at your son's house, but we found nothing. My priority will be finding your ex-husband. Any ideas about where he went?"

"Try Pamela Applebottom. She's an old flame of his. Dan and I ran into her when he first came into town. She seemed more than a little eager to hook up with him again."

Anita donned her hat and we each went our separate ways, Anita to her cruiser and Zack and I for my car. Our first stop was back at the garden center. Hiram Barley, Basset's ex-partner, had no alibi for the night of Basset's murder, but he had told us of his plans to sue Basset's estate for the money he believed Basset owed him. While that seemed a reasonable plan of attack to assure him he'd receive the money, lawsuits didn't always work out and they often took time. Was he willing to wait, or had he found another way to get his money, one that involved murder and another other approach we didn't understand? Yet.

"I wonder what the chances are of Barley being successful in his lawsuit against Basset's estate especially since we believe Tanya is his daughter and his rightful heir.?" I asked Zack.

"And there is another heir, you know."

"Yeah, that horrible man, Polander. And here's the connection between these two cases. Dan, the assumed shooter, also owed Polander money from way back, but Polander isn't the kind of man to forgive a debt even after all these years."

"But you don't believe Dan shot at us."

I shook my head. "I don't. Besides, it was so dark that night with the wind and rain. How could anyone aim with any accuracy?" I stopped and drew in a breath. "Maybe we weren't the targets after all."

Zack pulled into the garden center and parked. "Then who was? Any why?"

"The individual who has the most to gain from her father's death is Tanya." I unbuckled my seat belt.

"That gives her motive to kill Basset, but what does that have to do with the shooting?"

"Someone wanted her dead and out of the way. They could have tried to shoot her."

Zack looked at me, a gleam in his eye. "Where was Tanya the evening of the shooting? Could she have been in the park? With Robbie? And someone followed her there."

"Or someone knew she and Robbie were going there. Who? This is confusing. I can't believe Tanya killed her father although she would come into money at his death. Was Tanya the intended victim in the shooting? Nothing makes sense."

"Let's step back on this until we talk with Hiram Barley."

"Wouldn't he love it if Basset were dead and so was his daughter? No relatives to contest the suit," I said. But there was a relative. Zack and I looked at one another. We both knew who the other relative was. The illusive Mr. Polander.

Zack got out of the car, came around and leaned down to give me a kiss. "Good point. I couldn't ask for a smarter partner. Let's go, Nancy Drew."

The garden center owner told us Barley had arrived moments

before for his afternoon shift. We found him in the nearest green-house checking a woman's purchases. He strode up to Zack.

"I heard you're not even a cop anymore, that you got shot and had to leave the sheriff's department, so I assume you're here to buy flowers, right?"

"You're right. I'm not the sheriff any longer, but I am a consultant with the department, and the acting sheriff has asked I talk with you again about the Basset murder."

"This is harassment." Hiram turned to the customers in the center. "The police are harassing an innocent man. I'm here at my place of employment trying to earn an honest living and they're trying to pin a murder on me."

I approached Barley and grabbed his arm. "Fine. Let's talk begonias then."

Surprised by my intervention, he allowed me to pull him off to one corner of the greenhouse.

Zack followed us for a few steps but then stopped and let me walk Barley out the rear door of the greenhouse. Away from prying eyes and ears, I launched my attack.

"Wouldn't you say it would be easier to win your suit against Basset if he had no heirs? All that money in his estate and only you to lay claim to it."

Barley's face turned gray with shock and fear, then took on a look of rage. He shook his fist at me. "Who are you?"

Zack stepped out of the greenhouse. "She's my assistant. I suggest you back off. We suspect you were somehow involved in Basset's death. Maybe you didn't kill him, but you know who did. I've got the authority to arrest you now unless you tell us what you know." Zack didn't have that right, but Barley didn't know that.

"I don't know much, but I recommend you talk with that boyfriend of the gal who says Basset was her father. I think he had a hand in this." Barley's hands were shaking and sweat poured off his brow.

"How?" I asked.

"Married her, didn't he? If she died, he'd inherit all that money."

"And you'd end up with nothing." The murders were linked. Barley killed Basset and thought it would be easy suing for his share of the estate, but then he discovered Basset had a daughter, so he tried to get rid of her and her husband, but he mistook Zack and me for them that evening in the storm.

Barley said nothing for a minute, seemed to gather his wits, then said, "I want a lawyer."

"You haven't been arrested for anything, you twit," I said.

"We can remedy that." Zack took out his cell, connected with Anita. "The acting sheriff will be here in a matter of minutes. Anything you want to add before she arrives?"

Barley began to quiver, and the shaking grew worse until he plummeted to the ground in a faint.

Zack connected with emergency services and ordered an ambulance.

"Now we'll have two weasels in the hospital," I said.

Zack looked puzzled.

"You know, Stevens and this one." I gestured to Barley still unmoving on the ground, but now moaning. He had not hurt himself in the fall. He'd landed in a pile of fertilizer unharmed but smelling like a barnyard. I walked away for some fresh air.

The ambulance arrived before Anita. When she pulled up, she conferred with the EMTs who determined Barley should be transported to the hospital.

"From what you told me, I can't arrest him. There's no evidence he is involved in either crime." Anita watched the ambulance drive off with Barley.

"I know, but I thought threatening him might loosen his tongue. But it was an implied threat. He filled in the blanks and scared himself," I said.

"Barley did tell us something significant, however. He said Robbie was somehow involved," Zack told Anita.

"Involved in the murder?" she asked.

"We don't know. It's possible we weren't the intended victims in the shooting, that it could have been Robbie and Tanya, but in the dark, in the storm, the shooter mistook us for them. Zack and I were about to find Tanya to talk with her again." I could see Anita roll this idea around in her head, wanting to keep us out of the shooting part of the investigation, but also realizing it might be difficult get Tanya to talk with her.

"I know Tanya's not crazy about you, Maddie, but she'd be more willing to talk with you than either Zack or me."

"I can't let Maddie confront a possible murderer." Zack put a protective arm around my shoulder.

"We don't know she's responsible for Basset's death. It's equally possible she was the target of the shooter, and if so, she may still be in danger. I'll be safe if I talk with her at the real estate office. I'll bet she's there right now. I doubt Robbie will be with her, but Geoffrey and Abigail will be there. It's public. We'll all be fine. You can wait outside in the car, Zack." I tried to project confidence and eagerness to play detective, but inside I was trembling. It was one thing, I admitted to myself, to write about investigating a murder and another to be the one doing the sleuthing.

Zack grabbed my shoulders with his hands. His eyes darkened to a deep blue and his gaze swept over my face as if he wanted to both protect and encourage me. "Are you sure you want to do this, Maddie?"

I smiled, trying to keep my teeth from clattering with anxiety. "Oh, sure I am."

"Call the office to see if everyone is there," said Zack.

Geoffrey answered. "Abigail and I are here, but Robbie picked up Tanya to go to lunch."

"Where were they going to eat?"

"They like the burger place near here."

Tanya and Robbie. Killers or victims? Was one innocent and one a murderer?

My stomach rumbled. I was hungry also. "Let's grab a bite while we wait for Tanya to return."

"I'll be at the hospital checking on Barley. You two talk to Tanya when she and Robbie return." Anita left in her cruiser.

Zack and I headed for the burger place this side of town. Tanya and Robbie weren't there, and the waitress hadn't seen them. My stomach gave an insistent growl.

"We're here, so let's grab a bite. We can't work on an empty stomach," Zack said.

After we finished our meal, I called the office again. "Has Tanya returned?"

Abigail answered, sounding harried. "She called and said she wouldn't be in this afternoon at all. She told me she and Robbie wanted to take time for a short honeymoon. Spur of the moment thing, she said."

CHAPTER 21

AFTER ENDING THE CALL TO THE REAL ESTATE OFFICE, I called Anita.

"Barley repeated what he said to both of you, that Robbie was somehow involved in the murder. That's enough for me to locate Robbie and ask him a few questions, but not arrest him at this point. Where do you think they would go for a honeymoon?" Anita sounded irritated that Robbie and Tanya had slipped our grasp. "Our major suspect in the shooting is your husband, and my deputies couldn't locate him at his girlfriend's house. He's in the wind also. We finally get momentum in both cases and everyone we need to question disappears." She grumbled something unintelligible into the phone. "Listen. You two go home. It's my responsibility to sort this out." Anita ended the call sounding frustrated that our plan hadn't worked out.

I sighed. "I might as well call Jane and tell her I'll pick her up for the historical society's meeting this afternoon. Want to come along?"

Zack rolled his eyes at me. "You've got to be kidding. I'll take my afternoon nap on your couch. Drop me off."

Perfect. With Zack snoozing, and there being no historical society meeting today, another of my lies, I was free to pay a visit on Pamela Applebottom. I knew Dan wouldn't be willing to pay for a motel room if he could bunk with someone, preferably a woman. He wouldn't return to Geoffrey and Abigail's, and his wife (soon to be ex-wife) was busy with her new man. Pamela may have told the deputies he wasn't staying with her, but when she ran into Dan and me on the street the other day, she made it clear she wanted him in her life. The woman had terrible taste in men but look who was talking. I had my day with Dan back when.

I rang the bell at Pamela's house. She wouldn't be happy to see me, but she'd be even less happy after I talked with her.

She opened the door, but blocked the entry and didn't invite me in.

"I heard the authorities talked with you and you told them you hadn't seen Dan. Now we both know that's a lie. Where is he? The authorities could charge you for harboring a criminal, you know."

"I haven't seen him. He had nothing to do with shooting that acting sheriff. They have no evidence."

I pushed past her. "We need to have a talk, Pamela. I happen to agree with you. I don't think Dan did shoot Zack, uh, Sheriff Montgomery, but the county does have evidence he was at the crime scene. I know because I provided them with the evidence."

Pamela's hand went to her throat, and she gasped. "You are a cold woman, Maddie Sparks. How could you do that to him if you don't think he's guilty? You tried to set him up for the crime? Why?"

"I'm a mother whose son has been charged with murder, and I think there's a connection between the shooting of the sheriff and Basset's murder. I'd do anything to free my son." I looked around the living room. "Something to wet one's whistle? I'm parched."

I could outwait Pamela. I plunked down on her couch and perused the living room. The decorating was in as poor taste as was the clothing she wore, a too tight, green checked dress and a pair of those plastic see-through sandals that went out of style decades ago.

"I am not here to entertain you. Get out of my house." She pointed to the door.

I ignored her dramatic gesture. "I know Dan was here. I'd bet my social security on it. I may have found evidence he was at the scene of the shooting, but who's to say he was the one wearing that jacket, a piece of which got snagged in a tree, or that he fired the rifle?"

"That's what he told me!" In defense of Dan, Pamela had blurted out information that she could know only if he had been with her. Realizing what she had said, she sank into the recliner across from the couch. "I blew it, didn't I?"

"Yes. If I tell the authorities, and they obtain a search warrant for your house. I'm sure they'll find Dan's clothing here as well as the rifle. Am I right?"

She nodded.

"Do you know where he is right now?"

"No. He said he had to go out to meet someone, but that he'd be back soon. You missed him."

"Got a deck of cards?"

Her forehead wrinkled in confusion. "Why?"

"We can play gin rummy while we wait for him."

Pamela was no card player, and her coffee was undrinkable. After a few hands of gin rummy—I let her win one—it was clear Dan was not going to show.

Pamela began to cry. "Why would he leave me? He said he loves me."

Right. I'd heard that line many times. I considered calling Belinda and having her try to talk some sense into Pamela.

"It's time for you to make a call to the county sheriff's department and for me to leave. I've got pressing needs at home."

"Why should I call the sheriff?"

"Harboring a criminal, remember?"

"But you said you didn't think he shot at you."

"I was guessing. Now make the call."

I was right. I could outwait her. While Pamela was on the phone, I slipped upstairs to use the facilities, meaning I wanted to see if Dan's jacket was in her bedroom. She completed her call sooner than I expected. Without warning she came up behind me.

"Why are you searching my bedroom?" Her face was shiny and red from crying, but her tone had acid in it. I rued having let her win that hand of gin rummy.

"Oh, looking for the brand of skin cream you use." She almost believed me. "Is it in the closet?"

"The skin cream?"

"No. Dan's rifle."

"He took it with him when he left."

Oh, toads' toes.

I left before the sheriff's department showed up. I was doing Pamela a favor which I knew she'd never acknowledge, but I was giving her full credit for being wise enough to call in the authorities. I assumed she'd be smart enough not to let them know I had been at the house and was responsible for goading her into action.

I was feeling proud of the way I handled Pamela. When I got home, Zack was sitting on the couch with a look on his face that said I was busted.

"Jane called several minutes ago." He settled back into the couch waiting for my response to what he said.

"Oh, did she enjoy the meeting?"

"You are a poor liar, my love. Jane was looking for you, and not to accompany you to a meeting of the historical society. It doesn't meet today, does it?"

I looked down at my feet, not wanting Zack to see the look of shame on my face. Time to be honest with him. "The sheriff will be obtaining a search warrant to search Pamela Applebottom's house. That's where Dan was hiding out, but he'd left before I got there."

"You are a lovely woman who is too nosey and too arrogant for her own good, Maddie Sparks. If he had been there, he could have killed you. I know you don't think he was responsible for shooting me, but he's the sheriff's best lead in the shooting." Zack got up from the couch and came toward me. There was anger written all over his face. I backed up, shocked that he continued to approach. He reached out and grabbed my shoulders, then pulled me into his embrace. "I love you, but you scare the hell out of me with all your shenanigans. Promise me you won't go off like that again."

I leaned into him. "You love me?"

"Maybe. I don't know. You make me so crazy I can't think straight."

"Sorry."

"No, you're not. I think you like aggravating me."

"Well, only because you get over it quickly."

"Like now?"

"Are you still annoyed with me?"

"Yes, so let's go upstairs and settle this once and for all." Zack had an unusual way of declaring his love for me, but somehow, I didn't mind.

I grabbed his hand and pulled him toward the stairs.

"And no ringing phone is going to get in our way this time," I declared.

"Right. Listen, Maddie, I'd take you in my arms and carry you up the stairs, but my arm still isn't in good condition."

"The outcome for such sexual antics with folks our age isn't good."

Zack looked surprised. "You've tried a lot of antics?"

I remembered my attempt at trying out bending backwards over the couch back to determine if I could use it in my writing, and Sara found me with my legs in the air stuck on the sofa.

"Uh, no, but I do have a vivid imagination. Dashing into the bedroom while ripping off our clothes will do."

"Let's do it."

I ran for the stairs, Zack in pursuit. We were almost to the top, Zack with his shirt trailing off one arm, me with my skirt unbuttoned when someone knocked on the door.

"Go away. We're busy," I yelled.

"It's me, Tanya. I'm with Robbie. We need to talk to you. Someone is trying to kill us."

Oh, toads' toes and lizard livers. We were doomed as lovers.

I OPENED THE FRONT DOOR to a terrified young couple. They both looked around them as if they thought someone was hiding in the bushes or behind a tree, then they pushed into my living room slamming the door behind them.

"Have a seat?" I gestured at the couch.

Tanya hung onto Robbie's arm while he gulped, his eyes bulging out in fear.

"He may have followed us here. I don't know." He ran to the front window and peeked out. "I should have parked the car someplace where it couldn't be spotted."

Zack pulled Robbie over to the couch. "Sit down and tell us what's going on."

"I'll put on a pot of coffee." I headed to the kitchen but stopped and turned back. "We understand you were on your way for a brief honeymoon."

"We were heading to an inn for the night when a car roared up behind us, bashed into our back bumper, pulled around us and tried to force us off the road. Oncoming cars made the guy pull back. I floored it and took a right turn off the highway onto a county road, then another quick right. The car didn't spot my maneuver, so I continued to speed down some country roads and then back onto the highway. He was waiting for me there and took up the chase again. I drove into town and managed to lose him again. I pulled behind the post office. Tanya and I talked and decided to come to you."

"When he first started chasing us, we thought he was drunk or on drugs, but he kept up the pursuit." Tanya broke into tears. "I don't want to die."

"When did this happen?" I asked.

Tanya and Robbie exchanged glances. "Right after lunch."

"It took you long enough to come here," Zack said.

"The timing is perfect. Barley started his shift at the garden center shortly before we arrived to talk with him. No wonder he was so shook when I confronted him."

"I don't think this is the first time he tried to kill us either."

"He tried to run you down before?" Zack said.

"No. It took me a while to figure this out, but we think he meant to shoot us but shot you instead." Robbie popped off the couch and began to pace. "See, that afternoon, Tanya and I took a drive to the park. There was another car behind us, but I didn't pay attention because we were, you know, kissing and stuff. We parked and decided to take the trail up to the falls, but halfway up the sky started to get dark. Tanya is terrified of lightning. A storm was coming in, so we turned around and got back to the car as the rain started. I knew about the shooting but didn't think much of it until that car started trying to run us down today. Don't you see? We were at the park the night someone shot you."

"You think you were the intended victim?" asked Zack.

"More likely Tanya because she is Basset's heir, but marrying her puts you in the killer's sites also." I finished making the coffee and returned to the living room carrying a tray with the pot and coffee cups.

Tanya continued to cry into Robbie's shoulder. I handed her a cup of coffee. "This might help."

"With Tanya out of the picture, Barley's lawsuit would be easier to settle. We need to see if Barley's alibi for the time of Basset's murder is solid and find out where he was the night of the shooting. I'll call Anita." Zack took his cell and stepped out onto the back deck to make the call.

Tanya stopped crying and took a sip of her coffee, but she latched on again to Robbie's arm and clung to it, terror in her eyes. "I don't want his money. I never wanted anything from him but his love."

Robbie reached out and drew her closer to him. I'd figured Robbie for a loser, but he seemed to care about her.

"I never congratulated you on your marriage. I hope you will be very happy," I said.

Tanya sat up and gave me a tiny smile. "Thanks. We were on our way to Cazenovia for our honeymoon weekend when the car rammed the bumper and pursued us."

"Sorry about that, sweetie, but we're going to figure this out. Soon." Robbie pulled her into him and kissed her hair.

Zack entered. "I didn't get a chance to ask Anita about Barley. She wants me over at the sheriff's department right away. I briefed her on what the two of you experienced today, and she asked that you accompany me. Her deputies found Dan Sharps."

"Where?"

"Of all the places to hide out, he was sitting on a bar stool at Spoonies Bar, that dive west of here." Zack grabbed his jacket and gestured for Robbie and Tanya to accompany him.

"What about me?" I asked. "Don't I get to come along?"

"No. You sit tight. I'll fill you in when I have more news."

Zack returned to the house an hour later. "Did you go anywhere?"

"You told me to sit tight. I was right here. Why would I go anywhere?"

"Because you're nosy and like to be involved."

I had been on my computer checking to see if I could find any information on Leon Polander. We already knew they paroled him early, that he was Basset's half-brother, but there was no record of him once he was released. Was he in the area? If so, where would he stay? I decided to check the cheaper motels around. What I found was interesting but not good news for Dan.

The ploy I used to get information about Polander was simple.

"Hi. My name is Maddie Sparks and I'm looking for my brother. I know you're not supposed to give me any information about your guests, but he walked away from his rehab facility. He has Alzheimer's and the family is worried about him, so if you could check your records, you might be saving a life." If the desk clerk fell for my story, I then would give them Polander's name.

I was batting zero when I called The Timbers Motel and Housekeeping Cabins. I had gone through my tale of woe, but before I could give them Polander's name, the clerk said. "Sparks is the name? Yeah, we have a Dan Sparks registered here. Could that be him?"

I was flabbergasted and related the story to Zack.

"Dan registered at a motel?" Zack was as surprised at the information as I was. "Why, when he was staying at your son's place and then at Pamela Applebottom's?"

"Maybe it wasn't Dan staying there. Maybe it was someone else. Dan could have registered for someone then turned over the key to him."

"I'm assuming your mean Polander. Why would he do that for the guy?"

"Dan owed him money and never paid him. I know Dan told Polander that Geoffrey was supposed to pay him, but that was a lie."

"Dan was doing Polander a favor getting him that cabin."

Zack and I looked at each other, thinking the same thing. "Polander wanted to be in this area but out of sight because he was here to contact his half-brother, Basset. Their discussion went wrong, something happened and Polander stabbed him. Then he turned his attention to Basset's daughter, Tanya, thinking if he got rid of her, he'd be in line for the inheritance from his half-bother because there were no other heirs." I clucked my tongue. "It's a good thing you had Robbie and Tanya follow you to the sheriff's department. They're both in danger. Polander wants anyone gone who stands in the way of that money."

"You're right, Maddie. I'm heading back to the sheriff's department. They're going to need as many personnel as possible to search for Polander, beginning with the cabin Dan rented for him."

"Be careful." I reached up and kissed him on the lips.

"I will. There are ends I've left dangling here. I'd like to tie them up."

"Do you mean that?"

"What?"

"The tying up part." I giggled to let him know I was kidding.

"You are some woman."

CHAPTER 22

SOON ALL OF THIS WOULD BE BEHIND US. Dan might have rented the cabin for Polander, let him borrow this rifle and his jacket, but Dan was no killer although I wondered if he knew Polander had killed Basset and was responsible for the shooting. No. that couldn't be. Dan wouldn't have kept that information to himself. He was a man without courage, but he wouldn't help cover up a crime as heinous as murder.

I decided to take this time to write, so I went into my office to my computer, but before I opened my manuscript, I realized it had been days since I had read my email. A message from the vet's office popped up informing me of Spike's appointment for his rabies shot and annual boosters. The appointment was for today in a half hour.

"Spike!" I yelled up the stairs and knew that was the wrong approach for getting him to come down. I grabbed his bag of dried food and shook it. He appeared on the landing, giving me a look filled with suspicion as if he knew I was trying to trick him into coming down to be captured and put in his carrier. How did cats know these things? Wet food might work better. I rushed to the fridge where I had an open can, grabbed it, and spooned a glop into his food dish. He yawned and licked his lips but didn't move off the top step. I crept up the stairs with the dish in my hands making "kitty, kitty" sounds at him. He cocked his head to one side, and I reached out with the dish until I had it under his chin. The smell of tuna stew was too much for him. He let down his guard long enough to plunge his head into the bowl and began to chow down. I let him eat for a minute then I grabbed him and rushed down the stairs. Cat carrier. Cat carrier. Where had I put the thing? I checked my watch as I wrangled Spike in my arms and decided he could ride to the vet without being in his carrier. I dashed for the car and got in, settling Spike onto the passenger's seat. He gave me a look I'd never forget. Not anger, not a hiss or a growl or a mew of helplessness, but a look as if I had failed him completely. And I had.

I pulled over to the side of the road a few blocks from the house, thinking I could explain this whole thing to him.

"See, it's for your own good." The favorite line of frustrated and guilty parents everywhere. "I mean, you wouldn't want to get rabies, would you, or some other awful disease?"

Spike's eyes got bigger and bigger, rounder and rounder. The cat was doing cute on me to get me to change my mind. He blinked and let out a tiny "mew."

"Okay, okay. We won't do it today." I turned on my blinker and began to put the car in drive when the back door was yanked open, and a man jumped into in the back seat.

I felt something cold and hard against the back of my neck.

"Turn around and drive."

I looked over to see how Spike was reacting to the appearance of the hijacker, but Spike was gone. He must have slipped out of the car when the guy opened the door. I was alone with the man I suspected had killed Basset and tried to kill Zack, me, Tanya and Robbie. It had been years ago since I'd seen him and that was a brief encounter, but those eyes, those cold, flat eyes. No one I'd ever met had eyes so lacking in human warmth. I recognized him as the man who came to my house looking for Dan and the money my husband owed him. Leon Polander.

I gulped and tried to speak, but my voice came out in a squeak. "Where are we going?"

"Back to your place, babe."

"I'm not your babe." Where had that cheeky response come from? I was terrified. You'd think I'd try not to aggravate the man holding a gun on me.

"No, but you were Dan's babe. Now he tells me you're having a fling with the sheriff, as I hear it, the guy who was sheriff. Now I hear there's a broad in the position."

Babe. Broad. This guy was a feminist's nightmare.

I glanced in the rearview mirror, hoping I would spot Spike on the side of the road, unhurt and looking for a spot to hide.

"Don't get your hopes up, girlie. There's no one behind us who will rescue you."

I groaned. Now I was a girlie to him.

"You thought killing your half-brother would put you in the position to inherit his estate, but then you found out about his daughter. She had to go, too, didn't she? But you messed up on that one and shot the sheriff instead."

He jammed the gun into the back of my neck harder. "You're so full of it. Pull over in front of your house and don't make any funny moves. We'll walk in like we're friends."

I got out of the car, Polander following me, the gun jammed into my back. He grabbed me by the shoulder and with the gun in his other hand, he shoved the car door partially closed.

"You'll wear down the battery. The overhead light is on."

"Don't worry about it. We won't be here long. I'm waiting for somebody. I just called him. He should be here any minute."

That must be Barley, the other partner in this killing duo. I wondered how the two of them worked out the scheme for getting rid of Basset, Tanya, and Robbie. Killing Basset worked, but then Polander, or Barley? mistook Zack and me for Tanya and Robbie. How would they get rid of Tanya and Robbie? And me? And how could they cover up their involvement in all these murders? One of the partners would have to take the fall for the murders. Would it be Polander or Barley? In case Polander hadn't thought through all the ramifications, I determined it was my responsibility to inform him he might be the guy taking the rap for everything. It was the most likely possibility. He was the ex-con. Barley was a businessman turned garden center worker.

"He's going to frame you, you know, and then go to court for all Basset's money. If you turn yourself in, you can make a deal with the authorities. I suspect this whole scheme was Barley's doing anyway. He used you to do the dirty work, kill Basset and try to kill Robbie and Tanya."

Polander stared at me with a confused look on his face. "Who's this Barley guy?"

The front door crashed open, Robbie and Tanya pushing though it followed by Spike who slinked in behind them and dashed up the stairs. Smart cat. He must have hidden under one of the car seats, gotten out of the car when Polander left the door ajar and waited for an opportunity to slide back into the house.

Unaware, Robbie and Tanya had walked into the arms of a killer. Polander was certainly that, but he didn't recognize Barley's name. Had Barley used an alias when he and Polander worked together on their plan to rid Basset of his daughter, leaving his half-brother the sole heir? Assumedly Barley and Polander would have their legal representatives come to an equitable arrangement with respect to the assets of Basset's estate.

Tanya gripped Robbie's arm as he closed the door behind him. She blanched and sagged into Robbie when she caught sight of Polander. "You look like my father," she stammered. "You were the man who came into the restaurant that day."

"Wanted a cup of coffee to go. I didn't expect to walk into a place with cops in it. I skedaddled fast."

"I can see why Tanya reacted as she did. She caught a glimpse of you and thought Basset had come back to life." I realized that Polander's appearance the day Tanya and I went to lunch shocked her so much she fainted.

"I may look like my half-brother, but I'm nothing like him. And I got no use for a niece to foul up my plans."

"I don't understand," she said, looking up into Robbie's face in concern.

I didn't answer her but directed my attention to Polander. "Now that Robbie and Tanya are married, you'll have to kill both as well as me. Robbie would inherit Basset's estate as her husband."

"Maybe he can keep his mouth shut. How about that, laddie?" Polander grinned from ear to ear.

I expected Robbie to look as frightened as Tanya was and as terrified as I felt, but his face registered nothing. Perhaps he was working on a plan to rush Polander for his gun.

"And who are you going to blame for all these crimes?" I was attempting what all my protagonists did in these life-threatening situations—get the bad guy to talk while I figured out how to get us out of this.

"Your ex-husband might do," said Polander. "I was thinking Dan might be the perfect patsy, but there was the issue of motive. In the case of the sheriff and you, jealousy would work, but why would Dan kill Basset? I guess I hadn't thought through this one too well." Polander let out a chuckle.

"And you still had Tanya who stood in the way of your inheriting the estate," I said.

"Not my mistake." Polander's glance shifted from me to Robbie.

That one glance told me how wrong I had been.

Robbie nodded and slipped his hand into his jacket pocket, extracted a gun and pulled Tanya in front of him. Robbie's sudden move took Polander by surprise. He fired at Polander, who dropped to the floor, his gun falling from his grip. Robbie stepped over to him, stooped and picked up Polander's gun.

Tanya tried to fling herself back into Robbie's arms. The truth had not hit her yet. Robbie pushed her away from him.

"It looks as if I arrived in time to kill the man responsible for your father's death, my dear. Too bad he shot you and Maddie Sparks before I killed him." Robbie raised the gun to fire at Tanya, but a blur of yellow shot off the upstairs landing and onto his head. Blinded by fur, teeth and claws, Robbie whirled around. The gun went off, the shot felling ceiling plaster. I grabbed the cutglass brandy decenter off the liquor sideboard and slammed it into Robbie's head. He dropped to the floor. Both he and Polander lay still. I'd killed him. Not that I didn't have reason and I wasn't relieved to see him lying there, but I never imagined I was capable of killing anyone. In case Polander or Robbie wasn't dead I kicked both guns under the couch out of reach.

Spike jumped onto the couch and mewed. Tanya's eyes widened as she realized how close she had come to death at her husband's hands. "He didn't love me. He married me for the money. I never saw through him."

"He was devious. Spike saw him for what he was, though." I patted Spike on his furry head. "Time for your kibble. You did an excellent job, but don't think this means you don't have to visit the vet for your shots."

Spike tipped his head to one side and gave me a narrow-eyed look.

I called the sheriff's office. While we waited for them to arrive, Tanya and I sat on the couch. She covered her face and cried softly into her hands while I leveled my dad's shotgun at the two men lying on my floor. At this distance, I couldn't miss with a shotgun. But neither of them stirred.

Zack was first in the door and ran over to me, enveloping me in his arms.

"Are you okay?"

"Yup."

"Didn't I tell you not to get into trouble?"

"Yep. Blame Spike."

Spike, gobbling down half a can of cat food, made a grumbling sound in his throat. He was either vocalizing his extreme satisfaction with my choice of cat food or, more likely, pointing out the role he played in rescuing Tanya and me.

Burroughs arrived with her men and the EMTs, who examined Robbie and Polander. Both men were alive, but in serious condition.

"Your ex got smart and turned himself in. He'll do time as an accessory to attempted murder, yours and Zack's," Anita told me.

"I'm not even sure he knew Polander borrowed his gun and jacket." I wasn't defending Dan's alliance with a killer, just his stupidity at giving into Polander's demands.

"We'll let the DA determine the charges. Regardless of what they are, he'll need a good lawyer." Anita gave me a knowing look.

"Not Richard. Not with Dan's association with Polander and Polander's using his gun to shoot at Zack and me. It was Dan's rifle, wasn't it?"

"Dan brought the gun in with him. Ballistics says it was the one used."

"I'm certain Richard knows a lawyer he can recommend to Dan."

"Or, if he doesn't have the money, the court will appoint one," said Zack.

I laughed. "Or Dan might persuade Pamela Applebottom to pay."

Zack turned to me. "You hit Robbie with your mother's brandy decanter?"

"Well, it was my plan all along to take him down that way. I looked for an opportunity, and Spike provided it by distracting him."

Spike let out a shattering yowl of protest. I remembered his attack on Deputy Stevens the day of Basset's murder. The cat recognized both incompetents and criminals with apparent ease.

"Let me correct that. I mean, Spike took him down first."

I leaned closer to Zack and whispered in his ear. "The decanter move was an impulsive thing, but I don't want the cat to think I was incapable of protecting my family from murderers. I want him to feel safe here."

Zack put his arm around me and looked down into my eyes. "So now you're family to Spike?"

"I guess so, unless Tanya wants him."

Tanya heard me. "He likes you, and I think Spike doesn't respect me for my terrible choice in a husband. He'd be judging me every day."

The gal did make a bad choice with Robbie, but she seemed to be bouncing back from her near-death encounter. After everyone left, I made tea and Zack and I took our cups out back onto the deck off the kitchen.

I read hesitation in Zack, so I kept silent to let him talk first. As much as we had looked forward to the time when we could be alone together, I knew this was not the moment.

Zack finished his tea and got out of his chair. "I'm going to spend the night back at the B and B. If I stayed here, we'd be tempted to try romance, and we'd mess it up. I'll pick you up tomorrow morning and we'll visit Anita." He kissed the top of my head and left. I heard the engine of his car start and then drive off into the night. Was Zack right? Was it exhaustion that stopped him from taking me upstairs or something else? I remained seated on the deck until the moon rose, shining its shimmering light over my back lawn. It was the perfect night for love. The creek sang a babbling song as it spilled over rocks on its way downstream. A gentle breeze stirred the pine trees and night birds called to one another in the old maples.

Spike and I trudged up the stairs to my bedroom. I got into bed knowing that I was too stirred up to sleep. Spike curled himself at my side.

"My hero." I stroked his silky fur and took comfort in his purring. And then, it was morning.

CHAPTER 23

I CALLED GEOFFREY EARLY THE NEXT MORNING. Abigail answered the phone to tell me all the charges against Geoffrey had been dropped and the ankle bracelet removed.

"We're just exhausted after all this, but why don't you stop by this evening. And bring that sheriff guy."

"Zack."

"Yes. Him."

Geoffrey came on the line. "We can all get acquainted."

"I'm so relieved you're home. Are you opening the office today? And will Tanya still be working for you?"

"She's taking off a few days to recuperate."

"Won't that leave you short-handed?" The minute I said it, I wanted to bite back the words.

"About that . . ."

"Oops. Gotta run. I'm meeting Zack at Anita's office and I'm late." I hung up. I had promised to help the business and I suppose I owed it to them to keep my promise, but I would deal with that issue later. I stole a quick glance through the door to my office. My computer sat abandoned on my desk. I hadn't written since I found myself in the middle of this case. I stopped for a moment, then hurried on. There were still some questions about Basset's murder and the shooting.

When those had been answered, I promised myself I'd get back to my manuscript. Well, after Zack and I had . . . A tiny shiver worked its way down my spine. My life had become so exciting.

AN OPEN PASTRY BOX WITH DONUTS in it sat on the corner of Anita's desk. I helped myself to a chocolate-filled donut. Despite a good night's sleep, I still felt unsettled by Zacks's attitude toward us last night, but I told myself there was nothing that chocolate couldn't cure.

"So how did Robbie and Polander know each other?" I licked my chocolate-covered fingers and spoke through donut crumbs.

Anita held the box out to Zack, who shook his head, so she took the last one. She bit into the donut and then took a swig of coffee, swallowed and said, "They were related. Polander's sister—same mother, different father—was Robbie's mother. Robbie talked a lot last night when he regained consciousness. They wrote to each other while Polander was in prison. The plan to kill Basset was Polander's according to Robbie; he convinced Robbie that the two of them would inherit Basset's estate, but then Polander got word through his sister that Basset had a daughter. Polander changed up his plan to remove her from the picture, but he decided Robbie was the perfect person to help him. There was no reason to kill Basset unless Polander and Robbie were certain they were next-of-kin. Robbie started a relationship with Tanya, but Polander's early release from prison moved up their schedule by several months."

"Polander stabbed Basset, leaving Tanya's fate to Robbie, right?" Zack asked.

Anita nodded.

"I guess marrying Tanya wasn't part of the original plan?" I asked.

"Robbie said Polander wanted Robbie to get close to Tanya so he could find an opportunity to kill her."

"But Robbie decided to insure he'd inherit and not simply

through Polander but through Tanya, Basset's daughter and, better yet, Robbie's wife. Polander worried Robbie wouldn't go through with getting rid of his wife, and he grew to distrust Robbie's loyalty to him." My stomach lurched with the realization that Polander meant to kill both Robbie and Tanya when he followed them to the park and shot Zack by accident. "I always hated these summer storms in Upstate but this time the rain and wind saved Zack's life."

"And Tanya and Robbie's too." Zack added.

"I guess the DNA test proved that Tanya was Basset's daughter," I said.

Anita nodded. "But no will. Tanya said Basset told her he was thinking of making out a will when he got back from his trip."

"How is Deputy Stevens doing? Will he be back on duty soon?" I hoped Stevens would decide to leave the department.

Anita broke into laughter. "He resigned. He's setting up a blog with a few social media gurus on "Finding Bigfoot: Sightings in Upstate New York." He plans to go live on YouTube, so you might run into him in the woods if you go hiking. Or picnicking." Anita seemed to be warning Zack and me that the outdoors might not be the place to finalize our attraction for each other despite the perfect late summer weather.

"Didn't you tell him the sound he heard was a barred owl?" I asked.

"He'd never believe me, and I wouldn't want him to. This way I don't have to work with him." Anita arose from her chair. "I'm off to the hospital to see if Polander has anything to say to me. He's been keeping his mouth shut, but now that Robbie has given his side of the story maybe Polander will be more willing to chat with me. Either way, I've charged both with Basset's murder and attempted murder."

"I'm surprised Barley didn't have a hand in this. He's a horrible little man. The good news is that his lawsuit against Basset's estate will cost more than what he would glean from it. That seems like justice." I could hardly believe that it had been only a little over a week since I stumbled onto Basset's body. So much had happened in that time. I caught Zack staring at me, telegraphing a message I'd have to be blind to miss. I decided to be bold, so I reached for his hand. "So that about wraps up everything here, doesn't it?" I held my breath.

He saw the twinkle in my eye and read my mind. What would he say? "I guess you need to get back home. Your computer must be calling you for another scene in your manuscript."

"Oh, wonderful," said Anita. "Another in your cozy series?"

"Something like that." I tugged on his hand.

"I'm coming." He gave me one of his slow, easy smiles.

"You could stay and help me tie up loose ends here." Anita knew better. Over the days she had read the sizzling exchanges between Zack and me.

"Thanks, but you're the sheriff and I know you can manage this on your own. Besides, Maddie needs my help. She's stuck on a scene and could use my input."

ONCE WE WERE IN THE HOUSE, Zack took me in his arms and kissed me, slowly, wholly and completely. He lifted me onto the back of the couch and continued his exploration of my mouth.

"No," I said.

"No?" Zack stepped back and looked into my eyes. "Why not?"

"I've tried this, and it doesn't work."

"Tried it? With whom?"

"Myself."

"You'd better explain that to me. I don't get it."

There was a knock at the door.

"Gram? Are you there?"

"You might as well come in," I called.

Sara opened the door and stared at the two of us, me seated on the back of the couch, Zack standing over me.

"Sorry. I didn't know Zack was here."

"He was helping me with a scene I was writing. You know the

one."

She nodded. "Well. I'll leave you to it. I wanted to stop by to say hi."

"We'll be over later."

"Right." She opened the door to leave, then turned back. "I'm so glad Gram has someone to help her on these scenes. She's got a wonderful imagination, but I think it works better if there's someone else present to help with the details."

"Don't worry. He won't let me fall. Will you?"

"No more than I've fallen already, Maddie."

Sara waved good-bye and gently closed the door.

"Much as this seems an adventure, I think we should take it to my bedroom. Someone is watching."

We both looked up at the landing. Spike sat there, his gold eyes fixated on us, but they weren't judgey. In fact, I could swear he was smiling.

Cows, Lesley learned growing up on a farm, have a twisted sense of humor. They chased her when she went to the field to herd them in for milking, and one ate the lovely red mitten her grandmother knitted for her. Determining that agriculture wasn't a good career choice, instead she uses her country roots and her training as a psychologist to concoct stories designed to make people laugh in the face of murder. "A good chuckle," says Lesley, "keeps us emotionally well-oiled long into our old age." She is the author of the Eve Appel Mysteries from Camel Press as well as two other cozy mystery series and numerous short stories. Go to her webpage to find out more: www.lesleyadiehl.com.

www.ingramcontent.com/pod-product-compliance
Lightning Source LLC
Chambersburg PA
CBHW010540100726
47903CB00011B/3078